Praise for Susannah Marren's Palm Beach Novels

"Riveting . . . filled with betrayal, passion, aspiration, and deep emotion . . . *A Palm Beach Wife* doesn't pull any punches. I couldn't put it down."

ELYSSA FRIEDLAND, author of *The Intermission*

"A slew of family secrets, sisterly betrayals, and the suspicious drowning churn the Palm Beach waters in this wickedly entertaining novel by Susannah Marren."

MARY SIMSES, author of *The Wedding Thief*

"With a penetrating eye for tribal nuance, Susannah Marren returns to Palm Beach, where wearing the wrong shade of lipstick can be social suicide. *Maribelle's Shadow* explores how a mother and three daughters transplanted from nowhere play the ambition game with chilling skill."

SALLY KOSLOW, best-selling author of *The Real Mrs. Tobias*

"Another stunning novel from Susannah Marren set in Palm Beach. Exploring the intricacies and interplay of family loyalty, romance, and high society, Marren never ceases to amaze. This one will keep you turning pages!"

JACQUELINE FRIEDLAND, *USA Today* best-selling author of *He Gets That from Me*

"Sisters, husbands, scandal, business, and betrayal. This intriguing novel about deception, marriage, and the high society Palm Beach scene will keep you turning the page until the surprise ending."

SONDRA HELENE, author of the best-selling novel, *Appearances*

"Susannah Marren returns to familiar territory in her new novel, *Maribelle's Shadow*, navigating us through the glitzy, cutthroat world of the Palm Beach elite. Love, loyalty, and wills are tested as the mystery begins to come clear. An insightful look and welcome addition to the literature of mothers, daughters, and sisters—richer and more relevant today than ever."

ANNE WHITNEY PIERCE, author of *Down to the River*

PALM BEACH CONFIDENTIAL

Also by Susannah Marren

Between the Tides

A Palm Beach Wife

A Palm Beach Scandal

Maribelle's Shadow

SUSANNAH MARREN

PALM BEACH CONFIDENTIAL

MERIDIAN EDITIONS
WESTPORT, CONNECTICUT

Published by Meridian Editions
Westport, Connecticut

www.meridianeditions.com

This book is a work of fiction. All of the characters, organizations and events portrayed in this novel are either products of the author's imagination or used fictitiously.

Poetry excerpts by Susan Shapiro Barash. Reprinted with the permission of the author.

ISBN (paperback): 978-1-959170-34-1
ISBN (hardcover): 978-1-959170-33-4
ISBN (eBook): 978-1-959170-35-8

Art direction: Meryl Moss
Cover and book design: John Lotte

For the daughters

All of it has always been tricky
Then the ocean meeting the bay
Two bodies of water split
In search of the center.

Susan Shapiro Barash

Unknown Name

PALM BEACH CONFIDENTIAL

PART ONE

I said sure since you asked.
It was a safe hour. I thought
the sparrows weren't hollow.

Chapter One

2026

DUSK. Raleigh knows he is awfully close, recklessly near.

"Hey."

His lanky body divides her view of swaying beach umbrellas and the green water beyond. He's tan, wearing khaki shorts. She looks at his feet because her mother and her aunt have always said a man's shoes tell the story. But he's in flip-flops, there is no reading to be had.

Surrounding them are little children who stand beside their mothers as they pack up canvas bags, closing tops of water bottles, folding up chairs. All day long their mothers have slathered sunscreen, doled out sandwiches, warning their children not to wade far out. Now they gather them, calling *Clementine, Barley, Ida, River, Grayson, over here.* Women cover their pastel bikinis with matching saris, laughing a trilling laugh, patient in a way that happens in a small town. The demands don't seem as high in the Panhandle, a strip of northwest Florida bookended by Panama City and Apalachicola. Raleigh loves this exquisite part of the world. Until she was nine, she grew up a half hour south of Cape San Blas, in Kesgrave.

He lights up a cigarette. "You are?" he asks.

Raleigh places the scallop shell she's painting on her narrow drafting table. She's working on an order for twenty more, inside will be miniature seascapes, flowers, riverbanks. Her work is popular in tourist spots, gift shops along the shoreline. Without family money—and her separation from her husband—the cash is useful. She is empty, flat-out. The monthly stipend from Barrows, the family company, is on hold. Lucinda, her mother, likes to remind Raleigh that if she accepts so much as a dollar, it will be used against her in the divorce.

"I'm Raleigh."

"Raleigh, how'd you end up on this dune? I mean, plunked down midweek, making these?" He eyes the painted clam shells, an ocean scene in the center of a cockle shell. He holds up two. She has forked blue curls around the borders.

It's been a while since anyone has stared at her like this. It's confusing, she turns away. Although she hasn't been to a yoga class or Pilates since she arrived, she's fit from long walks. She checks her hair, messy, heavy, chestnut, setting off her face no matter how she wears it. Suddenly it's important to stand straighter, to have the smoothest skin, to not have the remnants of a Larabar around her mouth. Northern gannets and white pelicans fly above, and gulls skim the water. Her older sisters used to take her shell tossing, right by this jetty, aiming at the frothy edges, making wishes on them. The refuge of her childhood helps—she comes every few months for a week at a time.

Out of the corner of her eye, Raleigh sees more women and children leaving. Little boys weave around their lithe mothers. One young father starts shaking out the beach towels while his wife beams at the gesture. Their toddler daughter clings to her mother's legs. Raleigh winces. She once did the lovely young family cycle—an adoring husband with their darling young son—an incandescent triumvirate to the outside world. In Palm Beach where it matters a great deal. How she postured, swinging Caleb above the rolling waves at the private beach at the Breakers Beach Club with her lean, fine-featured husband. But she's no longer proof of the whole package, the image Lucinda treasures. While still part of the Barrows family, a Palm Beach family of some renown, she's the one who failed at her marriage. Raleigh's beauty remains; her talent as an artist remains, belonging to her unconditionally. On the toughest days or after a call with her lawyers about her divorce, Raleigh second-guesses the life she had.

"I'll buy this set."

"Will you?" She smiles. "That will be a hundred dollars."

Tilting his head, he takes off his sunglasses that might or might not be Ray-Bans, gives her two fifties. He comes closer. "I'm Porter, Porter Sanford."

It's as if they're indoors, with a ceiling and walls. It could be a black-tie party, a fundraiser, theatre before the curtain rises. Except his skin smells of the ocean, like he's a shrimper. His shadow beard is scruffy. Not the purposeful ones Raleigh knows from Palm Beach where men sport a rugged look without living it. He looks possibly thirty.

She watches him checking her out, her sarong and cropped T-shirt, her height, her weight. What men compute, believing they're subtle about it. She considers a disclosure; she has made a mess of things. She might explain that her son, Caleb, is eight hundred miles away with his father and a nanny, that she's the youngest of three sisters and the older two are enraged at her. The eldest, Maribelle, isn't speaking to her. Lucinda's wrath at Raleigh is brutal. Although Alex left Raleigh, her mother defends him. As far as Raleigh's affair, it isn't that Lucinda is against subterfuge, just against getting caught. Nothing sets Lucinda off like a poor execution. "You could have managed better, it was a poor decision to go with Samuel, your goddamn brother-in-law," she told Raleigh. "Unfortunately, Alex is a true believer, which makes him a punishing husband."

Porter scrolls on his phone. "The boat I've rented called *Moonlight* is docked right at Port St. Joe. I could take you for a spin."

The picture he holds up is of a twenty-four-footer fishing boat, late nineties model. The boat appears soggy, the dock worn; the planks are creosote.

A spin. Dread fills her.

"Very nice," Raleigh lies. "But I have to work on my shells. I'm on a deadline. Thank you."

His hand grazes her upper arm. His touch is smooth, like one of those boy/men who have one-night stands without exchanging a word.

"Okay, we'll stay on land . . . or a drink on the boat, keep her docked. Your choice," he says.

Your choice. "I'd prefer to be on land."

THE SUNSET is a deep orange with pink streaking through the middle when Porter leads Raleigh into the bar at Dune Lounge. A local band is warming up. Someone's strumming a guitar, Southern rock, maybe Leon Russell's "Tight Rope." Chords float toward them.

He holds up his hand to the bartender, fingers in a V. "Two Buds, right, Raleigh?"

Politely she nods, although she won't drink it. He seems

kind to include her in the drink order—or she's desperate to think so, starved for an up-close admirer. The light feels dingy, as if no one ever wipes the bulbs. Was it always this way? Over twenty years ago, when she was in grade school, her father brought the family there after tennis on the public courts. On those Sunday nights when they ordered pepperoni pizza, it felt brighter, cleaner.

Porter holds open his arms. "We could dance."

The bar is filling up, and women are noticing Porter. He's that type—someone will get there first. It doesn't happen often; historically Raleigh has always won the man. Still, prize or no prize, he could be anyone, from a serial killer on the run to someone Alex has hired to spy on her. Raleigh has had a sense of someone lurking in one form or another every visit to Kesgrave. Not that she can identify how she is monitored and watched, only the certainty it happens.

"No one is dancing," Raleigh says.

"Yet." He pulls her in. She decides it is worth it. Up close he banishes her sisters' wrath, her future ex's demands.

AN HOUR LATER they're on the terrace of her room at the Seabreeze Hotel, Main Street, Kesgrave. She ought to explain that she hasn't slept with anyone in two years; the trauma of Samuel, of Alex, lingers. Except when Porter opens the sliding glass door, she decides there is nothing he needs to know. Not tonight.

He looks at the queen bed with white percale linens, gives a thumbs-up. They laugh, then there's this pause. While two years is a long while to be celibate, an unknown man in her hotel room is lunacy.

"Tell me, why Kesgrave?" she asks.

"I wanted to see the area, I told you. I wanted to rent a boat. I wanted to see the architecture."

"The architecture?" She has one last chance to go into the bathroom and google him on her phone.

He puts his arms around her, begins the kisses.

Her fears are tamping down her raging pheromones. He is not like a Palm Beach polished man, some of whom are cardboard, others earnest enough. When the wealthiest come around, Lucinda whispers in Raleigh's ear, *your scandal is over, move on, find a very successful man.* Raleigh has explained to her mother that she can't—*it's my sadness, my shame*. Lucinda hisses back, *get over it.*

Porter moves to the desk, choosing a book-size canvas Raleigh has been working on, a couple in an embrace, the Gulf behind them. There is an exclusiveness about them; there is no arena beyond this moment. She hasn't quite conveyed it so far.

"This one is different from the others," he says.

"I'm mostly a painter. I do lots of portraits. Or I used to. I started this a few days ago, it's at Cape San Blas. I'm not finished."

"You're good . . . talented."

"How would you know?"

Porter laughs. "I only look like a local. In my previous life I went to Yale. I've taken a few undergraduate art history classes. I go to museums. I love paintings, photography, sculpture."

Yale? She nods. She'd like to believe him, how can she be sure? It's awkward. She has made assumptions about this man already, and an Ivy League school isn't among them. There's a nagging sense this is moving quickly, she hasn't been schooled in how to finesse a pickup.

He pulls out his phone, taps on it. "Beautiful Day" begins to play. He leads her around the room. Suddenly she's eight again, peering at Maribelle, her eldest sister, and her high school boyfriend Samuel, dancing in the living room before they left for the prom. Maribelle wore an elegant satin gown sewn by Lucinda, copied from a photo in *Glamour*, and Samuel looked handsome in his rented tux. As they headed out, he took the boutonniere out of the lapel and gave it to Raleigh. She fell for him that night, and for all the years he was married to Maribelle, she loved him.

Porter guides her into a dip and toward the bed. He lifts her up. His shoulders are thick, sheltering. He carries her bride style, carefully placing her against the wall beside the flatscreen. There is a scar over his right eyebrow, his eyes are medium gray; no other color mixes in. He begins with a wide kiss, the kind she used to know when she was single and sought-after. A time where every boy who approached her seemed promising and worth it. If she recalls correctly, she was a major kisser. She opens her mouth totally. What could go wrong? This man is alluring, foreign—his tongue tastes like papaya juice. Porter peels off his T-shirt. His rose tattoo on his upper right arm makes him more "other." She has a random lover in Kesgrave. Yet Raleigh feels Lucinda's reach, her sisters' judgment, as always. They would have a fit.

He stops. "What, what's going on? What's in your head?"

Sheer white curtains are billowing; the fabric is a synthetic blend. Without lamplight, her hotel room is in shades of sea green. She isn't really in the room anyway. She's an astral traveler. Outside it's getting darker.

"Nothing, I'm sorry, nothing."

He kneels down and starts undressing her delicately. Again, the sensation that she might be safe floats toward her. She's surprised; this isn't meant to be tender, merely finite.

"I can't," she says. "I'm concave inside."

He stands up, holds her tight. "Not to me. Let me show you why."

Again, the kisses. They have become line dancers, stepping out of the row together. His voice and touch are like the ocean after a nor'easter, on the third day, when the unrelenting rain and wind gusts have died down. The beach is radiant.

AFTERWARD his phone keeps dinging, and both of them stir—no one could doze through it. He goes onto the terrace, tucking it against the right side of his face. Raleigh suspects it must be urgent, sorrowful. Everything about his beauty becomes a kaleidoscope. Now back at the bed, she's quite still. Then he gets dressed while she's quietly staring.

"I have to go, Raleigh."

"What happened?" She gets out of bed, finds a beach cover-up on the dresser.

"Something terrible."

Who can determine the truth from the lie of a one-night stand? She believes him.

"It won't be okay."

Raleigh likes him much more than is reasonable. They've just met. "Porter, what is it?"

He puts his hands over his face. She shouldn't consider how much she wants him to stay, but she does. They take the five steps to the window.

Below it's like New Year's Eve. The band belts out

"Mr. Jones," people line the streets, some swaying to the song. Porter pauses.

She needs to know where he's going. Instead she says, "You don't have my last name." What is it? Once it had been Barrows, her father's name, then Morton, Alex's name. Today it is no one's name.

He's putting his cell and wallet into his pockets; the room crushes them. Still, she arches her back, edges to his side. When she kisses him, his mouth is hardly open and has no more flavor.

"I know you have to leave," she whispers. "But . . ."

"I saw you at the Pops bar on Monday night. I know who you are."

The band, now slightly off-key, is absurdly loud. Raleigh is uncertain that she heard him—did Porter actually say *I know who you are?* There is no quick text exchange, no selfie before he has to leave, no evidence of further contact.

Already he's at the door, and then he's gone.

Chapter Two

2026

Reeling Raleigh in is always a task. Today Lucinda must finesse a way to bring her youngest daughter back to Palm Beach. By asking Caroline, her pleasing middle child, to make it happen, there's a better chance it will.

Caroline relishes working for Barrows and is certain of the greater good. She, like Lucinda, prefers avoiding family drama and gossip at any cost. When Lucinda called her two nights ago, Caroline signed on at once. "It's about her divorce, isn't it? Raleigh *should* be in Palm Beach, Mom," she said.

"For lawyer meetings and more importantly, for Caleb, to show she is nearby," Lucinda said. "You'll do this, Caroline."

For this purpose, Lucinda impatiently waits in Caroline's library that overlooks the Intracoastal. Caroline's flight back from Savannah for the ribbon-cutting of the seventieth new Barrows location is delayed.

Lucinda paces, lifting silver-framed pictures of Travis, Caroline's husband, and their daughters, from the blond wood sidebar. The photo is several years outdated, Harper, ten at the time, wears lavender, and Violet, eight, is in pale green. As a young mother in this crisp version of family, Caroline has on a zesty print Lilly shift that matches both girls' dresses. Travis, a man who hides behind his sleekest eyeglasses, obviously took them off for this professional photo shoot and is left squinting. He is a requisite husband in his golf clothes. Collectively they are an ideal nuclear family living this sumptuous life in a high-worth town. Isn't that why Lucinda finds Caroline the most dependable, most satisfying of her three daughters? Not her favorite, though—Lucinda is too inscrutable for that.

Caroline sweeps in twenty minutes late in her suede Stella booties and floral dress. A tension infiltrates the room.

"I'm sorry for the holdup, Mom," she says. "And I know this is urgent."

Whenever her daughters call her "Mom," Lucinda knows it's important or they're forgetting her rule. She much prefers "Lucinda" from her daughters and their children. "Grandma" as a name is prohibited.

Lucinda only has ten minutes, but why make a fuss? As if on cue, Caroline smiles one of her "for the staff" smiles. "I'm sure you'll be pleased to know my last round of Barrows stops was a big success."

"I am delighted."

How perfect is it—Lucinda is always pleased—that Caroline is CEO and Travis is CFO of Barrows? Without this, where would Lucinda's place in Palm Beach be? There wouldn't be time to play cards, golf, tennis, even pickleball at the club, to say nothing of the luncheons, social and charity. Caroline and Travis' devotion, bordering on obsession, is invaluable; Lucinda only shows up at the office once a week. "We are on the verge of being a nationwide convenience store chain," Caroline likes to say. "The money rolls in," Travis announces at every family dinner.

Raleigh and Maribelle are another matter. Maribelle, as publisher of *PB Confidential*, the glossiest of the glossies in south Florida, wasn't interested in business. Since Samuel died and she left the magazine, moving to Santa Monica, she has even less interest. Raleigh never cared about Barrows—she is the "artiste."

Yet the risk of her divorce from Alex not going well—not working in her favor—looms ahead. Selling painted shells while galivanting around Kesgrave doesn't cut it.

"We've got to address the Raleigh situation," Lucinda says.

If there is a key to everything, Lucinda needs this figured out, tidied up. Raleigh has to be brought home from Kesgrave. The real issue is that her divorce is fodder for gossip, worsened by her future ex-husband's clichéd choices—presently dating the nanny and before that a nude model for his paintings. Raleigh and Alex were a fine enough couple, although they never embraced Palm Beach as Caroline and Travis have. Maribelle and Samuel positioned themselves well, but those days are long gone. Lucinda isn't about to work on Maribelle and her return to the island while Raleigh must come back.

"Let's FaceTime with her," Caroline suggests. She motions to Lucinda, and they sit across from one another on her butterscotch leather accent chairs. Behind Caroline are her curated books, not organized by genre but by jacket color. "Okay, I'll text to put it into play, see where she is."

Lucinda smooths her hair, runs her tongue over her lips. "One moment, Caroline, I'm not camera ready."

"Mom, this isn't with your friends, you're not being interviewed for *The Daily Sheet*. It's for Raleigh." Caroline's thumbs fly across her phone.

Raleigh's voice is heard within seconds as if she's in a tunnel. "Hey," she says. "I'm at the beach."

Caroline points. "Move over so we can all see each other."

FaceTime is a modern invention Lucinda uses but doesn't relish. She pulls her chair toward Caroline, peers at her phone, then pulls back a few inches.

"Hi, Raleigh. Mom and I are at my house. We need to bring you up to date." Caroline holds up her phone so the three of them are in focus.

Raleigh steps back. The water slaps against the shoreline. "Is Caleb alright?"

"Yes, yes," Caroline says. "He's fine. We just saw him this morning."

"Thankfully. So what's up?"

Lucinda is already annoyed by the call. This daughter isn't the practical one, and physical distance exacerbates it. "We need to talk about custody and . . ."

"Custody? What do you mean? Alex and I haven't even finalized a separation agreement."

Raleigh is shouting, there's a swooshing sound in the background. She is quite tan—has she not heard of sunscreen? Her hair, always wild, is thicker and crazier than usual. She seems alone, far from the world they know. Raleigh stands on the very beach where Lucinda and Reed first drank Southern Comfort in high school. Not that she would claim it—when has Lucinda ever owned that she's from Kesgrave? In a murky, gauzy way, she has no past—Palm Beach is her only home, none other. Mourning former days in a backwater achieves nothing; at least Caroline and Maribelle, even Bryant, get that. Raleigh seems to be the only one who can't put Kesgrave to rest. She's always played it like that—resistant to the social game in Palm Beach. All the more reason to bring her home. Lucinda does not want her there, filled with some twisted nostalgia.

"Listen, Raleigh, Alex is letting everyone know he intends to fight for custody of Caleb. He's hired Jonny Thiers as his lawyer. He's got a whole team of lawyers," Caroline says.

"I'm sorry, we have lawyers, don't we?" Raleigh asks.

Lucinda wishes she had a drink. She and Caroline share a glance. Outside a siren shrieks. An unwelcome sound in Palm Beach that unsettles residents. Lucinda looks toward the bookcase with pictures of Harper and Violet. Her cynicism rises quietly inside her—after enough years go by, Caroline will realize no one gets the children of her dreams.

"I don't believe you. Alex isn't that kind of person."

Lucinda decides on the hard truth. "No one thought so until now. Raleigh, you need to come back tonight . . . tomorrow. He doesn't have only the young nanny anymore but some Mary Poppins type too. He's playing the aggrieved, loyal husband who will do anything for his son while you're in Kesgrave, painting seashells."

Raleigh begins to cry, her face close to the screen, all spectacle and heartbreak.

"The real problem is Alex wants alimony. He wants you to pay him monthly."

Raleigh stops crying. "I'm sorry, what are you saying?"

Caroline holds up her phone. "Alex is getting nasty. You need to be there, at the meetings with your lawyers. You need to show up for Caleb, no matter what the schedule is with Alex in terms of days. You have to be nearby."

Lucinda sighs, aggravated. "Stop hiding, protect your rights. This is about Caleb."

"There are lots of little kids on this beach, Caro, Mom," Raleigh says. "It makes me sad."

"Right," Caroline says. "What about your own child? Are you listening to us?"

There's no answer. Raleigh sniffles more. Hasn't she always been one to split people apart while expecting forgiveness? Lucinda is tired, which is unlike her. She can't be jeopardized in Palm Beach. Her life is here. Her daughters are accountable for what they do, how they lead their lives.

"Let me make this clear, Raleigh," she says. "Around town, as you know, there's plenty of talk about who is married, who splits up, the terms—money and custody. It's one thing to have a soon-to-be-divorced daughter, but I also have one who is widowed. Early widowhood is tragic, a divorcée who fails at the divorce, well, that's something people judge. You know, where she is pushed around, loses access to her child, pays for the husband because she is from a family with means. People will be whispering about it. Worse, whispering about the mother with a daughter who did poorly. I won't be put at a lesser table at fundraisers because of your divorce."

Raleigh opens her mouth, shuts it. More crying.

"What Mom means," Caroline says, "is that you have to fight the fight. Divorces are common, the particulars count. We're with you, but you have to be there in person."

"I see." Raleigh's voice is small. "I remember my wedding . . . he said we could get through anything together."

"There's not enough time to be disappointed, to talk about what a complete prick Alex has turned out to be," Lucinda says.

Both her daughters pause. She doesn't usually speak like that, although they know how she thinks.

"This is where we're at, Raleigh. You just go forward." Caroline, the buffer, chooses her language well, yet she seems exasperated. Beneath her perfectly tailored liner and mascara, her eyes look worn. She has the air conditioning running high like she might be feverish for no reason.

Raleigh is still crying. Lucinda has an urge to mother her, although she admits she's not terribly good at it. Caroline's attempt to soften the news is sufficient. If it were only Raleigh's divorce in the mix, Lucinda might have more patience. Except there is her upcoming sixtieth birthday—two events: a luncheon, women only, and a formal party at the Boat and Oar Club for all. She can't have the news of Alex seeking alimony and claiming he's a starving artist getting around. Women take sides, and he's painted enough successful, admired portraits of them and/or their children. That he falls into the typical mediocre ex-husband bucket won't hold much weight. Lucinda can't afford for this to affect her friendships, for it to become the Raleigh camp versus the Alex camp—which is why some avoid divorce, choose lovers cautiously. Better to pretend you love your husband than suffer endlessly. The issue is that Alex asked for this, making Raleigh's battleground crystal clear. Lucinda needs her daughter home to save face, to put on a convincing exhibit. That would be wise.

Lucinda offers her best Palm Beach smile. "Get on a plane, Raleigh. Get out of Kesgrave and back to us. Soonest."

Chapter Three

2026

In the kitchen, Rosie is setting up fresh orchids in the double sink. Mostly Lucinda has her do this because in Palm Beach, it's what women in the estate section want on their coffee tables. The orchids are bought at Costco, but Lucinda uses Rapunzel Florists in CityPlace when she sends an orchid plant as a gift.

Rosie holds her arms out as if she is expected to serve something. "Mrs. Barrows?" Her eyebrows are close together—they need plucking. "Would you like iced tea?"

"Not now, Rosie," Lucinda says.

"We're good, thank you, Rosie," Maribelle adds. "We've just come from a big meal."

They walk into the library. The room is dramatic and still. After all these years in her Mizner mansion, there isn't a day that Lucinda doesn't admire the architecture and the bougainvillea that envelop her terraces. The library is the darkest of the rooms, filled with requisite shades of champagne couches, loveseats, side chairs. Only the Scalamandré pillows in oranges and turquoise light it up. Somehow this dash of Crayola coloring cheers her.

William is on his iPad, saturated by the screen. Sort of like Caroline's girls. Lucinda finds it surprising how they choose them over books. Except they're young and impressionable. At the lower corner of the bookshelf is *The Custom of the Country* that she's pulled, a title Lucinda looks at when she feels stressed socially. William doesn't notice what she reads.

"Ah, the sixty-year-old belle of the ball!" William offers up air kisses for both Lucinda and Maribelle. More social than personal, if she cares. "Can you believe your mother is sixty?" he asks Maribelle, his eyes still on Lucinda.

"Not really," Maribelle says. She's so nonchalant that Lucinda suspects she might be sarcastic in a guarded way. Still, having her eldest daughter home and staying with her, after almost two years in Southern California, is a reward, a long overdue visit that coincides with this milestone birthday.

"You are kind," Lucinda says.

As if that's enough conversation, William goes back to his iPad. Lucinda dreads the day he becomes part of the complacent old man in Florida syndrome. The ones who drive so poorly that family and friends avoid being in the car with them. Men who forget dates despite their calendars, fiddle with their hearing aids, and yawn constantly. Presently he is still tolerable—he knows the rule about no dental flossing if she's in a five-foot radius, and while the skin around his eyes has become grainy and his eyebrows curve downward, he remains attractive, falling into the category of good enough, which is an asset. She likes it best when he still works on his hedge fund—once the center of his life—and burns brain cells. In a broader sweep, she knows he's someone who will do the right thing.

Maribelle kicks off her wedges—at least she hasn't abandoned wearing shoes that add five inches. She's extremely pale, looking more like Raleigh than in the past, an odd twist considering what has happened between her daughters. Lucinda swats that out of her head to avoid any thoughts of tension in the family. She has worked carefully and constructed a life cleverly. Her birthday has a chance at bringing everyone together.

"My mother does not look sixty," Maribelle says.

"Well, it is happening," William says. "We'll fete her all the way. A roster of celebrations."

"It is bold to celebrate your sixtieth birthday in this town," Lucinda says. "Everyone lies about their age and what they've had done . . . and we are broadcasting it."

"And you've never had a facelift," Maribelle says.

"Hear, hear!" William holds up his glass of port. Port—really?

Is it a compliment? Lucinda can't tell. Bryant, six months older, has let her hair go white. She has no fears or worries—or few—when it comes to where she fits in. Why would she? Whatever occurs in her life is a reflection of what Lucinda yields. Bryant is everywhere Lucinda goes. For every party, celebration, or charity bash Lucinda attends, Bryant is her guest. She is close to Lucinda's daughters, as if they are hers. The grandchildren too. As a fellow shareholder, Bryant is in lockstep with the family when it comes to any Barrows gains.

Rosie stands at the doorway, a manila envelope in her hand. She waves it slightly. "Mrs. Barrows, this came while you were out."

"That's very plain. Is it an understated invitation? Are there others, Rosie?" Lucinda supposes not because it is the first week in February. The piles of creative, hand-delivered "for the season" invitations arrived in the fall through January. She checks her gold Cartier Tank watch, one of the last gifts from Reed before he dropped dead playing bridge. She has less than two hours before the Palm Beach Literary Society fundraiser begins, a charity event with a rather good cocktail hour. She'd prefer to arrive on the early side.

"It came for you." Rosie places it on the Biedermeier coffee table.

Lucinda nods, scrolling on her phone for missed calls and texts. "Thank you. I'm sure those are the menus for my birthday. I wonder when they're sending the votive samples."

Maribelle stands up. The envelope catches her eye, she lifts it. "Wow, how old-fashioned, obsolete really. Look at this cursive handwriting. It reads *Lucinda Barrows*, two inches high."

Lucinda has put her earbuds in. "I'm sorry, what did you say?"

"Nothing, I'm heading upstairs and fine for six o'clock." Maribelle puts it on the desk. A text comes in and she's distracted. She plunks back down on the couch.

Lucinda takes her tortoise reading glasses, the same pair she keeps in every room in the house and puts them on. She opens the envelope to find another envelope inside, a standard ten by four inches. The same handwriting, smaller, reads *Lucinda Matthews*, a name she hasn't seen in decades, having married Reed Barrows forty-two years ago. A name that smacks of Kesgrave, fishing fleets, gas stations, the storms off the Apalachicola River. Is it from one of Reed's relatives, a hometown third cousin once removed, writing to ask for money? This had happened before when Reed was alive, and he quickly sent a few thousand dollars here, a few thousand there. Anything to keep them far away, he'd say. Lucinda doubts many of those clannish cousins would seek her out now.

Still, the air feels tighter. It isn't distributed evenly; she could gasp for oxygen in the middle of the library. She walks to the card table on the opposite side, sits facing away from Maribelle and William, and begins to read.

"Mom, what are you wearing tonight? How dressed will you be?" Maribelle's voice dips in and out like bad reception on a phone call. Lucinda should go upstairs but can't draw attention to herself. Maribelle will notice, and there will be more questions—what exact time they'll leave, who's at the table the Barrows bought. Lucinda is oddly queasy; her heart beats unevenly.

The inside is printed in what looks like Helvetica.

KESGRAVE

I grew up in a place where nothing got fixed, from a broken screen door to a pitted boat bottom to a darkest secret. None of us had money; we wore cheap clothes and ate fresh fish. In grade school, we watched the fleets come in—we thought it entertainment, like swatting green head flies. We played jacks on the empty roads, those summer days. At least we had each other. My two best friends and I were together hours on end. We sat in each other's bedrooms, passing around Maybelline mascara and Revlon lipsticks from Kmart. Northwest Florida doesn't really have winters, but we celebrated the colder weather. Each of us had a father whose heavy boots stomped against the kitchen floor. They worked for the local builders, moving from one job to the next. Our mothers—called homemakers back then—seemed bored and were beautiful. They made sandwiches from jelly and called them "jam sandwiches," pretending to be fancy.

By ninth grade my friends and I had portable record players in our musty basements—listening to Elton John or Janis Joplin while everyone else liked Barry Manilow. We wanted bras and bell-bottoms, and we hoped to be kissed. We lied to our parents so we could meet boys on the beach on Saturday nights. We watched them tilt their heads back, chugging out of their grandfathers' flasks. We kissed those boys feverishly like it was a sport, one you had to win.

If we couldn't find someone's cousin or older brother to drive us to the river, there were empty garages to sneak into. Another spot was the Regal movie theatre. Once we were outed for saying we'd gone to see The Muppet Movie but had sneaked into Kramer vs. Kramer where a woman abandons her husband and small son for some unexplained reason.

I was the girl in the shortest minidress, I wore cowboy boots from Destin, bought at Kraft's discount shop. But as much as I tried, I felt like an outsider while they were set, they fit in, they would stay. Still, we three made a pact, drew blood from our fingertips to be sworn to one another. I had to trust them, didn't I?

You might ask why this confession now, where is it going. I want you to know how far I've come. I want to explain, finally, what happened, to tell you the truth.

"Lucinda?" William asks. "What is it?"

He and Maribelle are watching her.

"What are you reading?" Maribelle asks. "Are you alright?"

"Nothing, actually," Lucinda says. Her lie is obvious, and

defeat rises inside her. Had she known, of course she would not have opened it.

"I think it's meant for the office." She stands. "I'm going to get dressed for tonight. You might want to start, Maribelle."

Thankfully, Maribelle's cell rings. William returns to the iPad. Lucinda manages to get to the hallway and into the laundry room. Rosie is folding sheets with the precision of a navy officer.

"Rosie, where did this come from, this letter?" She holds it up for a moment.

Rosie lifts Lucinda's favorite lime and white floral pillowcases, usually a rather heartwarming sight. Lucinda gives her a minute, feigning calm.

"A messenger service. I'm not sure which one, Mrs. Barrows."

"Did you see the messenger? Or what the courier looked like?"

Rosie stares at her. "I did not."

Suddenly Lucinda is jolted in that way she barely remembers, an old, long-ago sensation rising in this moment. "Excuse me, Rosie."

In her guest bathroom she rereads the last line: *I want you to know how far I've come. I want to explain, finally, what happened, to tell you the truth.* The truth. The truth is dead. No one cares. Reed is dead. What would be the point unless she is being blackmailed years later? To what end—why would that be? "The truth" would be dangerous. Lucinda tears the pages into thumb-size squares and flushes several batches down the nearly soundless toilet. Once the last one has swirled and flushed, she kneels over the bowl and throws up.

Looking in the Lalique oval mirror, she pats her face with a monogrammed hand towel and rinses her mouth with Scope from the cabinet below. In the middle drawer she finds blush and a compact, kept there in case someone arrives early or late and she's downstairs, not at her dressing table, or when she is hosting an essential dinner and cannot go far for a touch-up.

As she enters the hallway, she sees William heading upstairs. His shorts with small green frogs embroidered over the light blue cotton seem frivolous, even if they prove he's a golfer, engaged in a sport. He is an original Palm Beacher, too Palm Beach for what is ahead—unless he is her fire extinguisher, a man to save the day. Reed is long gone, and William is her husband. *Husband.* Someone she needs—that's the discovery of the moment. Until now, William has done well to merely fill the right chair.

Chapter Four

1994

HALF-EMPTY CANS of Diet Coke are on the side tables, proof that a good idea only lasts an hour. The summer air in Kesgrave is heavy in a way Lucinda never appreciates or has gotten used to. By midday it blows off the river, past the banks into her tight, square living room. The open windows make little difference. The air conditioner is useless. They have to get a new one, but Reed keeps putting it off. Not that she will stay in this cottage forever—not another year, were it up to her.

"We shouldn't bake apples on the hottest afternoons," Bryant says.

She waves to stir the air. Lucinda notices how thin Bryant seems these days, willowy, not enough flesh for any amount of heat to bother her, or so it appears because Lucinda is in her last month. Her arms have lost their graceful curve and her face is full, making Bryant and Ruth-Ann, her two best friends, look prettier than they are. Their chins and cheekbones have become delicate, angular.

"But it's your favorite. You ate them every day for the first two girls."

"You suppose it's another girl," Lucinda says. "Isn't that what you mean?"

"Who knows?" Ruth-Ann smiles.

Ruth-Ann looks the best of the three friends, girlish, youngest in her short shorts with a tank top. In brown no less, a color that is popular but drab. Lucinda is too pregnant to be enticing while Bryant is the one who should be glowing—she's getting married in the fall. Ruth-Ann is not remotely interested in being a bridesmaid; she hasn't a thought beyond her photography. But her brother is the groom, so she must.

"It'll be a boy." Ruth-Ann sounds confident.

"We'll see," Lucinda says.

"I don't know," Bryant says, "you could have a girl or a boy and be happy, Lucinda. You've already got your daughters."

Predictions annoy Lucinda. "It's nice to be the right age to have a baby, that's all. Reed and I were kids when we started."

"You grew up together." Bryant sounds wise. Her fiancé, Bud, Reed's dearest friend, has been her boyfriend for ten years. Only six months ago they became engaged.

The knotty beige fabric on the recliner makes the back of Lucinda's legs itch. Reed favors the chair; it makes him feel he is in charge, a man who comes home from work and pushes himself into a vertical position to listen to news on the radio.

Bryant lights up a Virginia Slim—she's read they are popular. Lucinda taps her belly.

"You can blow that smoke over here. Once I drop this one, I'll smoke them on my own."

Everyone laughs. They'd been smoking together since junior high, sneaking packs of cigarettes from Ruth-Ann's grandfather's store. Back then Lucinda never liked it when they sat in the old dinghies near the cove to smoke—except for how they traded their secrets with every exhale. As the most coveted girls in Kesgrave, they believed anything was possible. For Lucinda it was heady stuff—she had worked her way into their sphere. She came from a poor family, a hard-to-shake fact. The only reason Lucinda fit in was her popularity and her looks. Bryant and Ruth-Ann had to be her friends, she wanted to be with them. They didn't worry about money or have to pretend things were better than they were. Lucinda edged in with her charm and wit, then became the leader.

The three of them would whisper their plans about leaving this hellhole in the Florida Panhandle. They'd secure scholarships—academic for Lucinda and Bryant, art for Ruth-Ann—travel to New York, Paris, Rome. Except instead Lucinda was pregnant at eighteen, and Ruth-Ann's parents wanted her to work in the store—her photography was a hobby to them. Bryant would follow whatever plan rolled out. She liked that the Humphreys—Ruth-Ann and Bud's family—were more successful than most, with their two convenience stores in the Panhandle. It was enough for her.

At least, Lucinda consoled herself, after her first two girls were born, she'd gone to Saturn, the local college two towns over. She chose to be a schoolteacher as a form of escape. She cared about her work and began to earn some money. When she assigned *Ethan Frome*, *A Tale of Two Cities* and *The Great Gatsby* to her students, she'd pretend she was teaching at a private school, as if the whole experience was happening elsewhere.

Ruth-Ann finishes wiping the lens of her prized Canon with a faded seashell motif dish towel.

Lucinda laughs. "Getting married isn't the hard part, it's after that. What no one tells you."

"Reed is a find," Bryant says. She looks out toward the river. "I mean he and Bud . . . I don't know better men."

"I agree," Ruth-Ann says. She lifts three magazines out of an Acme Market bag and passes them around, like a high school teacher handing back papers. "Here, let's start. We ought to figure out the menu, the hall, what kind of music. Plus we've got our flower girls."

On cue, Lucinda's girls, with Maribelle leading Caroline, run inside, both in braids with freckles in galaxies across their faces. Lucinda likes how, at ten and eight, they are mini versions of her, disparate from other Kesgrave girls. How else could they be? There isn't another mother for miles around who has Lucinda's style or aspirations. And her daughters are unlike each other. Maribelle is already a fashion diva. Caroline plays ball and fishes, bossing around the boys in her third-grade class.

Maribelle comes over to her mother, who is flipping through the pages of *McCall's*. "Are the flower girl dresses in there?" She begins taking out her braids, her hair flows crazily.

"Not yet," Bryant says. "Let's be patient."

"You'll wear matching dresses," Lucinda says. "Or dresses that go together."

"Why?" Maribelle asks. "Why is Caroline in the wedding?"

Caroline shoots her sister the finger while Lucinda and Bryant turn the pages. "Tell her, Mom," she says. "Tell her Aunt Bryant wants me there."

Bryant looks up. "True, I invited you both to be in my wedding. Walking down that aisle ahead of the bridesmaid." She speaks in her softest voice, the one that makes everyone feel they themselves are borderline hysterics.

"There's only one. I'm that person. Since my brother is

the groom," Ruth-Ann says. She swaps out her Nikon for her Canon. "Look at this!"

"Another camera?" Lucinda asks. "How many do you need?"

"It's digital," Ruth-Ann says. "I'm having a blast with the images, even if the quality isn't great." She starts clicking the shots.

Bryant turns the dial on Lucinda's radio to "I Will Always Love You" by Whitney Houston. "We should choose a few songs. Maybe this could be our first dance."

"First dance?" Maribelle asks. "What is that?"

"A ritual," Lucinda says. "One where the bride and groom go out alone on the dance floor and everyone watches. They are royalty for that night."

"Did you do it at your wedding to Dad, Mom?" Maribelle asks. She roots through her mother's makeup bag, then taps her face with pressed powder from her Maybelline compact.

Lucinda looks away. "No, no dancing the night I married your father."

"Why, Mom?" Caroline asks.

"We were in a hurry, that's what happened," Lucinda says.

"Six girls from my senior class got married before graduation," Ruth-Ann said. "One pumps gas, one . . ."

"Ruth-Ann." Bryant sighs. "Please."

"I'm just saying wouldn't it be nice to leave, at least for a while?" Ruth-Ann is earnest. "You know, get a degree, meet other people."

"You've always thought like this. You never wanted to be with a cool boy, the cutest ones at Pinestream, and make your bed here," Lucinda says. She's drinking a small carton of chocolate milk with a straw. She tilts her head toward the refrigerator and both girls jump up to get their own.

"What Bud loves to do is fish. Bud's a fisherman." Bryant speaks in a low tone.

Ruth-Ann stares at Bryant. "Don't say that to my brother. As far as our family goes, Bud's the legacy—the stores are like a miracle. There should be more. The sooner he stops shrimping, the better."

"He's not only a fisherman, unless you want him to be. He could go anywhere. Any of us could. Bud and Reed, they'd be able to build something up," Lucinda says.

Bryant looks away. "They should be back soon. We'll grill catfish for an early supper. The girls might start shucking the corn."

Lucinda fans herself with a copy of *Good Housekeeping*. "Don't you ever think it has to get better than this? That this isn't all there is?"

"All what is?" Bud stands at the back door.

Beside Reed, the two men are equally tall, over six feet, both in waders. When Reed takes off his baseball cap, Bud does the same. Although the rule is they clean up with the hose and soap before they come in, their hands always smell fishy.

The women and girls become quiet. When her daughters look at her, Lucinda nods. Maribelle and Caroline run toward Reed. Ruth-Ann goes back to her Canon, snapping every frame. Bryant and Bud look deep into each other's eyes—how it goes before the wedding. Lucinda, never religious, prays for a path out. No matter the cost.

Chapter Five

2026

MONEY IS EVERYTHING. Lucinda stands at the wide windows of Barrows headquarters, repeating this like a mantra. Below, in the lambent light, mostly women scurry in and out of the shops along South County Road. *Money.* It has always mattered most to her. In several weeks, Lucinda, who has earned her place in society, will be celebrated for her birthday. She will line up with the wealthiest of them all in Palm Beach, people she calls friends, those who wouldn't dare *not* be friendly. This matters too much to her for anything to be in jeopardy; there can be no threat to her social success.

She moves back into the center of her office, which once belonged to Reed, that dashing, half-disarming, half-annoying deceased husband. While every room on the Barrows floors exudes sophisticated mid-century furniture—Breuer chairs, an Ed Wormley card table, a Nakashima desk—it is the contemporary art, Rothenberg, Schnabel, Johns, that makes one catch their breath. In the mix is a requisite portrait of Reed by Raleigh. It's quite lifelike. Sometimes Lucinda believes the eyes follow her, like in a second-rate Halloween film. The atmosphere of her office implies a family steeped in collecting, sophistication, and wealth, as if they hadn't arrived a moment ago, as they say about newcomers (a presence of less than a half century) in Palm Beach.

In the family's brief twenty-two years on the island, Lucinda has become known for setting the stage. Country clubs, charities, yacht parties at sunset, one mansion per daughter before Maribelle became a widow and Raleigh's pending divorce. She has infiltrated impressively. Although at times a thankless task, she has done her best to teach her daughters well. Appearances win out, of course, and Palm Beachers have noted the smooth ride for the Barrows, the mothers and daughters stylish, real beauties. With Lucinda at the helm, there is no second-guessing, no regret. How ingeniously she has choreographed their lives, how masterful her skills. Beyond all wins—cards, luncheons, causes, golf and tennis matches—is the satisfaction of being a Palm Beach lady.

Estelle, Reed's onetime personal assistant who has seen everything, comes into the office. She twists her hands twice, a sign she's uneasy. Her neck has become craggy over two decades, and today her dress is wrinkled with a coffee stain on the cuff. Lucinda considers whether it is of value to mention this and decides against it. Estelle is the only woman Lucinda believes *should* go gray; her rationale is that coloring one's hair badly is worse than no hair dye. Not that Lucinda would ever be in either situation. Her own is well preserved—blondish streaks over darker hair with a surprising natural shine, falling to the shoulders—perfected by Didi at George's. She must appear youthful and ageless, particularly now that her daughters (secretly she and William) are hosting her birthday bashes.

By habit, Estelle begins lowering the off-white Hunter Douglas shades using a remote control. She's been in these offices so long she used to do it manually, a time drain compared to this invention. Lucinda watches her with pity and impatience.

"Mrs. Barrows, Ms. Bryant is in the reception area."

"Here? Have I missed something on the schedule? Do she and I have a plan?"

"There isn't a plan."

"That makes more sense," Lucinda says. "I mean, I'm at Barrows one day a week. It's pretty piled up . . . do you know what she wants?"

Estelle places the remote on the edge of the desk. "She says she has to see you."

"Has to?"

How unlike Bryant, who has always finessed calm and containment. She has never before barged into the office. Lucinda adjusts her Vhernier rose-gold hoops and Graff rose-gold pavé diamond bangles, checks her phone. In an hour she is off to Longgreens for her afternoon bridge game—a game she always wins.

"That's fine, Estelle."

THEY NOD without an actual hello. Bryant is the essence of understatement. Lucinda's favorite motto, "When in doubt, overdress in Palm Beach," is lost on her. Her cropped trousers and ballerina flats are a bore, as if she's doing errands incognito. Bryant spends her days volunteering for charities, favoring Mothers and Children as a cause, and pays little attention to the "scene." Nor does she inquire about the success of Barrows—she knows it steadily ascends. She's financially secure since Reed gave her a great deal of stock back in the day.

"You didn't drive over to talk about the centerpieces for my birthday, Bryant, did you?"

It's a reasonable assumption since Lucinda spends hours thinking about her beauty, her age, and her position in Palm Beach. At least once a day she discloses she's turning sixty to anyone who will listen. Mostly people say how young she looks. Forty-eight seems to be the consensus, which is satisfying if not quite a youthful number.

"Of course not." Bryant looks grim.

Lucinda does a sweep with her right hand. They should sit facing one another. She slides behind the desk, and Bryant sits across.

"Did you want Caroline to come say hello? She's just down the hall." Lucinda coughs slightly.

"I know that she's in the offices, but no need," Bryant says. "I've come to see you alone, privately."

"Okay." Lucinda frowns—almost, since her forehead doesn't really move. Bryant is so deliberate, which is baffling. "What is it, Bryant?"

"You and I, we've been together since kindergarten."

"Oh, I get it, we didn't do anything for your sixtieth two months ago and look at mine. We did take you to the Harbor Club, and I hosted two tables including your friends like Vivienne and Sunny whom I'm not fond of. You're upset. You're about to guilt me, say our grandmas and aunts were friends. The men worked together—those fishing fleets, the crabbing."

Bryant shakes her head. "No, I'm not. But I do remember everything. And your uncles, the worn-out motels, your father never having work."

Lucinda appraises Bryant. She isn't as pretty as usual; she's stringy—her arms have loose skin instead of tight muscles. The lines around her eyes and mouth show. If only she weren't holier than thou she'd go to Sienna Tram and have them Botoxed to oblivion. She could use some filler. Lucinda could get her an appointment tomorrow.

"Bryant? Will you help guide Raleigh with her divorce? It's a mess. You know, do your fairy godmother, unofficial aunt routine?"

"Of course I will. Lucinda, I'm here for you, for her."

Lucinda isn't listening; she keeps going. "Right, my wistful daughter, the one who couldn't follow the script, as facile as it was. Why not marry the right man and have an affair with an old flame, not your sister's husband?"

Bryant looks away. "I'll pretend you didn't say that."

Lucinda fidgets, so unlike her. Neither speaks for a moment.

"Has Raleigh reached out to you? Because I need her to . . ."

"No, that's not it," Bryant says. "I've come with news."

Lucinda can't recall a time when Bryant has been the bearer of meaningful news. It is Lucinda who disseminates news. Bryant is a staunch supporter of the Barrows enterprise (family and business), and she rarely leads in any manner. The friendship the two women share comes second to being the caring "aunt" to Lucinda's daughters. For years the girls have depended on Bryant for equanimity.

Lucinda is staring at Bryant. The light has shifted—a favorite hour of day at a certain age. Bryant's face is softened, more in repose.

"What is it?" Lucinda asks.

"It's about Ruth-Ann. I've come about Ruth-Ann."

A slick coat of fear comes over Lucinda. The room shuts off. She's there again with her best friends, on the beach in

Cape San Blas. Long enough ago to be forgotten. Has Bryant heard from Ruth-Ann? The thought of it—how wrong that would be, what Ruth-Ann would tell her—sloshes in her head. She had Ruth-Ann's word that Bryant would never know. She gathers herself together. "I haven't seen Ruth-Ann in decades." Lucinda ought to say she's sorry they haven't kept up, that's how life is.

"I know," Bryant says. "Nor have I."

"So what about her? Is she in town?" Lucinda asks. Yet she knows it isn't the case. This has to be serious. Bryant's eyes are colorless, her mouth is pulled.

"Ruth-Ann died. I read it this morning in *The New York Times*."

Dead. Ruth-Ann no longer living on earth. A flash memory of her those summers, her pastel printed skirts, narrow shoulders, flip-flops. How she only cared that her work was the best ever.

"Not a paid obituary. A real one, about her life. It turns out she was a big success," Bryant says.

She doesn't look at Lucinda. The slick coat of fear amplifies.

"Does it include her humble beginnings?" Lucinda asks.

"Nothing like that. It was about her talent as a photographer. She had a one-word name."

"A photographer," Lucinda says. "Is that how she managed a large obituary?" While the reality of Ruth-Ann feels fainter, like the relief of a receding tropical storm in Florida, Lucinda can't help but wonder how she deserved such an accolade.

"I thought you knew. I've followed her, somewhat. She'd done very well. She lived in college towns and taught.

I mean you can read it yourself. I tried to forward it and nothing went through. Google her."

Lucinda comes closer to Bryant. Although she has not seen Ruth-Ann in decades, that she died is a blow, that she's been plucked from what was once a threesome and now there's less.

"What name did she go by?"

"Calypso," Bryant says. "From Greek mythology. Calypso was a nymph and Atlas' daughter. Anyway, Ruth-Ann's photos are highly respected. She'd become an expert at . . ."

Like the ladies who lunch, Lucinda smiles one of her high-level fake smiles. "I'm sorry, Bryant, I've got to get on a call with the lawyers for Raleigh. If you want to wait for me in the conference room, we could leave together in twenty, maybe thirty minutes."

"Let's do that. I'm a bit sad, to be honest," Bryant says. She's fussing with her pendant, a moon on one side, a star on the other. With diamond chips. Simple yet symbolic.

A bit sad. Lucinda is anything but that. Rather, she's imagining how freeing a death proves to be on occasion. The secret dies too. What perfect timing.

Chapter Six

2026

WITHOUT HER SISTERS or Nicola or Bree, friends from the Academy, Raleigh enters the Lake Trail on Royal Poinciana Way. It's five o'clock, soon to be Caleb's dinner time. He's with Alex until tomorrow midday when they swap. Tonight she is meant to be sketching for the Lavendar family, the mother and her two daughters by the grand piano. Like the Renoir at the Met, Sara Lavendar said, where the girls have eyes only for their mother. Of course, why not? "Motherhood, the most revered and reviled profession," Lucinda likes to say. It wasn't until Raleigh was in sixth grade that Aunt Bryant told her that was not an original Lucinda observation; it came from Betty Friedan's book, *The Feminist Mystique*, a bible of sorts for her mother until she married William. Once that happened, the book was hidden somewhere or donated along with other titles so as not to rattle her second husband, whom Raleigh and her sisters label "the man who rarely speaks."

Along the water are egrets and cormorants while swallows fly overhead. Raleigh steps back; she has never appreciated birds. When Reed used to birdwatch in Kesgrave, only Caroline would go along. When they moved to Palm Beach and Reed birdwatched at the end of the day, Lucinda wanted the girls to try again. Although Lucinda rarely cared, it was Aunt Bryant who had binoculars and could identify the songbirds.

Most of the strollers and runners are long gone—in order to be seen, one has to go before 9 a.m. Her mother only goes at peak hours, yet Aunt Bryant usually avoids the tumult, which is why Bryant has asked Raleigh to meet now. Instead of it being a scene, another "who's who" walk, it's quiet. People are at home, costuming for a dinner party or a charity event, the best table at Tutto Mare, Coco's, Kyma. Raleigh and Aunt Bryant have not been on the Lake Trail together in months. She isn't sure why since no one has listened more patiently to Raleigh's travails than her aunt.

Streamlined boats glide along the Intracoastal. Raleigh turns away, which is absurd. There will always be waterways—they're in Palm Beach. She needs to heal, become Buddhist or something, learn to not be triggered. Her memory of Samuel on his Riva Rivamare that morning has to stop. Will she always be haunted, no matter what steps she takes toward a new life? Will she ever be game to get on a boat again?

"Ah, Raleigh, am I late?" Aunt Bryant is slightly out of breath. She dabs her eyes with a linen handkerchief that has her initials, likely a gift from Lucinda since no one else would bother with a monogram. She's in pale green yoga pants and a sweatshirt. Raleigh should have brought a jacket; the temperature is cooling down.

"No, of course not, Aunt Bryant, you're never late."

A voice from behind. "Am I late?"

Maribelle. Why is she here? She looks older today, as if she's drained by her return to Palm Beach. Apparently, she's become a product of the crunchy part of LA, in contrast to Caroline, who sports the highest cheekbones known to womankind. That Maribelle needs a touch-up by Palm Beach standards is obvious; she has gone au naturel. Raleigh is surprised Lucinda isn't all over it already.

"I am happy to be with both of you," Aunt Bryant says.

"I had no idea about this." Maribelle looks at Aunt Bryant as if she is alone with her. Raleigh doesn't exist.

"Nor did I," Raleigh says. "I'm not certain what's going on."

It's a valiant effort to get Maribelle and Raleigh to speak. A few people have come onto the path around them and pass by, fast and slow. Everyone seems to be paired—like in the morning, like how the world is.

Aunt Bryant has set her up; Raleigh is supposed to be alone with her, to share thoughts on Caleb, her divorce—a subject she talks about nonstop these days. Raleigh knows she's become a bore. Her best friends, including Nina and Lacey, stared at their phones and off in the distance at La Marina on Tuesday at a lunch. There was nothing they could contribute, plus Raleigh had said it all before.

Aunt Bryant, the orchestrator, is standing between them. She starts walking. Since neither Raleigh nor Maribelle would defy her, they join in.

"Tell us, Maribelle," Aunt Bryant says. "How is the climate in Marina del Rey? I've not been there for over a decade."

"I'm in Santa Monica, really. Two towns away, also on the west side. Not like the ninety percent humidity clinging to the palm trees in south Florida." Maribelle sounds unfriendly, remote. Although she has honed manners, clearly she has no interest in being there.

"Maybe today, but not always is it humid," Aunt Bryant says. "You remember that, I'm sure."

"It's humid enough of the time," Maribelle says. As if she never thrived or had a life in Palm Beach.

Aunt Bryant hastens her pace. Both sisters scurry along until it's a fast clip. "Well, sometimes you feel it and other times not. Probably like on the West Coast."

Maribelle looks only at Aunt Bryant. "The air in Southern California has a smooth, breeze-at-your-neck texture."

"Excellent," Aunt Bryant says.

"Well, the vista is reversed—the ocean is to the west," Raleigh says.

Maribelle's gaze is over the Intracoastal. "It's the vibe. On my lunch break I'm at Abbot Kinney or Montana Avenue where I watch in-love couples. In Venice Beach there are no men with paunchy bellies, no lumpy women. Everyone of every age seems taut and buff. They have runners' calves. Almost like I traded life in Palm Beach for a new set of standards in Hollywood. People are glamorous, hip, preserved in both places, still I prefer California—at least it's about creativity."

They're moving quickly, Raleigh and Maribelle facing straight ahead when they speak with Aunt Bryant.

"Are you dating, Maribelle?" Aunt Bryant asks. "Do you miss Palm Beach?"

What probing. Awkward, nosy, even if Raleigh and her sisters forgive Aunt Bryant anything.

"No, not one bit. At night I read poets, Edna St. Vincent Millay and Stevie Smith. Sometimes Thomas Hardy. Or play songs I was raised on that Samuel never liked, what you and Lucinda played for us. You know, Bon Jovi, 'Livin' on A Prayer.' 'Thank You' by Led Zeppelin, 'Touch of Grey' by the Grateful Dead."

"That wouldn't be happening here," Raleigh says. "Now Mom goes to symphonies and ballets."

Maribelle lunges forward, ignoring Raleigh.

"Well, you have a life engineered by grit, far from the Barrows clan," Aunt Bryant says.

Raleigh can't tell if this is a compliment or an observation. "How is it going with work in LA, Maribelle?"

She asks to be polite but knows something of it already. Lucinda couldn't resist telling her the remarkable news that Maribelle, on her own, had gotten a gig as a consultant for a new streaming series, *Florida Strong*, for an edgy venture. An ideal storyline—an ex-cop from the Keys investigates strange, inexplicable crimes. Maribelle is second only to the showrunner. Her authenticity as a native of the Florida Panhandle has really paid off.

"I hope it is very successful," Aunt Bryant says.

"It is and will be." Maribelle glares at Raleigh as she speaks.

Failure, grief, loss—they wash over Raleigh. Maribelle's stint in LA has brought an amorphous, flimsy relief. Were it not for Lucinda's birthday, Raleigh imagines her sister wouldn't be back. Not after staying at Lucinda's, where every room is in an off-white overlay, vogue, predictable, some of the fabrics stiff and bristly. While Raleigh, her life in flux, is designated to live at Caroline's, another home mapped out in white and off-white.

"Don't you ever miss *PB Confidential*?" Raleigh asks.

Maribelle says nothing. The three of them move faster.

"Maribelle?" Raleigh asks again.

"I believe Raleigh is asking if you miss being the editorial director, with that juicy gossip?" Aunt Bryant asks.

Maribelle stares straight ahead. "You mean the twisted

feature articles? I look forward to getting back to LA. Right now I'm working remotely to keep up with our series."

Aunt Bryant squints at her Apple Watch. "You'll be fine, Maribelle. Stay through the celebrations for Lucinda, that's what's needed."

"There's no other choice, is there? Besides, I do love seeing the family."

Her tone is chilling. Raleigh knows she is excluded from "the family" for these purposes. Maribelle's anger toward her seems to be rising daily. Raleigh has wrongly assumed that she was forgiven, somewhat. Foolish, really, since the last time the two of them spoke two years ago, Raleigh confessed to being Maribelle's dead husband's lover.

AUNT BRYANT'S CELL RINGS, and she comes to a halt. The sisters wait for her, looking out at the Intracoastal in opposite directions. The wind is forceful, shifting from the east to the west, yet the bigger boats don't rock. Maribelle zips her taupe vest.

"Of course I will. Yes, yes, no worries." Aunt Bryant holds up her hand to signal she wants another minute.

Maribelle comes closer. Raleigh imagines something magical will happen. She and her favorite sister will reconcile. They'll be confidantes again, everything forgiven and forgotten. The first thing they'll do together is a mani-pedi at the Eau, side by side, not a care in the world. Then Maribelle whispers, "Do you know what I think of to soothe myself, Raleigh? How soon I'll be boarding my Delta flight back to LAX. How living thousands of miles away from Palm Beach is like having wings."

"Maribelle, please." Raleigh begins to cry, quiet slurps.

Maribelle hisses through her whisper. "Don't you get it, Raleigh? If I ever thought I could get over what you did, I know now I can't. Being back, seeing you, it's like eating rancid tuna salad."

"I am sorry. I thought we were better, I thought you had made some peace . . ."

Maribelle is almost crying; her pupils are wide, her eyes dark. "You and I are not speaking. I'd walk through a pile of manure to keep away. I only keep up appearances for Lucinda and Aunt Bryant. We are not sisters anymore."

Chapter Seven

2026

As much as Lucinda savors winning at tennis, golf, and bridge at Longgreens, it is the hushed, lush women's locker room at the club that appeals to her the most. An elegant, immaculate room that suspends time. Cell phones aren't allowed, women discreetly shower, younger members gravitate toward the blow dryers and array of anti-frizz products in the "hair room." For those over fifty who are wedded to their biweekly blowouts at George's or Danielle's, the "makeup bar" holds the most promise. The question of who wears what lingers. Even the golf skirts are worth eyeing in terms of style and swing. No one dons anything from a discount store or Amazon—perish the thought. The lunch crowd, skipping the sports, is dressed carefully: Akris slacks, Roger Vivier flats, an out-of-nowhere Prada day skirt, Jenni Kayne cotton sweaters. For Lucinda the locker room is an unofficial fashion show, a cheat sheet; she sees it there first.

When Caroline calls, Lucinda picks up and sneaks off toward the far corner for a moment. "I can't talk," she tells her. "I'm getting changed for doubles."

"About the girls, I want to know if you'll be able to . . ." Caroline is speaking quietly.

"Later, Caroline. I only picked up to make sure it isn't a crisis of some sort." Lucinda rings off before Caroline can complete her request. She begins unzipping her dress, kicking off her mid-heel Manolos. This moment is a respite from her vexing—to varying degrees—daughters. Were she not preoccupied with her birthday celebrations, she'd be more irritated by Maribelle and Raleigh's cold war, ready for a new tact.

Under the most sympathetic lighting, Lucinda pats mineral sunscreen on her cheekbones and contemplates her next move. Two rows over, she overhears a conversation. The women aren't visible, yet Lucinda knows at once who they are. The thin, low buzz of the locker room, the calm of it, is punctured by Blair Jazzer, the CEO of Inright. As a glamorous working mother and wife in her early fifties, she garners attention. In hushed tones, she and Nellie Kean are sharing complaints.

Not that Lucinda knows Blair well, but she's almost always in *The Daily Sheet* and *PB Confidential* and at charity bashes. She's also been interviewed on CNN and Fox Business. Lucinda has read about Blair's work-life balance in *Forbes*, how she met her husband at forty and had her children late, as if it is an original idea no one has considered before. And now she is a new member of Longgreens after a very short membership consideration. Will the welcome be lasting? After all, she has a presence on an island where women value *no* career as much as they value *a* career.

According to Beebe Lestat and Mrs. Trask, Blair Jazzer and her husband have bought a high floor at the Bristol, where views of the Intracoastal and the ocean are endless, hypnotic. The new Jungle Road, as they say at cocktail parties around town. *How did that happen on the west side,*

Lucinda thought at first. When did people stop shuddering at the word "west" as in West Palm Beach? Rather than frowning at a property at the foot of the Royal Poinciana Bridge on the mainland side, they bought in. What was a wasteland when Lucinda and Reed first arrived in Palm Beach is now coveted.

"Already I'm convinced I'll only be here weekends," Blair is saying in her unidentifiable drawl.

"That should be plenty for you," Nellie says. "You have a great deal to do."

"I know, but George loves golf . . . my girls love the Inright jet."

Without checking the end of their row to see who is around, they lower their voices. Lucinda deciphers every few words.

". . . around Palm Beach she's someone, you know. I learned that from . . ."

"We all know her, but what *about* her? She must have played dirty. She comes from somewhere weird. No one knows how they got their money. Her family is very beautiful. Still, I'm telling you . . ." Blair sighs.

"Does anyone care, Blair? I mean, how do any of us get where we want to be?" Nellie says.

Blair laughs. "Well, we'll all go to her soirees—we have to. No one misses those."

"Why would we? She's a contender."

It's only the three of them there, too early for the golfers to have come in and the tennis players already on the courts. For those who only lunch followed by cards, the dining room is filling up. The air around Lucinda is nonexistent; she could choke to death and no one would notice. She faces the other way as Blair Jazzer and Nellie Kean exit. They are heading toward the open center of the locker room, a finishing area where double mirrors show front and back, where a crooked zipper or a bald patch for the older ladies gets fixed before venturing out into the club.

After they're gone, Lucinda unbuttons and rebuttons her shirt dress, rearranges her wallet and makeup bag, fussing about. Her palms are sticky when she whips her phone out, against the rules, and texts frantically. She decides to stick to the truth—how much more of that does she have?—when she texts Jolie Danes, her doubles partner and one of her oldest friends in Palm Beach. It's a rare kind of friendship where they could spend time alone together or with their husbands, Ned and Reed. After Reed died, Jolie stood beside Lucinda through those days as a widow where she was deserted by many. Too pretty, too much of a threat, Jolie told her. Then she introduced Lucinda to William, declaring, "You can stop now—this is a man who will do."

A situation at Barrows, racing back to the office. She taps, then deletes. *A situation at the house, racing back to put out the fire.* She taps and sends, knowing that to cancel twenty minutes before the match only works if it seems to be a family matter, a staff problem. That's how it is in Palm Beach, including for one's closest friends. As if any of it ever mattered.

In the full-length mirror to her left, she looks good—well preserved with the taut body of a retired gymnast. Her posture is excellent, a quality she has tried to impress upon her daughters and granddaughters, her slogan being, "Stand tall regardless of how you feel." She feels sick inside.

Beneath the lowlights of the lobby, clusters of women are coming in. They are blond, brunette, ash blond, their makeup exemplary, their hair natural or teased—shoulder length or shorter, their clothes designer, their bags Birkin or Chanel. Each appraises Lucinda as she heads out, acquaintances she wouldn't cross or exclude, what she would call the "thorny middle" of it. Lucinda offers her "running for office" smile.

Waiting in line for her car, she stands behind Jackie Lander and Berry Katell. She's about to say hello when pieces of their conversation float toward her. *So much strife . . . that family . . . her children . . . who knows . . . did you hear . . . sure, we'll go . . . the list is being cut . . .*

"Mrs. Barrows?" A valet comes over to Lucinda, holds out his hand for her car claim.

Her friends spin around, surprised. "Lucinda, aren't you in a game with Jolie, a lunch with . . ." Berry begins.

Jackie nods. "Jolie had reached out to us to join, but we're going to the Hive to shop for throw pillows."

Jackie's Range Rover Evoque is brought around. As the valets hold open the doors, Berry turns to Lucinda. "We hope things are shaping up for your birthday parties. How are the girls?"

Again Lucinda's campaign smile. "Everyone is well."

William's Bentley is being brought around. The door is opened, the three of them wave at one another as if they're in a subtitled foreign film and no one needs to speak.

ALONG THE A1A Lucinda speeds, swerving around the curves. Never get stopped by the local police, she likes to tell William, a man who gives generously to the PBA in order to speed. She taps her cell, Jolie picks up.

"What is going on?"

"I couldn't stay. I heard gossip, about me, Jolie. I might be having a panic attack."

Outside is devoid of technicolor, reduced to a sandy overlay. She gulps deep breaths. Lucinda doesn't recall when she last felt this level of anxiety. Maybe when she went into premature labor with Caroline or when Reed was dry-docking his fishing boat, left it to get a beer, and it was split in half by lightning seconds later. Or when they first got to Palm Beach and Raleigh, in fourth grade, was shunned. She was not invited to the important girls' parties and end-of-school celebrations. At once Lucinda honed her skills to make sure her daughter wasn't treated like that again. She and Reed joined the Breakers Beach Club, where Lucinda studied the mothers closely. She hosted unforgettable birthday parties for Raleigh there, inviting every girl in the class and her mother. She organized lavish spa days for Raleigh and her friends when they were only eleven.

"How are you so certain?" Jolie asks. "I mean, they talk about everyone—it's their raison d'être."

"Well, it feels like it."

"C'mon, you know better," Jolie says.

"Are people talking about me, Jolie? Just answer that."

Jolie sighs, maybe surprised or annoyed. "I told you, about you and everyone else."

Lucinda imagines Jolie sneaking off to the patio beyond the dining room for this call. The sky has gotten cloudy; the air inside the car is weighing on her chest. She has to risk expressing how it feels—Jolie is a true friend. If such a notion exists.

"No, me specifically. I'm having a sixtieth birthday party among the liars who never claim their age. I have two daughters not speaking, one widowed—not her fault—and one divorcing shoddily. I mean, women compete over whose daughter got the best divorce. I'm working on it, but it's messy. Maribelle wants to be in LA. She doesn't seem to care about having another partner . . . I'm losing my grip."

"Stop, stop it," Jolie says. "Just stop worrying about being judged."

"Really? Like I can. We're in Palm Beach. I'm not sure what you are talking about," Lucinda says.

She pulls into her driveway, turns off the engine. What an odd hour to be home. Usually she would be at one of the clubs or stopping by Barrows. She'll make use of the time, go into the library, start making calls to Raleigh's attorneys, search for what suitable men might exist for her single daughters, what influence she has for an introduction. If such men exist. Reach out to a few shops on the Avenue to see what's come in that's new—cropped pants, another long, flowy print number, the latest black sheath. Shopping always helps.

"I don't need to tell you it's an illusion, Lucinda. You're a master at it. You'll get your three daughters to bond, like it used to be. Make it a family reunion with Maribelle back."

"Thank you, Jolie." Her friend is making sense. Somehow Lucinda feels more assured than if she were seeking out her girls or Bryant for support. Which is not a common occurrence in any case.

"Of course. I've got to go. The cell police are milling about the club."

After Jolie rings off, Lucinda inhales, counts to six, exhales, does it once more. Beyond all else is the mirage of her cohesive, loveliest family. To that end, Lucinda ought to call up Tina De Lille, the new editor at *The Daily Sheet*, untrustworthy as she might be, to convince her there should be another spread about the Barrows family—nothing has run about them in at least three years. She might highlight

Lucinda's upcoming bashes, how Barrows thrives as a family company, her favorite causes. Nothing about the past. Seeing is believing, isn't it?

THE PATH to Lucinda's house is framed in white hibiscus, gardenia, and impatiens. White orchids hang from her palm trees. The only color comes from the purple bougainvillea. Were this someone else's entryway, Lucinda would consider it exemplary. Before turning the key, she spins around, knowing her home and flowers rival the best. She quite deliberately stages beauty.

She steps on an envelope that has been slipped beneath the front door. She turns it over, looking for a postmark, a date; there is nothing. Heading into her formal living room, a place they rarely use, Lucinda sits down on the piano bench and begins to read.

THE RIVER

I remember every detail of what we did after high school. We had been best of friends, and our mothers had been too. They knew the place well. No one left and no one new came to town. We had jobs, we got together on weekends. We went out on the boats, anyone's boat. My brother's dinghy had a 3.5 horsepower engine. The last year in Kesgrave had real seasons, Florida style. A long rainy winter into a cool spring, the kind where you wait a long time for summer.

Mostly I look back at how it was by the river when the tide came in, how we swam and waterskied, talking

> about our small dreams. It wasn't that I didn't want what they wanted—husbands, houses, children—more that chances were sparse and they'd gotten them. The other local girls were in line, every one of them. My mother said, you cannot leave, no one leaves, we would miss you, it wouldn't be the same without you. I believed her, I was that misguided. I never knew how far it was to the other side, until that one afternoon.
>
> I didn't understand then, but years have passed. I know it was about my brother. Once he was gone, there was no reason to be there. He had always been first, I'd never been first in anyone's eyes. Then it was over. The lies had begun before the burial.
>
> I still hear my brother's voice. It stays with me. I think of the dead, how it never should have been. I don't know if it's possible to right the wrong, still I ask you to consider what happened in Kesgrave. I believe that after you do, there will be a sense of justice, a path to settle the score.

Lucinda goes to the powder room and splashes cold water on her face. For the first time ever, she asks herself what her choices were. She knows who wrote these words. If only she knew who delivered them—who could be sending these and why? "Half an answer is no answer," Reed used to say. Her climb has been steep, and she has worked diligently to have no enemies. Frenemies undoubtedly, yet none of them know anything about her past. Only Bryant and Ruth-Ann knew pieces of it. And Ruth-Ann is dead, taken out of the equation.

Chapter Eight

2026

BEFORE she is by the window, Raleigh knows the sunset is over. Caroline is oblivious, tramping around her library in a tea-length pastel print, somewhere between resolute and ready to roll. Travis, in his custom-made navy blazer and khakis, stands at their wet bar, pouring himself a scotch. It's as if they're staged. Raleigh looks around, half expecting Maribelle to arrive, but her sister is at Lucinda's, avoiding her, no doubt.

"We're booked for 8 p.m." Travis finishes his drink with an awkward flourish. "We'll take my car."

He drives like lots of men on the island, braking, lurching forward at every stop sign. From the back seat, Raleigh sees how Caroline keeps fiddling with the air conditioner. Just like her sister, Raleigh used to sit beside her husband, Alex, off to a dinner or a charity bash, doing the same staccato gestures. A memory of driving alone to her secret meetings with Samuel for a tryst starts. Samuel's voice, Samuel inside her, still vivid although he is gone. *Who the hell sleeps with her sister's husband,* Caroline whispers when she is convinced Raleigh won't hear. *A person who cares only about herself,* Maribelle, the widow, the one Raleigh loves best and hurt the most, explains.

As the night settles in, Raleigh notices how lonely it feels.

Once Travis pulls up to The Marlybone Club, Raleigh sees Caroline's mistake, her misjudgment, whatever were her intentions. This is not where Raleigh ought to be—at a new social club, one that is coveted, private, with an edge. She isn't ready for "the game," if ever she had the skills. Her uneasiness increases as the valets move about like jumping beans.

Caroline twists her head to face Raleigh. "This was a Mizner mansion. You'll see, the rooms are super tasteful, European."

Her sister's description is like torture. Raleigh is unable to brace herself for a Palm Beach scene of this level. On a good day, she would need to be anchored in her life to withstand it.

"You're fine here," Caroline whispers when they head into the bar. "Sure, people are coupled, but they'll know some single guy."

Raleigh shakes her head. "Everyone is spoken for. Besides, it's a bad idea, Caroline."

Would Caroline be pushing Maribelle like this? It's doubtful since Maribelle has become quite independent. She exudes this strength. Raleigh admires how her sister is over the Palm Beach dictum. She'd love to know how she has managed—what being on the other side is like.

The women are young, luscious, chic. An endless, unwelcoming air sweeps by Raleigh. She thinks of the bar in Kesgrave, karaoke, everyone moving under a strobe light, people every age dancing together. Tonight nobody looks over forty, fifty at the most. The men are honed into lean, buff athletes, likely put on carbohydrate-free diets by their trainers, bench-pressing themselves into oblivion. Women are dressed mostly in Zimmermann dresses and a few classic designers. Maribelle might have once owned the same

Oscar with the intense flower detail that Gabriella Berlo is wearing. Raleigh isn't sure, as if the storing of such information in her brain has lessened. Maribelle's closet was the size of a studio apartment. She consigned her designer wardrobe when she left for LA. Could Gabriella have purchased the very dress that Maribelle unloaded?

Some of the flowy numbers tonight remind Raleigh of what people wore, including Caroline and Maribelle, right before Covid at the Opening Dance at the Harbor Club. Raleigh counts three to one blonds to brunettes, with long tresses. They make frantic gestures to aid their conversations; solitaires glitter. If ever this worked, she has no memory of it. Tonight she is exhausted.

Caroline's latest friends cascade toward Raleigh: Tina Steffens, Collette Nayers, Georgie Wyla. Caroline appears delighted; Raleigh likes how her attention slips from her. To the left is Maribelle's old crowd, Holly Lamm, publisher of *PB Confidential*, with Jacquie Quince, her new editorial director. The magazine was Maribelle's glory—how collected life was back then. How close the two of them had been with Caroline, an easy third, the most deliberate of the three. Raleigh isn't confused about that. Looped together, they had been enviable. The Barrows sisters. No one greets her. She closes her eyes, realizes she hasn't been to a Palm Beach event alone since she was in high school. She felt then what she feels now—that vomiting might or might not provide relief.

EVERY FACTION pauses to stare as a stranger wafts in. He's young and has more grace than any man in the room. From behind there is only his blazer, a hipper cut than most, stretched across his back. His hair is smooth against a sage collared shirt. He is a V, his waist narrow, his shoulders wide. Does anyone see his face, his profile? He is sexier, more striking than the wealthy boys three deep at the bar. The women in the reception area whisper . . . *not local* . . . *no one knows him* . . . *who brought him into the club* . . . *handsome, so handsome.* Then the next bevy of women at the bar . . . *to view the homes, the vias off Worth Avenue—Via Mizner, Via Amore, Via Bice—Whitehall* . . . *neoclassical Beaux-Arts* . . .

Because he is familiar, but it can't be, Raleigh follows him . . . until Allegra Dale, Raleigh's friend since seventh grade at the Academy and just married for the second time, stands taller, a ballerina en pointe, in Jimmy Choo stilettos, and taps his back. Guests pause, conversations congeal. Bartenders with their ripe biceps stop shaking dirty martinis and wait.

When he turns, people swallow the purified air. Like they are betting on a great gamble and are immediate winners. As if they've left their brains in the middle of the Southern Bridge and can no longer identify an outlier. Few among the guests care that he might prove perilous—Odette to Odile in *Swan Lake*, gossamer replaced by opaque.

Raleigh edges to where Allegra stands, convinced his eyes will stop at hers. They do, but his gaze moves ahead, like they've never seen one another. As if he isn't Porter and they hadn't met in Kesgrave.

Chapter Nine

2026

Raleigh is at Lucinda's house later than promised. Her sisters have already started a cheese tasting.

"Ah, you're here." Lucinda does this sort of half-fake smile. Raleigh hadn't expected her to be at home, draped in that ageless runway look, an Akris dress and matching blazer in a sand color that she favors when she's extra authoritative.

Raleigh looks at her mother. "I didn't know you'd be home."

"I've just gotten back. There was a Barrows opening in West Palm, for a double-sized location. I don't go often. I told Caroline I'd cover for her so you can be together, the three of you."

Obviously Lucinda is forcing this cocktail hour on them.

"Sure, sure. Thank you, Mom," Raleigh says.

Someone has rifled through the refrigerator and put out a platter. Her sisters are slicing into the St. Andre, a robiola, a block of Manchego and pouring Lucinda's wine. They hardly acknowledge her.

Caroline looks at Lucinda. "Are there more of the good crackers left for Raleigh?"

"I doubt it. This is the final one." Maribelle is holding a whole wheat cracker in the air, taking little bites.

"Raleigh, take something else to eat," Caroline says. "Since you're late."

Her sisters are sitting on mint vegan leather stools pulled up to the white quartz island. John Mellencamp is on Spotify, singing "Pink Houses." Caroline lowers the volume. Raleigh is an outsider; Maribelle and Caroline are crowding her out.

"Oh my God, I just got here. Please stop being rude," Raleigh says. She's sorry at once that her real thoughts have popped out of her mouth.

She'd like to ask how it is there's this lovefest. Maribelle and Caroline haven't been entwined for years. Yet to look at her sisters, they are not themselves. Neither has that Palm Beach aura. Maribelle is in black leggings and a tank top; her hair looks dirty but not like French women do dirty hair. Caroline has this torpid effect, as if when she isn't at work, there's no need for any style. She's in Crocs and baggy khakis. If clothes are costumes, which Lucinda taught them to believe, her sisters are not coming from anywhere good or heading that way.

Lucinda places her sweater and wide-brimmed straw hat on the counter. "Excuse me, girls, here we are in my home, a repository for family feelings. You could acknowledge Raleigh. Be more enthused."

Maribelle and Caroline pause. "Hi, Raleigh," Caroline says. "What will you drink? Some Spiked Pop, Perrier, a glass of wine?" Like she doesn't know what Raleigh's preference would be.

"Perrier." Raleigh opens a bottle.

Maribelle stretches her arms, then looks at Raleigh and away, like a feral cat. What about Caroline—is she taking sides? She and Maribelle seem chummy. Both sisters are practically guzzling the wine. Maribelle doesn't often do that; Caroline is the drinker of the three, wine only. Raleigh doesn't like any of it and turns it down at parties or feigns drinking champagne by asking the bartender to pour ginger ale into the glass. Her sisters have helped themselves to a Sauvignon Blanc, an everyday selection and not one of Lucinda's treasured bottles.

Maribelle and Caroline keep talking about *Florida Strong*. Caroline seems intrigued by whatever Maribelle says.

"There always has to be an alligator, sometimes more than one," Maribelle says.

The two of them laugh. Raleigh feels locked out, punished for the foreseeable future, maybe forever. Proof one should not have an affair with her sister's husband. The aftermath is beyond intolerable. Caroline should do something; Lucinda moves inside the doorway, waiting for her to make a gesture. Caroline comes through for Lucinda—she has stayed married to Travis, a man who plays golf and tennis, shows up, pleasant enough. Sure, he probably snores and gets poked to move into a better position. He's probably moody at home but can be ignored. Caroline loves working at the family company. Caroline should play savior; she knows what to do here.

Lucinda points her hand toward the empty stool beside Maribelle. "I won't have this joyless vibe. Everyone has to do better. If not for yourselves, for me. Your mother."

They're making Raleigh anxious. She walks to the refrigerator without an appetite and finds nothing to eat, not so much as a vanilla oat milk yogurt.

Raleigh raises her eyebrows. They are perfect or so Maribelle used to say, while everyone else seems to be threading theirs, tweezing or filling in the empty patches.

"Seriously, Lucinda." Maribelle frowns. Even Botox couldn't stave off lines in her forehead. Nothing about Maribelle is the same since she sold her house and every personal belonging and left town with Julian two years ago. Before that, she had been impeccable, her clothes couture, her accessories enviable. A youngish Palm Beach wife. She and Raleigh had been locked together, Caroline on the perimeter looking in. Now it's Raleigh on the border. Raleigh and Maribelle haven't been in touch beyond an obligatory holiday card or birthday text since the truth came out about Raleigh's affair with Samuel. For a long while, Caroline was the negotiator. Raleigh thought her sister would finally have a resolution, until today.

"Mom," Caroline says. "This is very stressful for me."

On the Intracoastal, two eighty-footers pass, so large and elegant they dwarf the water. Beside them, two small, whippy speed boats zip by, reminding Raleigh of Samuel. Water reminds her of him, of the accident. The day she met Porter in Kesgrave and he offered a ride on his boat, she knew it wasn't possible.

The playlist shifts to David Bowie singing "Heroes," a favorite of the Barrows sisters in better times. Lucinda says quietly, "Alexa, turn off the music." She turns to Caroline. "I'll need your help with your sisters."

Something about the tone as well as the request repels Raleigh; her mother doesn't ask for help. She is refined and collected, always in command. A reaction—like car sickness—sweeps over Raleigh.

"Why me?" Caroline asks.

Lucinda stares at each of them. "That's obvious, isn't it?"

"Not obvious exactly," Caroline says. "Why not you, Mom? Why not do it yourself?"

"I am asking you to do this," Lucinda says. In the strong kitchen lights that ought to be dimmed, she appears ever so tired. Maybe she looks sad, and Raleigh cannot comprehend that—her mother doesn't do sad. "It's simple, Caroline. You'll bring your sisters back together."

Maribelle's face smooths out in this unreal way. She's got this detachment about her. A recent effect.

Raleigh's lips become thin, and her mouth twitches, like it's not really hers. She starts crying in her tragic style. "I need it to win custody of Caleb. He's fucking five years old. I need Alex to not get alimony from me."

Maribelle shrugs, reaches for a brown bread square with gravlax and pops it into her mouth.

"Oh, okay," Raleigh says. "I get it, no one is going to respond to my pain. Try this, I'm sick of being the bad sister. I made a mistake, a huge, horrible, terrible mistake. I'm sorry. Isn't it enough that I've lost everything? My husband, my house, my clientele."

"No, Raleigh, it's not enough," Maribelle says.

Caroline reaches for the open bottle on the island. She pours close to the top.

Maribelle smirks in this twisted way. Maybe writing in Hollywood has gone to her head.

"Caroline, can't you arrange something, help Raleigh out with her divorce?" Maribelle might be sarcastic.

"I would if I could," Caroline says. Each word is measured.

Raleigh hates them, doesn't she? She lifts a water glass from the island and hurls it against the wall leading to Lucinda's pantry, a long toss for anyone. Maribelle finishes what is left in her wine glass and tosses it against the same wall. For a moment the three Barrows sisters are confounded.

"Sorry about the Baccarat, Lucinda," Maribelle says—

the new iteration of Maribelle, the one Raleigh doesn't recognize. "I'll go on the Avenue and replace them."

"I need us to get along like we used to." Raleigh is still crying. "To be there for each other."

Lucinda is viewing the drama. "We assume Raleigh is the desperate one—sobbing in the corner. If only it were that simple."

Briefly, the sisters are stumped enough by their mother's cryptic remark to trade glances, to be in the same sphere.

"I'm sorry, what's that supposed to mean?" Caroline asks.

A silent Lucinda, almost an oxymoron.

"Mom?" Maribelle asks.

Again, nothing from Lucinda. It's disturbing. It's awkward.

"I have to leave. I'm heading to Alex's for Caleb," Raleigh says. As if anyone cares about her schedule.

When she leaves, Raleigh has nothing to show for the time there. Some women kidnap their children during a divorce. Some soon-to-be-divorced women have mothers who throw money at the settlement to get it in order. Sometimes there are no solutions. The world is incredibly lonely; there isn't sufficient oxygen.

Chapter Ten

2026

Maribelle ought to cross her legs gracefully rather than sit in the passenger seat with her knees far apart. How has she become like this, Lucinda wonders—slouchy, lifeless, her black linen dress billowing. Maribelle has made a conscious decision to be other.

They head to Sunrise for dinner at The Polo Room, the two of them. The ocean is bluer than usual, there are fewer SUVs on the road.

"Don't you ever miss it, Maribelle, the island, the tranquility?"

Her daughter flips her head away from the water. "Tranquility? Are you saying that's what I had when I lived in Palm Beach, that it was laden with calm, there was this peaceful quality?"

"Not so shabby, Maribelle," Lucinda says. "You once had a house in the best location of our entire family, a husband, a career . . ."

"Mom, I came back for you, for your birthday. That's the only reason. I'm heading back to LA as soon as . . ."

Although it's one of those low-humidity afternoons, what is described as a "perfect Palm Beach day," there is that sense it's limited, precious.

"You had the most enviable job, Maribelle."

"What I love about being in California is that it is *honestly* tranquil." Maribelle takes her window all the way down like people did in cars together during Covid. Air rushes at her face. "My success is for real, on my own."

"Really?" Lucinda pauses. "Why not come home, go back to *PB Confidential*? You did well there."

"That's very unlikely," Maribelle says. "I have this new life. Without the shackles of . . ."

"I'm not sure what you are intimating."

"After a hellish time, I'm happy. I love Santa Monica."

Lucinda speeds up her Arctic Grey Porsche Cayenne SUV around the A1A. She knows better; the cops are lurking. Yet she steps harder on the gas. She glances again at Maribelle, born when Lucinda was only eighteen. Lucinda likes to say they grew up together. She wanted accomplished, stunning daughters, and Maribelle was the first. When she and Bryant sent Maribelle off to LA, it wasn't meant to be a permanent solution. Seeing her now, Lucinda knows she must have her back. Not as a defector or a guest, as the eldest daughter, to complete the roster. The Barrows family members need to be in Palm Beach and thriving—that's how Lucinda's reputation will stay intact. She cannot be judged; a woman flaunting—announcing—her real age is incendiary enough. Add to that how these letters are interrupting her life, unnerving her. She considers confiding in Maribelle, then resists.

Maribelle is one of her two single daughters with no proper prospects. Remorse kicks in, an emotion she only feels around four in the morning, a witching hour for migraine sufferers and anxious people. When the serotonin shifts in one's brain and there's no falling back to sleep easily. But being sentimental and remorseful in the afternoon?

"Mom?" Maribelle asks.

"I said I'm fine, Maribelle. Let's have a pleasant dinner."

When they arrive, the host, a young woman wearing a black minidress, hands Lucinda an envelope. "For you, Mrs. Barrows. It was dropped off a few minutes ago."

Lucinda, panicked, takes it discreetly. Maribelle is watching the bar, preoccupied. She goes over, air kisses a few people, which is promising. Except Lucinda is rattled. Who would know about her dinner reservation besides her daughters and William? Perhaps Estelle, who follows her calendar, has given out some information. That would be indiscreet, and she knows better.

Once seated in the front room, Lucinda looks to her left and right, offering a half-smile to the tables she knows. She waves hello to the Gilles and the Smaters, and they nod, their heads bobbing up and down. She tries wishful thinking. The envelope is simply an invitation. Still the room is rolling, chartreuse despite the cognac-colored leather and dark wood.

Maribelle plunks down. "Sorry, I ran into . . ."

"Maribelle, I'm going outside to get some air. I'll be a moment."

"If you feel ill, we can leave. You look drained. I didn't mean to upset you."

Lucinda stands up, straightens her shift, tosses her shoulders back. She's managed to fold the envelope in half, pushing it into her mini bucket bag. "Fresh air will do it. I'll be back shortly. Order us some wine."

Halfway down the street, Lucinda uses the light from her phone to read the letter.

THE DEAL

By now you know how we were bonded together as girls, the three of us. We'd made it through hurricane seasons, football rallies, the other girls in Kesgrave. We had shared so much. Because I was the youngest, they had taught me how to smoke cigarettes and drink beer. We weren't exactly equals. They didn't take my work seriously; they laughed at my dreams. I saved my money babysitting for the four Mercy kids. I saved to buy cameras. For "your hobby," everyone said—what else was a camera for? I will be a photographer, I insisted. They thought I'd read too many books and magazines.

That afternoon I had a camera strapped across my back. I was out looking for the blue jays, the mallard ducks—where the males were dashing and the females drab. There were hardwood trees and buttonbushes along the banks. I only planned on nature photos, to grab the light. In the years since, I've rewritten the scene in my mind, switching it out so we hadn't left each other, so I wasn't alone wandering. Instead we stood together, another happy if dull afternoon. We were dipping our toes, drinking Diet Coke.

I'd like to justify what I did, what I agreed to. In life I couldn't confront anyone. I didn't have the guts. I was a willow—I could be pushed, bought, whatever was required. Time stopped there, and I couldn't conjure up anyone's face or the house we lived in. In that moment I lost my memory, as if I'd been run over by one of the boys who drove into town on their Harleys.

They held out the deal like free candy at a matinee concession stand. I told myself it was okay. If you read every page I've written, you'll understand what I mean. You'll understand what I did in Kesgrave. You'll know why. What I saw came close to ruining me.

Lucinda folds the paper into a three-inch square as if this could downsize the impact. It isn't a demand letter or a blackmail note, yet she's being tortured. Who would send the letters, and why at this point in her life? She crosses her arms in a self-hug and taps her shoulders—something she'd just learned on ChatGPT to combat anxiety. After a few minutes, she's back inside.

Seated again, Lucinda acknowledges more guests, including the Dorie sisters and Denny Twain. More waves, fake smiles, one wink. She does her best—the terms of celebrity status in Palm Beach are not like anywhere else. Lucinda is known, respected, invited, and on occasion showcased, such as when Barrows underwrites a research center or a literacy program. Making a plea for Maribelle to stay in Palm Beach becomes more salient. That's why they're alone together tonight. The family must be whole, beyond reproach. That is Lucinda's first line of defense. She'll speak with her daughters later. She'll call another family meeting, insist there is no longer a cold war between Maribelle and Raleigh.

"Lucinda!" Maribelle says. "Mom, are you listening?"

"I am." Lucinda sees the two glasses of Sancerre have arrived. Carefully she roots around in her bag. The pill is smooth, tiny. She swallows it, takes a swig.

"What is going on?" Maribelle asks. "What is it?" She

looks afraid, apologetic, genuinely concerned. More like the old Maribelle, the one Lucinda and Bryant wanted to protect. Empathetic or not, she mustn't know anything.

"Getting through. That's it." The pill plus the wine will kick in shortly. The letters are churning, immediate, illuminating the past. They could ruin Lucinda, ruin everyone. A fall from grace of another order.

The server comes with their menus.

Chapter Eleven

1982

Lucinda, Bryant, and Ruth-Ann wear scratchy, cheap wool cardigans. Hers is rust, theirs are navy and tan. They wear Levi jeans that have no style or fit. In an hour they'll be going to the high school dance.

They're mostly at Bryant's or Ruth-Ann's. Their houses are nicer and their mothers less grumpy. Lucinda tries not to bring anyone home. But this time it's her turn to invite her friends over. Her mother seems tense, insisting the girls eat a five o'clock dinner of corned beef hash, which tastes extra greasy. Lucinda forces herself to swallow, washing it down with Dr Pepper.

"We have to hurry," Ruth-Ann says. This is her first dance. She's only in ninth grade. For Lucinda and Bryant, being seniors, there's no magic to it. Rather it's a path to stay out later with their boyfriends and avoid pushback.

There's little time to fuss with makeup; the dinner wiped that out. The "boys," Reed, Bud, and Ruth-Ann's latest crush, Chip Haller, will be waiting outside any minute. The plan is to lie to their mothers about supervising Ruth-Ann. Lucinda and Reed have already decided to leave the dance early. Bryant and Bud will prove better sports, going inside with Ruth-Ann and Chip, at least to start. Lucinda figures there's little risk and every reward in being in Reed's truck making out—and more. She and Bryant will cover for each other. It's going to be a fine Saturday night.

LUCINDA KNOCKS on the door of Bud's Chevrolet Impala. Ruth-Ann and Chip are already in the back. Chip puts up the hood on his gray sweatshirt and rolls down the window. The smell of Old Spice wafts toward them. Chip must be wearing his father's after shave, what the men use for special occasions. Ruth-Ann looks up, her face so hopeful. Lucinda must admit she's pretty with her wavy blond hair, those fine features. How she stands like a ballerina although she's never taken a lesson.

"You guys should go in when you get to the school," Lucinda says.

Ruth-Ann squints. "Aren't you coming?"

Bryant gets into the car. "Sure, we all are."

Lucinda shakes her head at Bryant, indicating she's weak and afraid. Why can't she say that they're going for a ride so she and Bud can have something for themselves. Not Bryant, always wanting to do what's right.

When Lucinda gets into Reed's truck, he's holding the steering wheel. She loves his hands, his neck, his chin. "Ready?" He asks.

She's annoyed that her plan might be compromised. Every minute alone with Reed counts, and a dance in the auditorium at Pinestream whittles away at their time. Besides, it isn't like they haven't gone to a few already.

The six of them file in. At once Lucinda sees classmates she'd like to avoid, including her cheerleading team and the other football players.

"Let's get to the back," she suggests.

Bryant, Bud, and Reed are smiling, waving as they go. Ruth-Ann and Chip seem reluctant to bring any attention to themselves. "My Best Friend's Girl" by The Cars is blaring, the dance floor is filling up.

Quietly Lucinda asks, "Reed, can't we get out of here?"

Ruth-Ann spins around. Despite the din, she has heard her.

"I don't think so, Lucinda. My parents think you and Reed are chaperoning me."

Chip is ahead, having found the snack table, loading pretzels and potato chips onto a paper plate. He might be okay; Ruth-Ann might be in good company. Not an easy find.

"Your brother and Bryant can do that," Lucinda says.

Ruth-Ann leans close to Lucinda. "Are you sure? Maybe I need more supervision."

"I think you don't need anyone," Lucinda says. "You'll be fine. Aren't there enough people in the room for you?"

Bryant and Bud are swaying to the next song, the Bee Gees' "How Deep Is Your Love." They'll stay the night, and Ruth-Ann, whether it goes well with Chip or not, is safe enough.

Reed has gone ahead to the soda table and is pouring two Cokes, not a good sign in terms of leaving. There's a strobe light that falls across him. She wants to be only with him. Doesn't he want the same? She doesn't get it.

Lucinda joins him, runs her tongue along her lips. "We could cut out if we go now and come back after a while."

Reed looks around, shrugs. "Okay."

They head toward the door through more waves, more

lower classmates coming up to say hi. Seniors are popular, especially when they're "the" couple at Pinestream, Reed as captain of the football team, Lucinda as captain of the cheerleaders.

Lucinda is leading. When she looks back, Ruth-Ann has caught up to Reed. She's tapping him on the back, ruining it all. Getting in the way. The only path to Reed being Lucinda's is to seal the deal. To get him to marry her.

Chapter Twelve

2026

MILOS, a glossy West Palm restaurant, faces the Intracoastal and beyond that, the island. Whenever Raleigh comes, she admires the gardens and view of the yachts. Tonight the bar is packed with a fluid young crowd. Long-legged women wear strappy stiletto sandals. Their dresses, mini or maxi, are in shades of melon or beige or in vivid floral prints. No one misses the chance to carry a Gucci, Fendi, or Hermès bag. Men sport blazers or chambray button-down shirts, white trousers tapered to oblivion, and sockless loafers that look like slippers.

Seated in the midst of it, Raleigh waits for Caroline, feeling old for the first time in her life. She has been youngest so very long. Her sisters are clearly older—some of Maribelle's friends have had facelifts, hair dye is a must. To add to this reality, Caroline arrives wearing a workforce dress, her hair in a blunt cut, boxy. When did her middle sister become corporate, and to what end?

"Wow, is there anyone we know here?" Caroline asks.

Being Lucinda's daughters, they don't so much as air kiss, let alone share a hug. The belief stands that an overt display of affection is tacky and unnecessary. Maybe that's why, when Caleb was smaller, Raleigh hugged him fiercely in public; it stems from growing up where an iciness prevailed.

"No one I know or recognize," Raleigh says. Their server opens a bottle of Acqua Panna and pours two glasses. "Are we waiting for a local or international celebrity to kick off the evening?"

"No, we're waiting for Maribelle," Caroline says.

"I thought it was the two of us." Why is it always the same circumstance, Caroline a tentacle of Lucinda, Maribelle unable to forgive Raleigh?

"To start, and then . . ." Caroline says.

The bar area is demanding; there's a chance of being swept up, pushed aside, something. Caroline slides off her stool. "Let's get to our table. There's nothing going on—for us, that is."

A host named Calvin leads them to the front room, the center table against the wall. They sit side by side, looking out, close enough to keep watching as if it's a Broadway production. A parade of Caroline's friends is en route to farther out tables near the dead fish display and vats of vegetables. Angela Thymes, Leesa James, and Sasha Sterrin suddenly appear, nod, do these narrow smiles. The din levels out. Caroline waves back without any hint of a Lucinda swagger, while Raleigh can't muster any reaction.

"I'd say the new people seem remarkably the same as those whom we've known all along," Caroline says. "But things *are* shifting. It's inevitable."

Their server is standing over them, clearing his throat. How long has he been there? He fans the menus, puts them at their place settings. He's tan, under thirty, on a path to something better.

They watch a woman standing on the fringes of the terrace. She lights up a cigarette despite the rules, blows smoke rings into the night air.

"Remember how Lucinda used to blow smoke rings?" Raleigh asks.

"I do," Caroline says. "Those thin cigarettes. Virginia Slims. Maribelle and I thought it was elegant."

"She stopped when I was in grade school," Raleigh says.

"Right, when she realized smoking didn't fit in with her plans for Palm Beach," Caroline says. "Déclassé. That's when she got a nicotine patch and did hypnosis to be someone who never smoked."

A man is with a woman on the terrace. She puts out the cigarette with her foot. A swarm of young men has arrived at the bar, the women, young and chic, make way for them. It's unclear if they know one another or are simply hoping to. Again, Raleigh has a sense that she's old, that life is passing her by. No one there has hired a sitter for a child at home or has been married and is working on a divorce.

Caroline is eavesdropping on the table to their left, a Palm Beach foursome. The daughter, in her Altuzarra print dress, is animated. The son-in-law—he seems to be that—balances this rarified world and free meal with how bored he is. He tries a smile as his wife describes their five-year-old. *After her first baby tooth fell out . . . every nursery school has that rule . . . a great swimming instructor . . . We prefer coed schools . . .*

Where might Raleigh fit in? She will not be sitting with a bland, well-meaning husband and Lucinda and William any time soon. Nor does she belong at the bar scene. Maribelle is on her way, and Raleigh dreads it. Her sister will be half-civilized in a restaurant, but she treats her like she's a thief in the night.

"Maribelle keeps at it—she isn't speaking to me still."

"Ah, Raleigh, you don't get it, do you? You can't always

cry to win. It doesn't work," Caroline says. "You've been very selfish, don't you see it? You can't have everything you want because you're youngest, prettiest, always delicate, the artiste. We're sort of sick of it."

Raleigh is astounded, misunderstood. "I'm sorry. I don't know why you're saying this, what you mean."

"I'm sure that's true. That's the problem. You're in your own world. Nothing seems to penetrate. You've hurt Maribelle, hurt yourself."

The terror of it, of what Caroline believes. The entire restaurant is about to fall on her. Raleigh has to defend herself, detail her side. "I want to explain, Caroline. I swear I can."

Caroline is twisting her hands, swallowing hard. "I have said a lot. I'm being harsh. I thought you should know how it is, the frustration for me. I understand who you are beneath, your goodness."

Raleigh is too confused to cry. "If you aren't on my side, who would there be?"

"Right, I get that." Caroline now twists her engagement ring, the replacement for the first one that wasn't a large enough diamond. Lucinda engineered the new one for Caroline's thirty-fifth birthday. When Raleigh was asked by Travis to ring shop, she made up an excuse. Maribelle went to the jeweler with him to select the stone.

Customers, holding their heads high as if it's a fashion show, are being ushered to tables inside and on the terrace. Raleigh wishes they were more distracting and she could escape her own thoughts. Caroline seems very nervous.

"Listen, Raleigh, you need some joyfulness. I don't know what will drive things forward. Would a younger man be interesting? Travis is a poster child for each grim result of what happens to men after forty."

Raleigh is about to confide in Caroline when Maribelle saunters toward them. She's much more like her old self when she was the editorial director of *PB Confidential.* She's wearing a lemony sleeveless dress, her arms thin, sinewy from weightlifting, a gym ritual that Raleigh detests. Despite Caroline's repeat need to clump the two of them together, Maribelle looks vaguely put out when she sees Raleigh. Her anger over Samuel will never stop.

Caroline picks up on it. "On the other hand, no one needs a rockstar. I'd just like you—and Maribelle, actually—to have romance in your lives."

"I don't know, Caroline. Before we talk about finding another man, let's talk about how Maribelle will be angry forever . . . and I'm her little sister."

"Eventually this will get patched up with Maribelle. You'll both meet someone."

Maribelle is nodding at the tables she knows, making her way to them.

Raleigh stands up, lifts her bag. "I'm sorry, Caroline, I have to go."

Navigating a path several feet to the right of Maribelle is doable. When Raleigh passes the bar, there are many scents canceling each other out. Among the crowd is Porter. He's in a cream-colored button-down shirt and jeans. He stands tall, disinterested, yet holding a glass. The youngest, prettiest women go closer, drawn to him.

He's facing away so she taps his elbow. Taking her hand, he leads her around the corner where it is empty.

"Why are you at Milos?" She needs to know. Why leave with her when he has choices. He knows what's ahead—girls, women after him, the many invitations extended to the latest commodity.

He's listening, yet his mind is somewhere else.

"Porter?"

"I was tipped off." He puts his mouth against her right ear. "Let's get the hell out."

APPARENTLY, he Ubered to the restaurant. They take her car to the Colony Hotel. In the elevator, he holds her carefully, longingly. They stagger to the room, entwined. Within minutes they are both naked; she can't think beyond it. He is tanner than when they first met. This one is a golf tan. His legs, from below his knees to his ankles, his upper arms, from where a polo shirt covered them, are paler. Proof he is infiltrating; he's been asked to play, he wears the uniform. She'd like it not to be so—she wants him separate, beyond the Palm Beach template. She wants it to feel like it did in Kesgrave. It's plenty that he's the intriguing young man who has come to town.

He traces her jawline with his right hand. "We're only in this room," Porter says. "Nowhere else do we exist."

"And we're a secret because of my . . ."

Porter puts his finger to her lips. "We're a secret because it's better like that."

He starts kissing her crazily. Is it nothing more than sexual attraction, tucked into hotel rooms after trading cryptic texts? Is this all Raleigh is good for? Has she become a pro, thanks to Samuel?

"Agreed?" he whispers.

"Agreed."

They're principal dancers in a pas de deux. It's the safest Raleigh's been since the accident.

Chapter Thirteen

2026

MIDNIGHT is an odd hour to drive by one's soon-to-be-sold home, once shared with her future ex-husband, yet Raleigh does it. Porter had asked her to stay at the Colony and the idea of his arms around her all night long (if that ever truly happens) nearly persuaded her. Instead, she's on her way back to the guest room at Caroline's. She's been schooled by the divorce lawyers to be "impeccable" until the deal is finalized.

Raleigh drives on List Road, slowing down in front of the house. She's somewhere between nostalgia and disbelief that this is her life—she no longer lives there and has no surety of where she'll end up. What is clear is that she won't be with Caleb every day of the week, no matter how her divorce plays out. Although Lucinda aspires to put Raleigh back "on the map" in terms of next husbands, Raleigh is too beguiled by Porter, a man who is merely passing through, with a room at a hotel. What he owns or needs would probably fill two suitcases while she would require forty boxes excluding wardrobe cartons, to make a move. She should care about that disparity except she doesn't.

Raleigh turns off the engine and searches for the keys, hoping they might be in her bag. The exterior lights are on as if someone inhabits the place. Out of some twisted nostalgia, Raleigh goes in. She cares most about the room where they both painted early on, before they had a studio. The walls are now a stark white, what Ginelle Parker, their real estate agent, insisted upon for staging. I hope you're listening to Ginelle," Lucinda had said. "We want this house sold quickly." The empty walls are like ghosts of her work, portraits Raleigh was commissioned to paint for happier families than the one who lived here—or at least a better pretense of an intact family.

The minute she turns, she knows someone is there. Alex.

He faces west, where the daytime views take in the Intracoastal. "What are you doing here?" he asks quietly.

"Me? What about you? Who's with Caleb?" she asks—but she knows. Alex is constantly covered, with two sitters on call.

"I remember when we were a team," Alex says without looking at her.

"I remember too," she says.

She once thought Alex and Caleb were plenty, more than enough. Tonight she despises that she ever saw Alex's face. Sharing a child with him is beyond punishing.

The first time she ever slept with him she was wearing Lucinda's vintage Frye boots. They had left a party their mutual friend Thad hosted. When she kicked them off, they thumped against the floor, so noisy it interrupted their tempo. "Cry Me a River" by Justin Timberlake, downloaded from Napster, was hushed for a moment. Alex was six foot two with a runner's build and an artist's sensitivity. He had real talent and was from another world—someone who grew up in Philadelphia in a privileged banking family. In theory, Raleigh's husband was the anti-sycophant from Kesgrave—refreshing after her brothers-in-law who had glommed onto the rise of Barrows. Life seemed bohemian when Raleigh and Alex first married and lived in Savannah, until Reed offered to buy them a house on the north end of Palm Beach. Alex welcomed the idea. He thought the island was exotic at best, a bit clannish at worst. A free home was worth more than Raleigh's pleas that physical distance was a salve.

"We're being bribed," Raleigh had told Alex.

"We're being freed to paint without financial stress," he assured her.

Who knew that after they'd brought Caleb into the world together, after her affair, *despite* her affair, he'd become such a consummate dick? Had she missed it throughout?

Regret chips away at her. The same story over and over. Raleigh trespassed and slept with Samuel, Maribelle's husband; she stole time with him as if sleepwalking. The morning of his drowning, the trance ended. Ever since, it's as if she stands out of reach, unable to get back. Regret is such a terrible emotion, worse than guilt, really. "I only regret what I didn't do," Aunt Bryant has said over and over—Raleigh has never asked what fuels her aunt's remorse. Once Caleb was born and Alex's contemporary paintings started to take off, Raleigh was exhausted, restless. Lucinda sensed it and her solution was to take Raleigh and her sisters to Paris for a long weekend.

"I don't think I can leave Caleb," Raleigh said.

"Of course you can," Lucinda said. "I'll send Rosie over to stay with Alex and Caleb. Your nanny isn't enough support. If you are unhappy, you will get on an early flight and turn around."

Caleb. How could she fly across an ocean with her son

that young? Still she did, with Lucinda and her sisters. The entire flight over she had anxiety attacks, imagining that once they landed, checked into the Ritz, and shopped along Rue St. Honoré, she would get back on a plane. She told herself that at any juncture she could ditch Lucinda's agenda, the boutiques on the Left Bank, the Louvre, the Musée d'Orsay, the shopping and eating and people watching. The franc was strong, and Lucinda was delighted. For Raleigh it was painful, and each call with Caleb made her worse. He cried and screamed, "Mama, Mama!" like she'd committed a crime.

"Do you miss Alex?" Caroline had asked her.

"Not exactly. I miss the nights with Caleb asleep in the next room."

Had Raleigh missed Alex, would her life have remained manageable? "Can't you love him enough?" Lucinda asked when Alex filed for divorce. "It would be much easier."

Raleigh had answered, "It doesn't matter, he's over me. Too little too late."

Alex is watching her; he's saying something. She has to be friendly, civilized. They're side by side, yet he's foreign, as if they were never married, never ate fries with mayonnaise together or shared a bed. She has no memory of what he smells like in the morning, if he drinks coffee black or with almond milk, whole milk, heavy cream. He is a hidden man, the father of her child. That he is very attractive is academic, similar to admiring an actor on a Netflix series or a professor in college.

He coughs politely. "If only you weren't a cheater, Raleigh." His face isn't balanced anymore. The space between his upper lip and the bottom of his nose has widened.

Cheater. Such a nasty word choice. There were others to consider—unfaithful, lost, lonely, desperate, hungry-hearted.

"I feel sorry for the next guy. Once a cheater, always a cheater."

Defending, explaining how it really happened, is tempting. She's been warned not to engage in any personal conversation with Alex. Besides, who would understand the Samuel part except for Aunt Bryant?

"Sure, there will be a next guy." Alex sighs. He's staring at her like she's pretty, not sane or grounded. As if she deserves nothing.

Aunt Bryant predicts there will be another, that moving on to new love after old is the reward. Although she herself lives like some unnamed order of nun since Bud Humphreys, her fiancé in Kesgrave, died.

"We should go, lock up the house," Raleigh says.

A memory surges in technicolor, she and Alex and Caleb, at what was their home. They were having breakfast, Caleb in a highchair, Alex scrolling on his phone. She was making French toast while counting the minutes to get into her studio—as soon as Caleb was at preschool. It was ordinary, it was extraordinary. It was.

"Oh, Raleigh?" he says. "I'm watching you. I'm after the same things you are. Except I deserve them. Caleb should be with me. I'm not off in the Panhandle selling tourist art, trash dipped in bright blue paint."

She is at the front door, away from the family life she once had; she turns to him. "You know, Alex, it was the idea of you, not the actual person, that worked, if it ever worked. But we share Caleb—he's our son. We should be kind to one another, do the right thing for . . ."

"Fuck you, Raleigh. I wish I'd never laid eyes on you."

She imagines Porter, his mouth on hers, his entire body, how he pronounces words, names. Mid-century architecture is his favorite. He reads James Joyce. He smells like washed seashells after they dry. She has no idea where to put this relationship that has spun into her life.

"Never tell the next man about how vicious Alex has become," Lucinda warns her repeatedly. "It will only get in the way of a second chance."

Chapter Fourteen

2026

TODAY at Café Flora on the Avenue, Raleigh has the chance to tell her mother and aunt she has met someone. She doesn't plan to reveal much, only to get news out that she's moving on. To have Porter exist in real time. "Reinvention," Lucinda likes to say, "is the best tool." When Lucinda texted to beg off, stuck in a menu meeting, Raleigh was relieved. Lucinda, Maribelle, and Caroline judge her, while feigning they are open-minded. Aunt Bryant truly is open-minded. The family always said that in a past life she must have been a schoolteacher or a nurse; she's that sincere. Lucinda on occasion undermines Aunt Bryant's goodness: "She's not holier than thou—she happens to have a good handle on the role." Raleigh loves that Aunt Bryant acts like a real saint.

When Raleigh first came to this restaurant, she had just graduated from the Academy. "Isn't eating here like being transported to a small, beautiful town in Italy?" Lucinda had asked, pivoting in her chair to take it in.

Aunt Bryant is per usual, in rose-gold progressive glasses, reading her phone when Raleigh arrives. Her lime-green cardigan is a statement; the lunch will not be heavy and grim. Upbeat is the mode. "Raleigh, you look well."

"Thank you." Raleigh has cleaned up. She's in narrow-legged navy pants, a finest cotton T-shirt, and a tan chunky bootie. She shakes her hair out of a ponytail, which is very Caroline or Maribelle. Maybe she is more similar than she likes to believe. She hopes so because of Porter. She has to be prettier, chicer than her recent victim single mother gig.

"I'm sorry I couldn't do a dinner," Raleigh says. "I'm sketching at night, for a portrait."

"A new commission, excellent," Aunt Bryant says.

"Yes and watercolor, my favorite." Raleigh looks around, relieved at how empty the place is.

"So why are we meeting beyond the crowd—anything special, or simply an overdue hour together?" Aunt Bryant asks.

"I wanted to see you and Lucinda."

"I'm sorry she isn't coming. How unlike your mother to simply cancel." She's waiting for Raleigh to explain why she needs an audience. A server comes over cautiously. Aunt Bryant puts her hand up like she's a traffic cop, and the server backs off.

"I'll tell you. We'll talk today."

"You seem secretive," Aunt Bryant says. "Maybe we should have just gone to my house."

Raleigh looks left and right. "No, no, this is fine." She pauses. "I've met someone, Aunt Bryant."

Aunt Bryant beams. "Is it someone we know?"

Raleigh's stomach churns, how it gets when Alex changes the calendar with Caleb for no reason. She tosses her head. "That's what my mother would ask. Is it important?"

"Not really. I surely didn't mean to sound like that." Aunt Bryant sits straighter, more rod-like. She takes a lip gloss from her bag, runs it over her lips. "I don't care where he's from. I only thought it might be a family we know."

"Then what?" Raleigh raises her voice slightly.

"Then I'd tell you to be very discreet. In my circles, I hear Alex is out to get you."

Raleigh decides not to tell her about Alex's latest behavior, his unrelenting anger. "Well, this guy is not local. He's touring Florida or something."

Aunt Bryant waves at a table of four women across the courtyard. Another group of women arrives—another exchanged wave. Sometimes she's more Lucinda than she lets on.

"Touring. Tell me more, Raleigh."

"Life seems different because of him. Has Lucinda said anything to you, anything she's noticed about me?"

"Nothing," Aunt Bryant says. "She's very preoccupied. Have you seen it? I don't know if it's because she's turning sixty or if there is more to it than that."

Raleigh is disappointed. She wants her news to supersede Lucinda's birthday. But what could be more serious to Lucinda than turning sixty? "I don't get it. She's been lying about her age for years. Lately she's been insane over the menus for the luncheon, every detail, and for the dinner dance. I wish it were over already. It would be such a relief."

"Of course, of course," Bryant nods. "Now tell me about this man. Gorgeous, smart, young, old?"

"A few years younger. He gets around, I'm sure. I don't know exactly why he's here. He's an architect. People come to Palm Beach to see the houses, the Breakers. I heard my old friends from the Academy are curious about him. Like Jilly Meil, you know she's getting divorced."

"Is she?" Aunt Bryant asks. "I had no idea."

Raleigh has said enough; she can't jinx this. She won't mention Kesgrave, how drawn to him she is. "I know nothing except he's Ivy League. That's useful information, I guess."

"Oh, Lucinda will love that."

For a few seconds they both laugh.

"I'd like to be careful, to keep this quiet," Raleigh says. "I haven't told my sisters. Well, I haven't told Caroline, and I doubt Maribelle cares since she still isn't speaking to me."

"They'd understand," Aunt Bryant says.

"Would they? Not really."

Aunt Bryant nods carefully. "Does this man—you don't have to name him—does he know who you are?"

"We haven't been together that many times . . ."

"Oh, I know. I know that cautious feeling."

"Do you?" Raleigh can't fathom that. Her aunt has been part good witch in *The Wizard of Oz*, part Miss Havisham in *Great Expectations*, and part a martyr for family—for her sisters, herself, Lucinda, for Raleigh's entire life.

"Never mind that. I meant who you are in Palm Beach. Does he know you're a Barrows?"

A Barrows. How depleting it is to be a Barrows. Some days it makes her want to leave the island, buy cheap wedge shoes online, sundresses on Amazon, paint only decorative art. And move down the coast—if not to Kesgrave, the Panhandle. That would upset her mother beyond if she were to date the wrong man. She hopes.

"No. Somehow, I've managed not to tell him. I want to be with him for who I am, not some nouveau riche soon-to-be-divorced woman with a child."

Aunt Bryant sniffs. "Those labels are never yours, Raleigh. Whatever this man knows or doesn't know."

WHEN RALEIGH heads south to pick up Caleb after confiding in her aunt, she has buyer's remorse. Sharing news of Porter hurts her head; she can't see him as clearly or feel him as deeply. It lessens her handful of memories: the hotel room in Kesgrave, the day he came off the tennis courts at Longgreens with Chip Darren and they feigned not knowing one another . . . she saw his muscles that are natural, not like he has a personal trainer. She cannot describe him to anyone or it becomes murky—his touch, his voice, how he steps through the room. Nothing in her life has ever been sacred before, nothing has been so painstaking. She knows that she'd go to great lengths for this man, that there is some danger around him.

Chapter Fifteen

2026

ALTHOUGH LUCINDA rarely admits to an error in judgment, Carla Barnes might prove a disappointing choice of a divorce attorney for Raleigh. As the situation unfolds, it's apparent Carla hasn't got those dimples of steel necessary for her daughter's pending battles. That Lucinda herself never appreciated Alex's vengeful side is proof she also hasn't guided her daughter to the right lawyer. It would be best to change to one of the guerrillas from Boca, but the stretch of matrimonial litigators from Palm Beach to Miami is interconnected. There's a price for disloyalty, especially among the stars of their boutique law firms. They are meant to appear civilized, understanding while capable of flipping into sharks if need be. Raleigh's weepy despair over custody of Caleb is almost distracting for Lucinda. She wants to avoid it like the paper wasps back in Kesgrave. Instead she needs to be sympathetic. While it is her daughter and her grandson whose happiness is at stake, this is also not good for the Barrows family, let alone the business. Being pitiable is almost worse than being ordinary. Who dares to divorce one of her daughters? That's where Alex should have known better. For the fiftieth time, Lucinda wonders how things with the girls and with Barrows would have played out were Reed still alive. She would have foisted the strange letters she's getting onto him. Reed who remained a duck hunter until he died, the Panhandle there beneath his Palm Beach veneer. A man who could twist anyone's arm.

Raleigh is right on time, crunching her tires on Lucinda's pavers. Lucinda gets in and slams the passenger door. They sort of nod to one another as Raleigh begins unnecessary swerves around the A1A. Raleigh has always been the worst driver of her three girls. Why didn't Lucinda agree to meet her there or drive herself?

"The Southern Bridge will be up," Lucinda says.

"That's beyond my power."

Her car is a miasma of candy wrappers, *I Can Read* books, and a beach towel strewn across the back seat. It isn't as if Caleb is with Raleigh enough for this, as if she and her son share a daily drive. That's the whole point, to make her daughter the custodial parent, to keep Alex from having hours and influence. This early divorce meeting kicks off a strategic plan for Raleigh.

"Alex has a girlfriend."

"Okay," Lucinda says. "He would by now. I only hope she's kind to Caleb."

"Kind to Caleb? That's rich, Mom. Alex is with our nanny, tooling around Palm Beach with her," Raleigh says.

"Gabriella, your nanny?"

"Exactly." Raleigh speeds up rather than slowing down as they approach the bridge. She does a quick screech to a halt.

"Well, that will work well for your custody plan—it won't be in his favor. If you don't run around with someone, Raleigh," Lucinda says. "You cannot fall for someone at this point."

Raleigh is silent. They're stopped in line with the other cars until the bridge goes back down.

"I can't and Alex can?" she finally says.

"I know it's unfair. I'm sure you want an adventure, still people are judging. Alex is a man in Palm Beach, and men get to have more power. Not that they should. You, the wife he ousted, the one who had an affair, need to be celibate. Let's win this divorce case. Don't jeopardize your custody battle. Later you can look at the choice of young men around town who might work for you."

"You're worried about how it would appear in Palm Beach. You're worried about gossip." Raleigh sounds surprisingly indignant.

"No, I'm not," Lucinda defends. "That's not the issue."

"I don't believe you. It's always on your mind. How you appear, how we—your daughters—appear. Mom, Alex is out there, having fun. He's vengeful, confident. I'm not allowed to have a life?"

She's met someone. It's in the lilt of her daughter's voice, her shoulders against the car seat, the slightest softness of her lips, in profile. This is the daughter who will never get that double chin that runs on Lucinda's side of the family. Yet there's a fatigue around Raleigh's eyes, even if her sadness has lessened. Sadness is something Lucinda can't tolerate—there's little room for it; didn't she learn that years back in Kesgrave? The more reason to get Raleigh's divorce in order. Her daughter has to win. For everyone's sake—Barrows are winners. That's their global message. Raleigh deserves a chance at happiness, that's the personal, less major reason.

"We should cancel this appointment. Carla is not the

right lawyer for you," Lucinda says. "I doubt she's sharp-witted enough. Things can be stacked against you easily, Raleigh."

"I'll be punished forever for Samuel, for hurting Alex—if that's what I did."

"Who cares what happened or what you have done." Lucinda sighs like she's exhaling a cigarette, how she used to do it. "What matters is what's ahead."

How she wishes it were that facile, erasing a past, no trace. For Raleigh there isn't a shot of that. They're in a fish-bowl, where Samuel's death and the fallout of the affair have a lingering if not front row effect in Palm Beach.

The bridge is going down, cars in the left lane are lurching forward. Raleigh is close to the BMW sedan in front of her. Lucinda begins a text to Sybil Trask, asking the name of the divorce lawyer her niece used from Lauderdale or was it Miami. A text comes back at once. *Beyond expensive and I don't usually mention cost. Worth every cent.*

Being compassionate toward her daughter would work while instead she's suspicious. "You are with someone right now, that's it?"

"Unexpectedly."

Lucinda sucks in the air once again before she does a long exhale—double dipping on her thoughts. "What is ahead for you is clear, especially with this suddenly monstrous ex of yours out to win. He's becoming a famous artist on top of it. Women at the card games at Longgreens talk about it. Eventually, of course, there should be a right next husband for you, Raleigh."

"I'm sure you prefer your daughters married," Raleigh says.

"Yes, absolutely." She points to a parking spot.

Raleigh pulls over on South Country Road in front of Classic Bookshop. Mothers of little children push strollers, walk hand in hand toward a playgroup or morning program. They have that attitude, as if they're doing something monumental, out and about as young mothers with high-earning husbands. Women who naively believe in a solid future, youth, family, success. As if the role is brilliant. One mother has a small son, maybe four, who is laughing and squealing with their blond labradoodle. Lucinda imagines Caleb with Alex and that damn nanny and their rescue dog, Arlo, a hound Caleb adores. Days filled with drop-offs and pickups while Raleigh is disenfranchised.

"Right, Maribelle is supposed to be remarried soon and I'm supposed to find an eligible man on your timetable. Ever since Maribelle showed up content to be single, not dating, there's this bizarre take on it. As if you believe she's *other*—she's crossed over to the dark side."

"Maribelle is a free woman. For you, Raleigh, it's a timing issue. At the moment, the long-suffering single mother card is the best one to play."

Lucinda leans forward and turns up the air on her side. It blasts at her. Her phone dings; she reads the text quickly, dictates a response.

"Yes, my youngest daughter. Raleigh." She fishes for a pen in her purse, scribbles frantically on a notepad. "I've got it. Thank you. I look forward to seeing you tonight at the Leners."

Hanging up, Lucinda googles, points west, then south.

"Let's get on the 95. We're going to Gregory Dent. He's excellent for the biggest and trickiest cases."

"We don't have an appointment. We have to cancel Carla," Raleigh says.

"We will. Just head toward Miami. I'll find out which office this lawyer is in today," Lucinda says.

"And barge in, like that?"

"Rather like that. Directly to the best." Lucinda tries to recall if Carla belongs to Longgreens or the Harbor Club, one of the dinner clubs. She shouldn't alienate her. It won't work in her favor. Saving her daughter and youngest grandchild will require time, wisdom, always money. "Look, we'll retain both of them. We need the ammunition. I'll pay for this, Raleigh. It has to be done right." Raleigh's driving is slipshod. It puts Lucinda on edge. "Pull over. I'll drive the 95."

On the highway, Lucinda glances at Raleigh, texting furiously, almost smiling. She has that glow, the kind great sex elicits. If she isn't heeding her mother's warning, there's no need for a recount. Only for the divorce to be on track.

Chapter Sixteen

2026

WITH RAIN SLASHING across the island, the twentieth-century gallery at the Shelteere Museum is busy for a Wednesday morning. Women stroll with women, their heads tucked, holding conversations as important as the place. Lucinda is positive these pairs are trading secrets as they linger over the O'Keeffes and Hoppers. Then the few couples of every age. Some men wear pastel Hokas and rain parkas, while younger women are in yoga pants and sweatshirts. What gets Lucinda's attention are the seasoned wives, those who have won at the game, in neat puffer vests and expensive jeans or jeggings.

Jolie is late, which is rare—too late for Lucinda to confide in her about yesterday's divorce lawyer search for Raleigh. Instead, Lucinda is concentrating on where they're meant to meet—at the members' desk. Will Jolie be waiting there, not gliding around? Then she appears, put together as ever, moving through this calm space, in contrast to Lucinda, who fears, despite her best efforts, that she's losing her looks, her style. For someone who is always ordering others to straighten up, she's secretly a hunched-over woman today. Her makeup is smooth and subtle, as always. Isn't it? Yet when she smiles, her face is not brighter; there's no amount of product that could make a difference. She only hopes no one has caught on, no one whispers that something has changed about her. Her Birkin bag and bird-themed scarf must camouflage her mindset. She can't be simply pretty enough, rich enough, powerful enough—she is Lucinda Barrows. She needs to be chic and exuberant. How else can those hand-delivered letters fade in importance? Instead, she is worried constantly. Who is sending them and always the question why? She shudders at the idea of someone else getting copies. Then two of her daughters are not speaking and off-track for youngish Palm Beach women.

"Here we are!" Jolie is delighted to see her. Although she hasn't the kind of money Lucinda and her family have amassed, Jolie doesn't care. While lifestyle matters to Lucinda, Jolie is impressively unencumbered by it.

"We'd best hurry."

They begin the two-step that every other viewer has chosen, heading into the room with Corots, Courbets and Lucinda's favorite, a Rosa Bonheur—not only because she was a woman artist but for her depiction of lions. Lucinda can't focus; her anxiety is rising.

Jolie is watching her. "Let's get to the boardroom."

AT TIMES Lucinda wonders if, in her next life, she'll skip being on these boards. At the moment, she chairs the Aquatic Preservation Board, the Arts into Schools Board, and the Fashion Palm Beach Initiative, while serving on six other boards. When asked, it's hard to resist; these accolades are a path to social ascension. Yet today she wants escape.

"How long will this run?" she asks.

Jolie stops for a second. "A recap of the new calendar—events, programming. Not exciting."

Lucinda needs to get into the washroom and take a Xanax. That would help, except at once they're whisked off to tables covered with white cloths, and breakfast is about to be served. The waitstaff is formal, old-school. Women are already seated—friends, acquaintances, those you would not cross. To her left is Lucinda's wine tasting club, to her right is her bridge game, and behind is her Monday pickleball "group." They might be staring at her from every direction.

Until a few months ago, Lucinda knew women talked about her in respectful, envious tones. Today, she is no longer sure—she might be losing prestige. Only last Friday at Longgreens, ready to play nine holes before lunch and cards, she was slighted. When she arrived, she wasn't on the chart for her golf game. It wasn't feasible to not be included. Livid, she complained to Janine, the golf pro.

"This is a mistake that must be fixed," she said.

"I'm sorry, Mrs. Barrows," Janine said, without looking up from the schedule. "There is no mistake. Mrs. Detrix called and asked for you to be switched out."

Although Janine was able to get her into another game, Lucinda barely knew the women; they were new members, two from Boca. She had to act as if being excluded and pushed to the side had no greater implications, taking her back to when she and Reed first arrived in Palm Beach over twenty years ago. As if being one of the best female golfers and one of the richest weren't enough. Lucinda was off kilter, shaken. Worse, later in the locker room, she'd heard the toxic whispers. Were they talking about her? She couldn't be sure. She imagined how it would go—*The daughters? Two not speaking . . . after the accident . . . Maribelle is back . . . a shame she left PB Confidential . . . Raleigh's divorce. Messy . . . only five years old . . . the father . . . excellent portraits, wasn't Raleigh the portrait artist . . . he's contemporary.* She knew without proof how devastating this would be.

Jolie taps her arm. "Lucinda, wasn't that your suggestion?"

The conversation has taken off, and ideas are moving fast. Lilly Coles stands up to describe a mother-daughter-granddaughter benefit luncheon for next season. "Let's do that," she says. "Everyone here has a daughter or two, a granddaughter in college, high school."

"How about a mother-daughter lecturer team—does something like that exist?" Sandra Wiley asks.

These women stand as testimony to Lucinda's idea, her very theme. The one she has been sharing foolishly in the locker room of Longgreens, the Harbor Club, Boat and Oar. She's witnessing their claim of her concept of next year's luncheon at the Shelteere. They have stolen the notion she was about to present.

Jolie taps her again, tips her head as a signal Lucinda should say something. Lucinda is steeped in the realization that nothing is hers anymore. She can't speak.

Jolie stands up. "We could do it with curators, art, maybe poetry and art together. Lucinda, didn't we talk about this, how lively it could be?"

Lucinda tries out her best Palm Beach smile with no effect. Like her lipstick is painted on her face. In a moment, Sidney Loree, leading the subcommittee, will take an unofficial count of yays and nays. A preliminary reading.

Lucinda's brain fogs; she is not mildly disappointed, she is deeply unnerved. She stands up, murmurs she's not well, a migraine, and unfortunately has left her rescue meds in the car. She leaves, believing the women are whispering about her. Jolie follows her.

"Jolie, you see how I'm treated," she says.

Without a word, Jolie opens her umbrella, holds it over both their heads. Lucinda is close to falling from grace.

Chapter Seventeen

2026

WILLIAM, rained out of golf, has pulled into the garage when Lucinda parks beside him. Together, after a peck of a kiss, they go through the kitchen door. Rosie is cleaning out the refrigerator, an array of apples, pears, goat cheese, and oat milk yogurts are on the counter.

She shows Lucinda an envelope, like the others. "Mrs. Barrows, someone put this under the front door, and it triggered the alarm. The alarm company called, and the police came."

"That proves it works. The alarm is set from the ground to the rim of the door," William says.

Anxiety, the kind Lucinda tried to shed during her brief ride back from the Shelteere, creeps in.

"Did the camera get a picture?" William asks. "I'm sure it did."

"It doesn't matter, William." Lucinda tries to sound normal. "We don't need to do anything."

"I'll take it, Rosie. A letter addressed to me, isn't it?" He holds out his hand.

Lucinda stretches her hand out farther. "Or to me."

Rosie forks it over as if it's a reward. The three of them are standing beneath a hued light, meant to be kind to women of every age who are guests at their home. A murky, temporary solution for crepey skin.

"Maybe first see that the pool isn't overflowing," Lucinda says. "They were here today, and I always like to make sure."

"I checked," Rosie says.

"Thank you, Rosie. William, can you verify the temperature is at eighty-four? The pool gets cold quickly during heavy rain. Maribelle will swim laps tomorrow." Lucinda knows he'll do this; he loves scrutinizing a home that's already in top order.

She clutches the envelope, another installment that is meant for her. A confessional, an apologia. Is she the only audience? Once William is gone, she rushes into the main bedroom. The shades are open, a sleazy, grayish cast emanates from outside. The rain becomes stronger, reminding her of how flooded Route One would get, back in Kesgrave, the Panhandle, during an unrelenting rainstorm. In the past, she tells herself—yet it is disquieting. She walks into her dressing room, closes the door. In the mirror, her face is hollow, drawn. She begins to read.

THE CITY

I thought I was cheating on Kesgrave those first days in the city. Like being saved from an abusive lover while still loyal. I took my map and toured. I was in sneaks and jeans, doing the width of it, east to west. I had to see both rivers to know I'd survive. They framed the buildings. Since there were waterways, I could manage.

I wasn't ready for the crowds. Even on Sundays, people were everywhere, shoving, yelling, always rushing toward something or someplace. One humid afternoon I photographed a series of women. Maybe it would not be about men again. I'd seen such awful things. The women were exquisite—their jawlines, how they walked with purpose. Few of us came from around there; we were transplants. What struck me most was that no one seemed afraid. I wondered who they were, what their secrets were, where they were going, who they loved and who loved them. How did they become savvy—how could I become one of them? I knew nothing. I had just gotten there.

At night I'd wake up to sirens, to voices of people who walked the night long, many with their dogs barking. My brother's death was this hole in me, yet duller in the city. I didn't know how to get started. I had no friends, no connections, only a portfolio and a dream. Plus the money they'd given me. I took classes at The New School and got lucky. I had a mentor, and I became his apprentice. Then his lover. I told myself he loved me for my talent, and maybe he did, maybe he didn't. Either way, he got me started. He gave me so much, including you.

I had a small solo show. The reviewers loved my pictures, the angles, how I captured light, illuminated profiles. Proof I existed beyond Kesgrave, proof of life. When I thought of home, of everyone, I pushed them out of my mind. Except Lucinda, Bryant, and I had been like sisters. It wouldn't go away.

Once I became established, I made plenty of friends, but I was guarded. I had promised to be. I thought about the dead.

Folding up the letter, Lucinda opens the safe where she keeps her jewelry and locks it inside. William knocks on the door.

"Lucinda, are you okay? Can I come in?"

"Just a second." She sucks in her breath, double-checks the safe door, counts to ten.

"The rain isn't letting up. Might I interest you in a few *Saturday Night Live* skits in the library?" He knocks again; he's ready to walk in. An invitation to a shared stormy afternoon in Florida. Sex might or might not follow. He is her husband, after all. "Lucinda?"

"One sec, William, please."

Lucinda moves toward him, sucking in more air, remembering she was indigent as a girl in Kesgrave. Her mother cleaned houses and motel rooms. Her father had no steady work as a shrimper—he drank too much. Cousins and friends knew and thought less of her. A life she fought to leave behind. The first step up was Reed, followed by Barrows becoming a local chain. Suddenly they had money in a poor town. They were rewarded for their efforts.

Except she couldn't totally shake the weight of it, the trade made for the payoff.

Chapter Eighteen

2026

Boat and oar club has always been Raleigh's favorite among every membership Lucinda and Reed sought when they first moved to Palm Beach. While those who belong praise the building, location, and food, it is the mix of precision and allure, the terraces overlooking the ocean, that appeals to Raleigh. "The north end of the island is most beautiful," Lucinda always says, "with those wide, dramatic beaches and slight cliffs." For her Gilded Age white tie birthday party, it is the obvious choice.

First to arrive, Raleigh, in a seafoam skirt and white T-shirt, finds a chair. Kit Carter, in her yoga pants and Hokas, saunters in and immediately hovers over the table settings. Hired by Caroline as the party organizer, she is Raleigh's friend from the Academy. They did ballet and hip-hop together in fifth grade.

Kit starts taking items out of her bag—a Bakelite barrette, her phone. She finds a pen and pad, opens it up. "We cannot use their napkins."

Raleigh turns toward them. "Really? I mean the tables here are always pretty."

"No, no, your mother wants another effect. Don't you agree?" Kit parades about the vast, empty dining room, assessing its potential.

"Sure." Raleigh walks beyond her, along the margins. Although she has arrived ahead and in her family, who gets there first has significance, she is in no position to have an opinion.

"She's chosen *The Gilded Age* as a theme, you know, like the series."

Raleigh nods, the tide is coming in, it's distracting. "That works for a big birthday dinner."

"Your mother also mentioned *War and Peace.*" Kit keeps moving from table to table. The linens are a light amber. She holds up swatches of pale blue and lime green and darker shades of blue and fuchsia as options. She fishes around in her large canvas L.L. Bean bag, pulling out pastel and primary shade napkins, hand painted, some with an amorphous flower print.

Raleigh half likes both ideas for the theme. "Maybe we'd better wait 'til my mother gets here for everything, Kit. She's pretty fussy."

Kit claps. "Remember when we got caught smoking in her mini-Versailles gardens at the house? We were in eleventh grade."

"Totally. She grounded me, but I was relieved. I missed Jess Corsage's sweet sixteen."

"I was there—you missed little."

They both laugh. Since Kit is her only Academy friend who never married and doesn't seem to care, it's a relief being in her company. "You must have some single friends now," Aunt Bryant coached Raleigh recently. "You'll find them."

WHEN LUCINDA and Caroline come in from the office, the mood shifts to pure business. Lucinda has been obsessed with her luncheon and the evening party to follow four days later. When they were speaking yesterday, she told Raleigh that getting these festivities right is like walking neck high in manure. Today she's coiffed and fashionable in a coral boucle jacket and wide silk pants. No matter what, Lucinda has a complete focus on place settings, guest lists, and assigned seating. There could be a tornado approaching the island and she'd remain in this mode. It is Caroline who follows her around the room, looking wiped out, as if she's just missed a train or plane and has no recourse.

Kit carefully lays out the napkins as if she's at the card table. Lucinda fingers the fabrics, frowning at the color scheme. Rosie arrives, rushing in with a large shopping bag, nods at everyone, and without speaking, starts unpacking Lucinda's personal pale blue linen napkins with her monogram, *LBM*, stitched in a deeper blue.

"Well, those are quite perfect," Kit says. "Do you have a hundred and twenty-five of them? If not, we'll use one for every other place setting and fill in with what I've brought."

Lucinda tosses her head back, takes off her Lafont progressives, a pink cat-eye frame from fifteen years ago. Raleigh remembers when Reed bought them for her in Paris. She was alone on that trip with her parents. Today Lucinda's eyes look tired, the skin beneath puffy. Not as usual.

"Kit, dear," Lucinda says. "Let's you and I decide on the flowers and the final menu. Besides lobster rolls, arugula salad, and chicken paillard."

"I have a call today with the Free Forever Bakery. The gluten-free cake will be a replica of the new Barrows in Atlanta," Caroline says. Her phone rings. She holds up her hand, steps back to take the call. Raleigh steps back with her. A moment later they head toward the women's locker room.

THE SPACE is much bigger than at Harbor Club or Longgreens. Raleigh plunks down on the beige linen sofa in the parlor area. Across from her on the wide quartz vanity is a bowl with Bayer Aspirin, Extra Strength Tylenol, and Benadryl.

"I can't be here much longer," Raleigh says. "You guys can do the table settings or whatever's next. It isn't as if we haven't discussed this ad nauseum."

Caroline sits quietly on the love seat facing Raleigh. "Mom wants us here."

"Where is Maribelle? Why is she late?" Raleigh asks.

Her face is composed, Lucinda style, but Caroline is sucking in her breath. What they've been taught—to feign repose when the situation is anything but calm.

"She's not coming." Caroline stares at the long communal vanity where hand cream, mouthwash, and cotton balls are placed.

"I'm sorry, what is that?"

"I thought you knew."

Raleigh looks closely at Caroline. She really is a pro. "You knew I didn't know, Caroline. Why is that?"

"Because you two are still not speaking and Lucinda doesn't want to deal with it. She says it's ruining her week." Caroline stands up, puts her bag on the vanity. She starts combing her hair with a neon green wide-tooth comb. She has the best hair in the family at the moment, although it's always a seesaw among the three sisters. Who has the best clothes, shoes, totes, hair, reading selection. Except Raleigh and Maribelle aren't in the game now; they barely speak.

Raleigh gets up to be next to Caroline. In the mirror, by her own standards, Raleigh appears drained. She could use eyeliner, the kind that has no parabens or preservatives. Maribelle told her about it ages ago, and she can't remember the brand. Raleigh bites her lips, hoping it will bring some color to her face, like a princess in some book she read decades ago. She could be conflating two tales, and it wasn't about a princess.

"Since you're here, stay, weigh in on the table designs . . . something."

"What do she and Kit want me for? They know what to do," Raleigh says.

"It was Mom's idea. She asked us to come," Caroline says. "She could have brought Aunt Bryant or someone from her bridge games if she needed anyone's opinion."

"Exactly," Raleigh says. "Isn't the décor, the music, the theme very specific?"

Caroline shakes her head. "Whatever."

Raleigh starts lifting her hair with her fingers. Despite how heavy it still seems, she's losing some each day. The stress of the divorce, Alex asking for alimony, that she and Maribelle are not speaking, all of it holding her back. She feels some kind of internal psychic click, as if she is literally moving to the other side of the feud with Maribelle. She is courting with being Zen about it.

"I'm relieved Maribelle's not coming."

"Are you?" Caroline snaps her bag shut. "Let's go. We can't keep Lucinda and Kit waiting."

LUCINDA'S tobacco-colored Vivier kitten pumps tap across the wide-planked wood floor that is original and impeccably resurfaced. "Raleigh, a word?"

"Sure," Raleigh says.

Caroline moves along quickly to the other end of the dining room where Kit is on her cell, her arms in the air.

No one is around and still Lucinda steers Raleigh toward the wall. They face the ocean. An unusually rough tide churns up, the sun has gone in. Lucinda places her right hand on Raleigh's elbow. In her best pretend nice tone, she begins. "Raleigh as you are aware, these festivities for my birthday *must* go well. Lately it has been a crazy salad. William is not as malleable as he used to be, nor quite as presentable. I don't want to be pegged as having an old, waddly husband, but he could be headed in that direction. I wasn't included in the top thirty for Blair Jazzer's fiftieth birthday luncheon. I'd like to say it's age driven—her list is younger—except I know who was invited, and that's not the case. No one in our family can be fodder for gossip. I cannot have you and Maribelle *estranged*."

How Lucinda pronounces "estranged" is like she recently learned the word and wants to put it to good use. Or she wishes she were from England.

Lucinda clears her throat. "Your feud with Maribelle . . . about Samuel . . . the affair, whatever, is old news. Over. Is that clear? You'll both have to put it behind you."

Raleigh tugs her skirt down and wiggles her toes while looking impassive, appropriately remorseful. "I'm not the one. Maribelle won't spend time with me or be in the room if I am."

Lucinda takes her phone out of her pocket, begins texting. It isn't clear if she's reaching out to Maribelle or answering a text. Her breath rises and falls. "Here's how it's going to work. You and Maribelle will no longer carry on your private war. There is a great amount at stake." Lucinda frowns, runs her tongue across her upper lip—a sign she's determined. "By the end of today you will be speaking, and that is how it will be from hereon in. We cannot undo the past. No one can. God knows I'd give anything for that to be the case."

Since when has their mother become a sentimentalist, someone who second-guesses? "Okay, I get it," Raleigh says. The sky is getting darker, although the Palm Beach weather report predicts sunshine.

"Raleigh, I need a commitment to this plan. I know something is up. I won't have it. I'd like for *PB Confidential* or at least *The Daily Sheet* to do something for my birthday parties. *Confidential* should put us on the cover."

Lucinda is delusional—her birthday isn't newsworthy; it's merely important to her and within her circle. Even in Palm Beach it doesn't seem to be worth printing. Besides, it's doubtful that Maribelle has the clout to pitch any storyline, let alone their mother.

Across the room Caroline is earnestly considering the color scheme for the luncheon while Raleigh has done next to nothing for her mother's birthday. She's too stuck, something has to give. Mostly Lucinda needs the feud with Maribelle to end.

"This isn't taxing. Appearances are everything, you know that. Besides, you and Maribelle have always been close. She practically raised you. You've heard my wishes, yes?"

"I'll do my best." Raleigh sounds watery, wishy-washy. The desolation of days without Maribelle is real. If only she could vouch for her sister.

Chapter Nineteen

2026

SUNDAY IN SEASON at the Breakers Beach Club is filled with snowbirds who come for the winter months. Lucinda relishes weekends there and while Raleigh most often declines the invitation, today she is with Caleb. He loves Lucinda's cabana at the ocean, the hot dogs and fries for lunch. She always sneaks in a Coke or Sprite, claiming she's the grandmother, she's allowed.

All afternoon Lucinda smiles, seeming almost relaxed. She's been maniacal lately, Caleb distracts her. He is disarming today in his bathing trunks and polo shirt. He sits still whenever Raleigh reapplies sunscreen and adjusts his baseball cap. He wades in the ocean and swims in the large pool. In her pink and melon print sarong and white maillot, Raleigh is on best behavior. With everyone buzzing about, from Lucinda's friends to her sisters' friends to her own from the Academy, it's a reprieve of sorts. The energy and beauty provide enough diversion.

By five o'clock, Raleigh rushes to have Caleb ready for his father, and the temporary high of the day begins to disintegrate.

"Mommy, what's wrong?" Caleb asks. He sounds wistful. She's busy wiping the sand off his Crocs.

Raleigh doesn't answer. She's sorry to be leaving. It has

been a relief to be only with Lucinda and not her sisters, although she never used to think like that. And rare for her mother not to include the entourage—Maribelle, Caroline, her family, and Aunt Bryant. Samuel was always there, of course, when he was alive, as Maribelle's husband, as Raleigh's covert lover. Raleigh herself with Alex and Caleb completed the supposed family picture. Today was unusual and fading fast. In anticipation of returning Caleb to Alex for his allotted time, she is sickened, sorrowful.

"Mommy?" Caleb looks at her. He's got those round brown eyes, more Alex than hers, but his mouth is hers, full lips, a wide smile. His face is symmetrical, ideal for a painting. She ought to sketch him now as a kindergartner because it's fleeting, gone in a snap.

"Mom!"

"Oh, Caleb, I'm sorry, Potato. Let's go to the lobby. Dad will be there."

She collects her beach bag, his backpack, with two books about food trucks and a miniature football, tugs on her floppy wheat-colored sun protector hat, and takes his hand.

Lucinda, also in some weird hiatus-type trance, comes up from her walk with William along the shore. "Caleb, dear, I'm sorry to see you go." In grandmother mode, she leans down, kisses him goodbye. Raleigh tries to recall if her mother was ever sorry to see her go and can't.

"Raleigh," she says. "Thank you for the day together."

Maybe her mother is on Prozac or one of the other SSRIs that make people calmer. Could it make them warmer and kinder?

William, in his requisite Lacoste medium-blue shirt and khaki shorts, winks at Caleb. "Is there anything you'd like next week, Caleb? More gummy bears, a chocolate lollipop?"

Raleigh shakes her head. "Thank you. We're good."

Her mother comes close and gives her a stilted hug. Her diamond heart necklace glistens—the one she promised Maribelle when she married Samuel (then reneged), promised to Caroline when she married Travis (then reneged), and didn't bother to offer to Raleigh. Apparently, it mattered to her—Reed chose it for her at Tiffany's on their first family trip to New York City. Her three daughters love the necklace; they were there when he surprised her with it.

Raleigh is confused—it's awkward. "We'd better go. I don't want Caleb to be late."

THROUGH THE LONG, regal lobby with vaulted ceilings, Raleigh swooshes by guests and tourists moving in both directions. Everyone looks familiar and strange, like it's a mirage and she's a teenager again, hanging out at the Breakers. Whenever she was dropped off with her friends, Lucinda and Aunt Bryant spoke of the Mediterranean style elegance, while mostly it was incredible fun to be there. She's moving toward Alex, holding Caleb's hand tightly, stunned to see Porter walking in her direction.

"Raleigh?" he says. He's in a linen shirt and a bathing suit, carrying a brimmed straw hat. "Hey, how are you?"

Raleigh is jumpy.

"I didn't mean to frighten you. I guess I keep showing up."

Raleigh might listen to anything he says—his voice is that polished.

"I didn't expect to see you." She looks down at Caleb. "Porter, meet Caleb, my son."

Porter kneels, holds out his hand. "Hello, Caleb. I'm pleased to meet you. I've heard about you from your mother."

Caleb steps back, then forward. Porter touches the tip of his baseball cap. Caleb puts out his hand for his little boy handshake. "Who are you?"

Porter stands back up. "I'm your mother's friend. I'm at the Breakers admiring the architecture, the property."

"We were with my mother at the beach club," Raleigh says. She's relieved she didn't run into him there. Besides, he would have had to be a member or a guest of one to access the cabanas.

"Nice," Porter says. "Caleb, what did you do there? Did you catch crabs, a fish or two?"

Caleb laughs. "No. I ate hot dogs and had a cupcake. I swam."

"Are you a good swimmer?" Porter asks.

"I am, I swam the whole kid pool."

"Did you? I'd like to see that," Porter says. "We could have a race."

"You can. I'll tell Mom. She'll make a plan to bring you." Caleb looks happy, earnest.

A pool of sunlight shines over them. Both her son and Porter are lovely. Caleb's eyes travel to the left side of the lobby, and his mood changes at once. Raleigh watches Alex's fast approach. His gait is quicker than it used to be. He is arrogant—it precedes him. Whenever they meet to exchange Caleb, he seems in a perpetual state of low-level rage.

"Dad! Daddy!" Caleb shouts. "Over here."

Alex has already noticed the three of them. He pushes

ahead of other people, through the lobby, in order to reach his son.

"Caleb!" He shouts, scooping him up in his arms. "My boy!"

Caleb, raised above eye level with Raleigh, laughs. Porter waits.

"Alex, meet Porter. Porter, Alex."

The two men nod, neither holds out a hand.

"Hello, how are you?" Porter asks in a well-mannered voice. Although Raleigh hasn't a clue how, he has been raised well enough.

Alex puts Caleb back down and takes his bag. "We are set, my boy."

As chiseled as ever, with a bone structure Raleigh used to admire, Alex is now more muscular, like he goes to the gym religiously. Porter, standing there, is every bit as attractive on a classic checklist and more so. Not even close. Raleigh is sorry that the two have met.

"We'd best be off," Alex says. "We've got dinner plans at Cucina with the Lawrences and movie night after that. We'll watch *Robo-Dog*."

Raleigh bends, gives Caleb a tight hug. "I love you. I'll see you on Tuesday. I'll pick you up from school."

Alex and Caleb walk toward the entrance. After six feet, they turn around. Alex leads Caleb back, coming close to Raleigh. "Let me underscore the situation, Raleigh." He has lowered his voice, still Porter and Caleb can hear. "If this friend of yours wants anything to do with my son, it won't be happening. I'll stop him or any other man on your path. No one comes near my son. I am his father, is that clear? Understood?"

He turns and yanks Caleb's hand, heading again toward

the entrance. She waits for Caleb to look back at her, but he doesn't.

"I'm sorry about that," she says.

"It's not your fault," Porter says.

She only imagines what he's thinking, what a mess it is to witness.

"My ex, he's very . . ."

"I saw that," Porter says.

"I wish you hadn't."

Porter touches her shoulder. "Where are you going?"

Raleigh's trying not to cry. "This minute?"

"Let's go to the Colony."

"Sure," she says, except she hasn't brushed her teeth in hours and has no real clothes in her beach bag. She needs a minute. "Sure, let's."

QUICKLY, in single file, they cut through the Colony pool, around the lounge chairs, and on to Porter's room. The room she wants to be their world, with a balcony and limited square footage—a bed and desk on the ocean side of the island. She knows it by heart, the crisp white bedding, the palest blue walls. He hits Spotify on his phone, "Sad-Eyed Lady of the Lowlands" plays.

"Why did you choose this?"

"It makes me think of you," he says.

"I'm not only sad, Porter." She is half lying.

"I know that."

He takes her hand, starts a slow dance. She puts her face against his neck. She might be okay were she able to stay with him, moving to a song Aunt Bryant, a Dylan fan, loves. The only reason Raleigh has heard it. When it ends, he stops the music as if he's waiting, deep in thought. They sit down on the edge of the bed. She ought to say something about the Breakers.

"I want to apologize for this afternoon. Caleb likes you."

"I like him. Not sure about his father."

Although it wasn't quite choreographed, she is glad he met Caleb but wishes he hadn't met Alex. An image of Caleb eating lamb chops with mint jelly while missing her slips in and out of her mind. Next, her head fills with Porter and what she doesn't know about him—while he's witnessed her plight an hour ago.

"I care about you, Raleigh. That being said . . . I'm not sure this is a good idea. You have a kid. You have a divorce ahead of you. I'm around to view the architecture, the place. I never meant to meet you."

That same coldness fills her as when Samuel used to say he loved his wife, her sister Maribelle—as when Alex used to say she could do no wrong. Then Samuel drowned, and Alex decided she was very wrong, wrong enough to divorce and to spite.

"What do you mean? We did meet, and we do matter to each other. You asked me about my son, and unexpectedly today you saw him," Raleigh says.

"If only you could take the 'Barrows' out of Raleigh Barrows," he says.

"I don't exactly know why that's the problem," she says.

"Right, it's about your married name too. Could you erase Morton while you're at it and come as Raleigh?"

As Raleigh Morton, she and Alex had brought Caleb to the Colony for a literacy fundraiser. It was held on the patio and beach. A clown painted the children's faces. She and Alex linked arms and shared a laugh at how delighted their son was, twirling in circles. Self-reproach saturates her. Alex is a spoiler who has fallen in line with the meanest of ex-husbands in town.

She puts her arms over his shoulders. "I'm here, Porter, for you, with you."

His eyes are closed, his chest against hers. His breath is perfect. He undresses her slowly while they're kissing harder, holding tightly. Nothing else counts, only she and Porter, swept up together. For the moment because they can't resist—similar to breakup sex, except they've never been a couple.

Chapter Twenty

2026

LUCINDA comes to Barrows straight from a bridge game at Longgreens carrying a Kelly bag. She's in an ecru sheath, not a recognizable designer, possibly one of her "cheap and cheery" dresses from a generic source.

Despite the sophistication of the Barrows offices, with an assured ambiance, there's an unpredictable gloominess today. She isn't sure why Caroline asked for a meeting here, which red flags what her daughter wishes to discuss.

Lucinda is arranging photographs and framed articles on the side bar when Caroline comes in, placing her iPad on the conference table.

"These are dusty, aren't they?" Lucinda asks.

Caroline sighs. "I'm not sure, Mom."

"Please, call me Lucinda. Your sisters do."

"I call you Lucinda when I'm talking *about* you," Caroline says.

"Ah, often I hope and in glowing terms." Lucinda keeps fluttering around. "What can I do for you, Caroline? You insisted on meeting today."

Caroline appears unhappy. "I'd say I requested, not insisted."

Lucinda circles the room, running her hands along the furniture.

"Mom . . . Lucinda, what are you doing?"

"Checking. That's it."

"Okay."

"I'm checking we aren't being recorded," Lucinda says.

"Excuse me? Why would that be?"

"Let's sit down. I know our schedules are tight. There's a three o'clock with Raleigh's attorneys, both teams. I've asked them to come, meet in person."

"Estelle told me. I have a marketing meeting at the same time."

Lucinda settles into the Reed chair. Beneath the mid-sixties lighting, she doesn't look well. Her dress is loose; her profile hasn't that sharp jawline; she's drained. If this continues, it could become Lucinda's greatest fear—a slack face, a double chin, a turkey neck to follow. She knows her eyes lately are flattened, like she's been given bad news. Her posture requires effort. She isn't holding her head and shoulders back in her exaggerated style. She gazes around as if she hasn't been there before.

"Mom, I mean Lucinda, did you know that I once saw you like you are today, years ago, back in Kesgrave?"

Lucinda twists her body and face toward Caroline. "Really? I don't recall. How would you compare this to Kesgrave? We are in Palm Beach. In a few hours I'll drive back along the A1A to my beautiful home. You will do the same later, returning to your daughters, your husband."

Kesgrave. Lucinda hears herself pronounce it as an obscure word she's unexpectedly come upon.

"Correct." Caroline checks her phone. "Shall we discuss the key objective for today?"

Her gestalt is corporate. Lucinda, instead of bracing for

a distasteful conversation ahead, considers if her daughter needs a makeover. She's stylish, though not enough for their circles. Presentation means a great deal in their sphere. Lucinda nods. "Sure."

"Well, you have the same vibe as decades ago, in Kesgrave. I was fourteen. Your bedroom door was wide open. You and Dad were arguing on the stairway. You stood at the top of the landing. Dad was halfway down. It was around three in the morning."

"I have no memory." Lucinda opens her bag and takes a buttery pink pashmina to put around her shoulders.

"Don't you?" Caroline asks. "Your voices were strident. You kept saying *the river* that day. You were shouting at Dad. I couldn't see your faces, only your backs. You wore an aqua silk slip nightie. Dad wore boxers with the Champion logo. It was the only time I ever heard you cry."

Caroline should stop. This prelude isn't necessary. "I don't remember," Lucinda says.

"None of it?" Caroline asks. "In the morning, Maribelle and I woke Raleigh and got her ready for preschool. We let her wear whatever she wanted. A clashing ensemble, a red sweatshirt with magenta leggings—from T.J. Maxx, which you disdained. You let her wear it, to fit in with everyone else. *Until we get out of here*, you used to whisper. I know Raleigh heard you."

"Why are you—why are we doing this, Caroline?" Lucinda asks.

"I need to finish, to explain how worried we are about you now. That morning when you came down to breakfast, your voice was like you'd been chain smoking. Your eyes looked like they are today. That's why I'm telling you."

Lucinda wishes her daughter were less expressive, less of a storyteller. Every detail rings true, and yet there's no point. "I've come to tell you something. It sort of meshes with what you just talked about."

"What is going on that you seem as unhappy as back then?" Caroline asks.

"I'm okay. Do I seem other than that? Are my timing and lighting off?"

"Yes, actually," Caroline says. "You're tired. You've never been tired."

"Very. It has been, it *is* a long haul, Caroline. Listen . . ." She doesn't continue. Once she describes the letters, they become true; it cannot be taken back, wished away. An anguish sets in, the mood overwhelming the space.

Caroline leads her to the couch. Lucinda's knees graze the coffee table as if she's in the wrong place, not in the choreographed conference room where hundreds of meetings have occurred.

"What is it?"

"I've been . . . I'm being . . . I'm getting these letters. Someone who knows me has written them. They're in an order, entries in a diary, to destroy me by the end. I haven't told anyone. I can't drag William into it. Maribelle is preoccupied. She's single, alone. Raleigh is getting divorced, upset."

"You're confiding in me."

"Exactly," Lucinda says.

"Okay. What do you know, and how is it obvious that someone is out to destroy you?"

"I know it. I am very sure, Caroline," Lucinda says. "Someone from my past has written these. They're out to get me at this late stage. After I've overcome so much."

Caroline frowns genuinely confused. "I don't get it. Your past? You're talking as if you have some dark secret."

Lucinda looks away. "I keep thinking of hand-me-downs, being poor, how mean girls could be."

"I'm not sure what . . ." Caroline says.

"Nothing, really. Never mind that." Lucinda opens her right palm. She's holding a Miniature Black Caviar Jar pill-box by Judith Leiber. Caroline and her daughters gave it to her last year for Tylenol, antacids, Benadryl.

"What are you taking, Mom? Maybe we should tell Travis about the letters. Go to the police?"

"No, I don't think so. Not Travis, not the police. Not yet."

"Why not?"

"I can't say."

Caroline lowers her voice like Lucinda has a migraine. "Tell me anything. Some ghost in your closet? Some crazy-shit admirer? Let's protect you and our family."

Lucinda takes out a pill and swigs it back, washing it down with Saratoga water, poured ahead of their session. Dread creeps in; she waits a beat.

"Wait, what are you doing? What are you taking?"

Lucinda laughs her fakest cultivated Palm Beach laugh, the one she saves for charity lunches or doubles in tennis at the Harbor Club when she should have won and hasn't. "Nothing, really. A pill to ease things."

"Meaning?"

"Xanax."

"Since when do you take medication, ever?"

Lucinda purses her lips; she feels foreign. "Since someone is out to get me, to ruin me."

Caroline waits, counting to ten or more. A mother

in every way. "Do you know who is writing these letters?" she asks.

"I do. I knew the person once. It has to do with Kesgrave. I'm sure of it." She won't explain anything more. That Lucinda has chosen to confide in Caroline is more than she can bear.

Chapter Twenty-One

2026

Raleigh stands beside Lucinda in the center of her mini-Versailles gardens, looking out at the Intracoastal. The air has that Florida feel to it, how it was in Kesgrave when she was young. The boats, including a Benetti motor yacht, are heading south. While her mother loves the open water, Raleigh notices Lucinda's high anxiety this afternoon. If Raleigh has inherited a rising sense that nothing is ever free of danger, her older sisters have apparently missed that gene. Neither Maribelle nor Caroline acts as if beauty and safeness might be mutually exclusive.

Lucinda waves her arm, tugs her lemon-colored cashmere sweater at the waist, straightens her ivory wide-legged pants. She takes off her sunglasses; her eyes are kohled, Cleopatra style. Not an effect Raleigh has seen her mother go for. Too heavy-handed and out of character.

"Are you okay, Mom?" she asks.

Lucinda sighs. "Why does everyone keep asking?"

Raleigh doesn't face her mother. "I don't know, you seem wretched."

"Well, I do have my birthday coming up, and I keep asking myself why I wanted it to be a major celebration."

Because of who you are, Raleigh would like to say, but she resists. Something about Lucinda is concerning—she seems to have been drinking, which never happens; it would be absurd. "The parties will be really nice."

"They have to be better than that. They have to be splendid," Lucinda says.

"Oh, they will be. Your friends, your daughters, and your grandchildren will all be there."

Lucinda taps her Hermès Oran sandals against the slate floor of her terrace, nodding as if she hasn't heard her. Didn't she summon Raleigh for a specific reason—conversations about progress on her divorce, healing the Maribelle rift, wardrobe questions, always? The daylight isn't direct. It twists around the garden. Raleigh waits.

"Ah, yes, all that." Lucinda gives her this odd, watery smile. She lifts a glass of iced peppermint tea from the wrought iron table with latticework. Next she reaches into her pocket for a pill and scarfs it down.

Rosie appears. "Mrs. Barrows, you have a phone call. The landline. It is Mrs. Jolie. She says you aren't picking up your cell."

"My cell, where did I leave it? Rosie, will you check my car?"

"Mom, you never forget your cell. What is going on, Rosie?" Raleigh asks.

"I don't know." Rosie sounds weary.

Lucinda heads toward the house without glancing at her pink roses, her yellow and violet pansies in a maze that Raleigh has not seen before. "Nothing, nothing is going on," she says breezily. "I'll take the call from upstairs."

Rosie shrugs.

Raleigh's head is cluttered with how altered Lucinda has become. How unlikely that anyone has the skills to repair it.

"Am I late?" Caroline asks, walking in her purposeful

style across the terrace, avoiding spray from Lucinda's favorite, the "dragon" fountain. She is in her weekday best, a Veronica Beard knit dress and mules. Raleigh knows Caroline has not yet spoken with Maribelle about their rift. She hopes today's conversation is not more of the same: Lucinda's unending quest for her eldest and youngest daughters to reunite. "Where is she?"

"Mom's on a call on a real phone," Raleigh says. "She could be a while."

"Actually, that's fine, Raleigh," Caroline says. She gestures toward the inner hedges that are low, contrary to many of the mansions in the estate section. "We have some privacy. Thankfully we're not at a club or a restaurant."

Although the conversation hasn't begun, Raleigh already wishes it wasn't taking place. "Privacy? Honestly, Caroline, Mom is acting bizarre. I don't know if you've come with a surprise or some news bomb, but I can't do much more today."

"I wanted to speak with you alone. Good that it's quiet—this won't take long. Where's everyone?"

"William is off at a member-guest golf tournament in Boca."

"William? That's the least of it. I meant Maribelle. Is she around?"

"No," Raleigh says. "She is not."

They sit down facing each other. Raleigh puts on her fedora. The gulls swoop in a circular motion, like planes that can't land. Out over the water, the Royal Park Bridge is up, a Sunseeker slowly passes beneath.

"We have a situation. It has to be discreet. No one knows about it. At least I hope not."

Caroline pours a glass of peppermint tea.

She is chummy, friendly, playing the warmer sister, which was not true until Maribelle became icy. Raleigh knows that Caroline is hell-bent on something serious. After this she will go directly to Barrows for scheduled meetings, compartmentalizing whatever is on the table in this moment.

"What are you talking about?" Raleigh asks.

Caroline tosses her shoulders, straightens up. "A problem with Lucinda. I'm asking you to find out what's going on."

"What do you mean?" Raleigh asks.

"You've no idea?" Caroline pauses like she's at the gym at Longgreens and needs electrolytes before bench presses. Taking a minute before challenging her strength.

"I'm not sure what you're saying, Caroline. You mean how strange Mom's become? She could be drugged or something."

"Exactly," Caroline says. "I suspect . . . I'm worried that Lucinda has done something awful. That her life is in jeopardy, or her status or our lives. That she's being threatened."

"Are you sure? Wouldn't she be the one threatening someone?"

"She came to the office and confided. When she got there, she was freakish, loopy. I thought she'd slept in her dress and heels. Her makeup was caked. I had to get her to wash it off, start again. She was not her impeccable self. I don't want to betray her—she hasn't told anyone but me about letters being dropped off at her house. I haven't seen anything. She kept saying she has to find out who delivers them, who is behind it."

Raleigh stares at their mother's cone-shaped topiaries, perfected by Lester, the gardener, who follows instructions prudently. Every Thursday morning at eight, Lucinda shows him photographs on her phone. He somehow understands her better than most people in her life. She's always raving about the results that stun her, she is always pleased. Could her grounds, her house, her entire manufactured life in Palm Beach go up in smoke?

"That's crazy. Crazy talk," Raleigh says. Although Caroline is the sanest in the family and rarely exaggerates.

"Well, she's drugged-out half the day these past few months. Haven't you noticed? Xanax, Valium, something to ease her pain."

"I did notice," Raleigh says. "She pops pills. She's never done that—she doesn't believe in it."

Caroline holds up her hands. "I know. Maribelle knows. We've talked about it. The problem is bigger."

Raleigh can't listen. She's watching a Riva Rivamare speed past on the Intracoastal. Two young women in bikinis are visible, dancing on deck to a beat she can't hear. The entire Intracoastal looks curvy, as if the water might spill over. For an instant she mistakes the man at the helm for Samuel. She tries to shake off this memory and wonders if she'll ever break free.

"Raleigh?" Caroline is irritated.

"I'm listening," Raleigh says. "Who is sending these threats, these letters?"

"I want you to find out."

"What? Me?" Raleigh laughs. "Sorry, that's absurd, Caroline. I'm not a private investigator. I'm in the midst of a . . ."

Caroline looks at her cell, slides her forefinger around her screen. "Listen, you'll have to go to Kesgrave. We'll say it's for your art. You're trying to get more business with your little shells or whatever you were doing there instead of portraits in Palm Beach. Wait, better yet, you've been asked to do a local portrait or a few portraits. Lucinda and Maribelle will buy this story. You like being there—it works. For a few days. It makes sense. There's real peril, and we must find out. I know it's from the past."

"Peril?"

Caroline sighs. "Raleigh, we can't reveal a thing until you get back. We'll sit down, figure out next steps."

"There's nothing left of us, of Mom, in Kesgrave," Raleigh says.

"True. Lucinda has eliminated evidence of life there. Every spinning wheel in the land, *Sleeping Beauty* style. A wheel still exists—that's the problem, it's resurfaced."

Raleigh shivers. The family was there for decades, maybe centuries. Kesgrave cousins are abundant, not that they have kept in touch.

"What exactly am I looking for, Caro?"

"I don't know, it could be very bad or simply humiliating. You know how unhinged Lucinda is about her image. Whatever it is, it's making her sick, scaring her. She's like an addict. She'll end up in rehab. Can you imagine anything worse for her than that?"

"Isn't Maribelle better for this?" Raleigh asks.

Caroline takes Raleigh's hands in hers. "I don't think so. You're smart, you're winning, you'll find people we knew, people who knew Lucinda. You'll figure things out. Please do it, Raleigh—you're the one who's been going to Kesgrave."

"Whatever I can or can't find, I'm flattered that you believe in me," Raleigh says. "I don't want to disappoint you." Beyond that, she'll get out of town and away from Alex, who has Caleb for the next three and a half days. Away from

Porter, who is a heart smasher. She'll do it for her mother's sake, for Barrows.

"You won't." Caroline starts scrolling for flights to get Raleigh to Kesgrave, the Panhandle.

RALEIGH AND CAROLINE walk from the gardens into the hushed library, on to the foyer with its eighteen-foot-high front door. They pass the kitchen, where Rosie and Daisy are speaking loudly about cutting melon and papaya.

When the door is opened, Maribelle is in the driveway. She steps out of an Uber, her recent mode of traveling around Palm Beach, rather than borrowing one of the six cars in the garage. Raleigh can't see who the driver is, man or woman. In LA, cars drive without drivers, headless horsemen of the twenty-first century. Maribelle wouldn't do that. She's laughing as she gets out, an overfriendly gesture. Her dress is deep plum, gathered at the waist. She's thin, stunning, a return to how she once was. Had she arrived five minutes later, or had Raleigh left five minutes earlier, this could have been avoided. Instead, Maribelle slams the door and faces the house. On Lucinda's carefully paved, manicured driveway, they gaze at one another. A thick, impenetrable stare. Sisters. Raleigh raises her hand to greet her and Maribelle does the same—a truce gesture, albeit brief.

Raleigh has been given a purpose, for the greater good. If she can help their mother, it will affect everything "family" to follow. Including the Maribelle feud. Won't it?

Chapter Twenty-Two

2026

CAROLINE AND RALEIGH leave while Lucinda is on her call with Jolie. Jolie who is kind enough—or to flip it, callous enough—to describe Michaela Rael's private water aerobics class. That Lucinda wasn't invited to.

"At her home," Jolie keeps saying. "She can't invite everyone."

"You were invited," Lucinda says, sounding like an eleventh grader.

"She is my sister-in-law," Jolie says. "I called to see if you want me to get you on her list."

Since the Xanax has kicked in while Lucinda and Jolie hammer this out, her final decision is not clear to her. It's the underlying problem that gnaws at Lucinda. She is loath to lose her hold socially. This problem is crystal clear. She isn't on everyone's short list anymore. The fallout could prove singular, especially on the eve of her birthday. With a generous guest list, Lucinda has always erred on the side of inviting many rather than forgetting anyone. An approach that should garner friends and avoid enemies.

Ever since arriving in Palm Beach she has not wanted to offend anyone. Her only goal is to be important, sought-after. To have standing, a moneyed life—which brings her to the nagging question, what faux pas did she or one of her daughters commit? She has spent the past twenty years being a leader, not a follower. If the letters are being sent to others as well, she is in a worse bind. The biggest threat would be if they are delivered to Bryant. Lucinda pulls herself together. She will get through; she will find a path.

William's golf game is over, and he expects they'll lunch together by the pool. It has slipped her mind, while William and Rosie seem to know about it. On a Saturday afternoon, if not at Longgreens or Harbor Club, it's a reasonable plan. At the top of the stairs, about to descend to greet William, Lucinda overhears him speaking to Rosie.

"Is Mrs. Barrows alright?" he asks. "I thought she would be with her daughters or doing a few laps."

"She's not with them. She's gone upstairs. I'll find her if you like," Rosie says in a noncommittal tone. She's the best actress of any in Lucinda's inner circle.

"No, no, I hear you. I'll meet you outside, William," Lucinda trills. She sounds unrecognizable, as if there's a ventriloquist working with her, salvaging the moment. She takes the steps slowly downstairs. On her way to the terrace, she stops in the library and collects a copy of *Buddenbrooks* that she's been rereading. A story of the decline of a remarkably wealthy family makes her feel less isolated these days.

For William's sake she emerges, finding him in the gardens. Lucinda is looking half-whole. She can't do better than that. Her hope is that love remains blind and he won't notice.

"Well, hello," she says.

"Where are your girls on a Saturday?"

She tolerates his peck of a kiss. He's getting a pot belly, a minor one, yet it's annoying. At best he'll be part of the crowd of men who get away with it due to other attributes—

good hair, decent bone structure, fine clothing. If only she cared, if only she had the bandwidth to take action. It would require subtlety, and she's short on that these days, alas.

"Busy. Plans, friends, tennis," she says. She places *Buddenbrooks* on the edge of the grill. She won't retain what she reads anyway. She's become a sieve. William is smiling at her, a benign, sincere smile. His good nature is inherited, no doubt; he's from a long-standing, upstanding Palm Beach family. He represents a buffer for Lucinda.

Daisy comes out carrying two salad niçoise platters and a baguette. Rosie follows with two water glasses. Beneath her right arm she has discreetly tucked an envelope. The same one, by the same sender as every damn one that's come before. With a smaller envelope inside and her maiden name in that specific cursive writing. Lucinda takes off her sunglasses for a moment.

Rosie, onto the game, nods. "Mrs. Barrows, could you come into the kitchen to approve the crème caramel for dessert? I've overcooked it, I'm afraid."

"William, would you mind?" Lucinda asks.

"That's fine, Lucinda. I'll wait to begin."

Lucinda races to her dressing room and tears the envelope apart.

CHANCE MEETING

When I met him he was wearing a pale pink shirt made of fine cotton and a gaberdine blazer. He was surrounded by women, then made his way to where I stood in the Great Hall with two classmates. I was relieved he wasn't as tall as the men back home—as if shorter was a recipe for humility. At the college, he was liked better than other professors. He was pure urban life, not lured by the tides, the river. He did not know what it was to swim in the Apalachicola. The word shrimper meant nothing to him. That was uplifting.

He had been my professor the last two semesters. We began our affair easily, we belonged together, it was meant to happen. He had a wife; he was promised to her. I kept hearing that. I decided he didn't need to know about Kesgrave. I was tired of varying versions, banal explanations, unconvincing threads of a story. I only said I'd grown up in the Panhandle. I offered no more, no part about my family. Or my friends.

Our second year together I was pregnant. I told him he had no claim on this baby unless he became available. I knew our child would be talented, smart, photogenic. I'd keep that baby safe, I'd make our baby mine. At this point, you'll want to know how I loved him. Totally. The good men, they fall to the side, the same as the bad ones. No matter where you're from, what you've done. I longed for him always.

A year after you were born, your father and I ended up at the same party unexpectedly. He wanted something, some piece of raising you. He offered money, he wanted to see pictures. I said no. I was ascending with my work. Women were having children without fathers—the world was slightly more forgiving. There was no way to redeem my past, but I had you. I had this career. I had the photographs.

Before Lucinda adds this letter to the others in her safe, she rereads the last page. "*There was no way to redeem my past, but I had you.*"

Who is the "you" in these letters? She tries to remember what Bryant said about Ruth-Ann's obituary. Was she not listening carefully enough, so relieved at the news that she couldn't think it through? Of course she could google her, yet the idea is revolting.

Lucinda locks up and opens her makeup drawer to apply blush. She should get back out to William, who waits patiently. How opposite of Reed this second husband is—muted, unperturbed. Back in Kesgrave, Reed was compelling from the get-go with his engulf and devour quality. By the time Lucinda was in tenth grade, there was no existence unless Reed was at the center. Their life together was as if they'd gotten on a two-person bumper car, rounding the curves as best they could.

Since receiving the letters, when she conjures up Reed, the vision is bathed in dread. She's walking in quicksand. She could be swallowed whole at any juncture. All because of some concealed person out to get her.

It is suddenly quite warm out. Those little welts on her collarbone are starting. A chill radiates in spite of the rise in temperature.

Chapter Twenty-Three

1994

A DAY AFTER THE ACCIDENT, there is no telling what is next. Lucinda and Reed are bound now in a way they've never known. Beyond the two daughters they share and the child about to be born, there is a phantasmic wire tugging at them, coiling them to each other. Lucinda knows it will never be what it was the day before, never again.

She begins breakfast. Anything will do; her children could eat oatmeal or jam sandwiches—she isn't able to think about it. Reed is standing outside the door, sloping, his entire body empty, like when they take the stuffing out of the scarecrow in *The Wizard of Oz*, and he is nothing until they replace it. She and Reed in that limbo space. She hopes not to go into labor. She is in her ninth month, her baby fully formed at this stage, that far along. Isn't it true by the end, in the days before they're born, they keep growing? As if she is entitled to give birth, to get on with being an ordinary young mother living in Kesgrave, trying to raise her children the right way, loving her husband less than she thought she would.

The kitchen phone won't stop ringing, and Lucinda won't answer. She knows it's Bryant, alone, Bud dead, shockingly gone.

"We should get that," Reed says. His face is pallid, squiggly lines are etched into his cheeks, his eyes hooded, as though he's been drinking, when he's had nothing. A crust forms around his mouth, and his beard smells like dog dander.

"Daddy, Daddy!" Caroline jumps up and down in the living room.

Neither daughter has freshened up. Lucinda always requires it except for this morning, she can't be in charge.

Reed opens the back door and stands on their screened-in porch. Maribelle follows him.

"Daddy?"

He lights up his pipe without answering.

Caroline follows Maribelle. "Daddy?"

Still he pays no attention, as if he doesn't care, like they are someone else's daughters. The fleets are about to go out, and the general store, Humphreys & Barrows, isn't opened. It was Bud who did it most days, and here it is after eight o'clock. The fishermen will be waiting for their coffee and blueberry muffins, eggs over easy on a hard roll with bacon, catsup. The endless night Lucinda and Reed shared has blown into morning, totally dismal. This unrelenting Bud death hovers over them.

The yellow wall phone rings again. Lucinda picks up. No sound, then Bryant breathes deeply. Shouldn't she be hysterically crying?

"Bud knew how to swim in an undertow, in anything, any storm," she says. "He had his life saving certificate." Her voice is harrowed into a dullness.

"It was an accident, Bryant," Lucinda says. "We get how that is around here."

Reed comes back in, the girls tugging on his sleeves. The baby begins to frolic around, pummeling at her ribcage. Lucinda has heartburn; she needs Tums.

Reed takes the phone from her. "Bryant, why don't you come over, be with us. Have breakfast with the girls."

Maribelle and Caroline listen.

"Is Aunt Bryant coming over for breakfast?" Caroline asks.

Everyone would prefer Bryant's company, knowing how Lucinda despises the early morning. How she isn't half human until 10 a.m.

Bryant sniffles, loud gulps, so odd for her. "I will."

The weight of it is terrifying. There is no escape, no solace in the invitation, only a reminder of how it is and will be without Bud.

When Bryant comes in, the girls circle around her, cautious, curious, as if she's floated onto the shoreline and dragged herself to them. There is no rushing to her, jumping up and down at her arrival. She's hunched, sorrowful, an old woman overnight.

Lucinda ought to do something, to console Bryant. The idea of Bud gone makes her nauseous. The baby starts kicking in a defiant way, a reminder of life after death. Bryant sits down on the kitchen stool, made of ersatz leather, cracking along the seams. An ugly color, somewhere between maroon and a deep red. It had been Reed's mother's, a castoff disguised as an heirloom to be handed down. The strangest day for her girls is beginning. They settle down in front of the television, aimlessly watching *Sesame Street*. Rules tossed away, grief filling in the spaces. They know they will be missing school.

Lucinda comes close to Bryant, about to put her hands on her shoulders and make a trite comment. Whatever people say in times of loss. Loss beyond death. Bryant stands up.

"I was supposed to spend my life with him," she whispers. "He promised."

Lucinda wonders what will happen next, the years ahead without Bud. She is sick in her soul for everyone.

PART TWO

Do you remember how

we found a way out?

Chapter Twenty-Four

2026

TWO DAYS LATER in Kesgrave, Raleigh watches the sun slant across the emerald-green water; the sand is a powdery white. Since Caroline organized the trip, she is staying in a suite at the Henderson Beach. More Palm Beach than expected, although not quite the Palm Hotel or Brazilian Court. When she checked in and saw a lobby filled with young, cool wives, their children and husbands, her stance became wife-like. A newly minted version of what she was once good at, sexless, pretty, the hollow interior of it. Three months ago, when she walked into the Seabreeze, a beachy, local hotel on Main Street, she postured as carefree—single with possibilities. In truth, she was recovering from the loss of Samuel, the shock of her impending divorce. Returning unexpectedly to Kesgrave this afternoon, Raleigh realizes it's no longer about any of that. Porter is whom she misses.

Everything Porter draws her in—that he listens to music Lucinda and Aunt Bryant taught her: The Rolling Stones' "Wild Horses," Jethro Tull's "Aqualung," Bruce Springsteen's "Thunder Road." He goes to the Shelteere, visiting both Contemporary Art and the Old Masters' galleries. She has heard from Nina and Bree that he is invited to the clubs where he is excellent at singles tennis, a scratch golfer, a sailor. He is not in the club life; he exists beyond that realm. Nothing about him reminds her of anyone she has ever known, as if she's been given a key out. Away from Palm Beach men, the socially connected ones. Porter remains other, honest and sincere. Or so she believes. At this hotel she imagines watching the sun set and rise with him, morning sex, jokes to tell.

She pours from a bottle of Acqua Panna water. Her phone dings—Caroline.

Settled in? About to meet the first batch?

Fine, Raleigh texts back, disliking how Caroline counts on her. Her mother and Maribelle too, without knowing it. Ironic after having been practically brainwashed to obliterate Kesgrave. Her mother and sisters, Aunt Bryant take this path. Raleigh, as the family knows, romanticizes the place, while they pretend it never happened.

Back inside, she lifts her laptop from the chair and scrolls through the schedule, attempting to be geometric, balanced. Caroline has organized it well. "Dig around," she told Raleigh. "I've compiled a list—teachers, the mayor, cousins. Try to meet them."

Doubt infiltrates. Caroline could have found some private eye, somebody no one has met, to investigate. An unprejudiced, real investigation. It's flattering that her sister trusts her. Whatever was buried, now it's stirred.

Another text comes in. Her meeting has been changed. She is to meet Mrs. Packer in a half hour.

ALONG THE BACKROADS in a silver rented Jeep, the facade of Pinestream rises, flustering Raleigh. A massive regional high school that her sisters attended. By the time she was nine, Lucinda and Reed had shut down their Kesgrave life and moved to Palm Beach.

"Are you sure your favorite teacher has something to say?" Raleigh had asked Caroline. "I'm on a tight schedule."

"Mrs. Packer knows a lot. She knows everyone. I promise you can go early to the town hall if she has nothing for us," Caroline said.

During class time, between bells, the main building is hushed. It feels a heavier load than Raleigh expected. Maribelle's and Caroline's days there had merit; they were A students, cheerleading captains, prom queens. They had told Raleigh that moving through these cinderblock hallways as the pretty, rich, smart Barrows daughters wasn't a party. Lucinda was complicated and extremely visible. Isn't that why Raleigh is in Kesgrave today?

She passes the door where her mother once taught AP English. On Raleigh's seventh birthday, Maribelle had brought her here. They stood at that door, waiting for Lucinda to remember. She had promised to arrange a party at Chuck E. Cheese. Instead, Maribelle cobbled together a celebration with three other little girls at the house. There was no apology from Lucinda. She said, *You're seven, you'll live. There are mothers who bake birthday cakes, Hallmark-wrap the gifts. They remember. What I don't forget is teaching. I don't forget our Barrows stores.* What would it be like, Raleigh used to wonder, to have another mother, not Lucinda?

PINESTREAM is still poorly laid out and cavernous. On the front walls are framed accolades of the best students. That old feeling surges over Raleigh, that she'll see her sisters' names all over the place. An embarrassing and satisfying experience. Maribelle aced every award and recognition—National Honor Society, valedictorian, editor of the yearbook. Caroline too was a star—track and field, drama club, student council president.

Samuel is showcased among the athletes. There he is, smiling into the camera as captain of the football team and the wrestling team. The next grouping has a picture of Samuel with Maribelle, homecoming king and queen that same year. Raleigh remembers the shape of Maribelle's deep blue satin gown, Samuel's ivory boutonniere as they left for the dance that night. Samuel had plucked the flower from his rented tuxedo and handed it to her. "Someday you'll be the queen of everything," he told her. She knew then she would adore him always.

Fucking Samuel.

"Well, Raleigh Barrows! How great it is to have you visiting Pinestream!" Mrs. Packer's voice is behind her.

Raleigh spins around. Her sisters' favorite, a former close friend of Lucinda's, is now an older woman. Everything about her has aged. Her hairline is receded; dark brown has turned to gray. She doesn't look resilient. There are those lines in her face that you don't see on Palm Beach ladies; theirs are eradicated through myriad procedures. She might fall into the woman's arms.

"Mrs. Packer!"

"I hear you have a few questions. Follow me."

Early for any lunch shifts, the cafeteria is overly bright, glutted with fluorescent lighting. Mrs. Packer, who looks as if she likes fast food, buys two packaged Drake's Coffee Cakes, one Coke, and two waters. They sit at a table overlooking the football field. The scoreboard is gigantic; it must be blinding when it's on and the numbers keep changing. Far off, the bleachers, made of splintered wood, look the same as when Maribelle and Samuel used to take her to the games. When Raleigh looked away, the two of them would kiss, over and over.

Raleigh and Mrs. Packer do small talk—weather, climate change, the undertow in the Atlantic—before Raleigh moves on.

"Mrs. Packer, you know my sisters haven't been back home in many years. I've only come a few times. I left Kesgrave in grade school, so I'm curious."

"Oh, I know. I heard that you, the little sister, were around a few months ago, doing some painting. And a great beauty. Lucinda's daughters are that, as was she. Raleigh, why are you here now?" Mrs. Packer crumples the wrapper of her coffee cake, holds the second one toward Raleigh. She shakes her head.

"I wanted to learn more about my parents. My father is gone. Lucinda—my mother—never talks about Kesgrave."

"Does she know you're visiting?" Mrs. Packer asks. She takes a worn thermos out of her bag. She smiles; her teeth are crooked. Weren't they always? Lucinda used to say Mrs. Packer ought to drive to Destin or Pensacola and get her teeth straightened. True to that belief, Lucinda, Maribelle, and Caroline had done just that. Not Raleigh. She didn't have the same experience in Kesgrave. She was much younger; she became a Palm Beach child and ended up with an orthodontist on Sunset, two blocks from A1A and the ocean. No wonder Raleigh thinks Kesgrave is novel and picturesque while Maribelle and Caroline don't see the allure.

"Yes." Raleigh is uneasy. "She'd like me to learn how she grew up in the Panhandle, about Barrows. I'm talking to people who knew her and our father."

Mrs. Packer exhales, looks at the laminate table like it's interesting. "Your mother and I grew up together. I was a grade ahead. Everybody knew everybody. She and I both came from decent families, but there was no money. We took loans and started college at Rickens in our mid-twenties. By then your mother had Maribelle and Caroline. We began teaching together after that. I never had babies, while she kept at it."

"Maribelle raised me," Raleigh says.

"I'll bet. Your mother was ambitious, getting the one position four of us wanted, teaching senior English. She won that round."

"I guess my mother's like that, " Raleigh says.

Mrs. Packer pats at her mouth with a cafeteria napkin. "I don't want to be negative. Your mother and I taught for years, we . . ."

"Sure, I get that. Still, she always had to be best, ahead of everyone."

"Right," Mrs. Packer says.

The janitor passes by with his mop and bucket, splashing disinfectant. The smell of Clorox and lemon rises.

"This might border on gossip, but is there anything else about you and my mother?"

Mrs. Packer looks away. "Why would you ask that? There must be other people you'll speak with, classmates, cousins. I don't know how much you've kept up with Kesgrave."

"Not much."

"Do you ever hear from anyone?"

"Some cousins." Raleigh won't elaborate. Reed's side of the family has reached out from time to time. Reed always sent them money. After he was gone, Lucinda did. *Make this go away*, she used to say. *Throw money at it.*

"Well, your cousin on your mother's side, Kirby Kirks—I believe his mother was a Matthews—is now mayor. Like his father before him. Maybe that should be your next stop."

Raleigh checks her phone. "Exactly what I've planned."

Before she can thank Mrs. Packer, the woman places her hand on Raleigh's forearm. "At least the mayor won't have the same Lucinda stories as I do. You know your mother and I shopped for our prom dresses together. We were both invited. Lucinda was going with Reed, of course. I was going with Andy Cramn. I'd put a dress on hold down on Main Street at Gizzi's—I was saving my money. It was a peach color, a smooth fabric that hugged the body. She told me it didn't look good and to keep shopping. We were the same size back then. The next day she bought it."

Raleigh is not surprised yet feels defensive. "I'm sorry, I don't know what to say."

"No need to say a thing," Mrs. Packer says. "I'm glad to have finally told that story. At least I wasn't screwed like Bryant. Now that's another category altogether."

"Bryant? What about her? She's in Palm Beach with my mother, with our family. She's our godmother, an aunt to us."

Students are beginning to come into the cafeteria from both entrances. The clanging of trays and their chatter begin. Raleigh is standing with Mrs. Packer under more unnecessary fluorescent lights; it's almost painful.

"Is she? Bryant was always a saint. She left Kesgrave the same person she was when she was a girl and lived here. Your mother became fancy. I remember how she got that sapphire ring from Cartier. Reed bought it for her, although she chose it. She'd had her eye on it. She told me the whole thing when we were in the teachers' room. Then she wore the ring to school—can you imagine? But where else was she going? A four-carat sapphire with diamonds around the stone. You know, very classy."

"She still wears it from time to time," Raleigh says. "I remember when she got it."

Reed had wanted to surprise Lucinda, but there was no putting that into play. As a little girl, Raleigh was in on the secret. Her father called it "Operation Sparkle."

"What an incongruous piece of jewelry for Kesgrave. To wear while Lucinda was teaching made it worse," Mrs. Packer says.

"What I remember is how happy she was with her sapphire ring. In Palm Beach she wore it a lot with my father to parties and charity dinners."

"Of course she did," Mrs. Packer says.

They're heading toward the side parking lot where Raleigh has left the Jeep, where her sisters used to park their cars. She is about to thank Mrs. Packer for her time when she comes nearer to Raleigh.

"It's good to see you, Raleigh. For months, years, after your family left Kesgrave, I tried to reach your mother. My letters were sent back with 'Return to sender' stamped on them. I know I had the right address. I'd say it's bad karma to turn your back on the past. That's how I look at it."

Chapter Twenty-Five

2026

Augustus avenue, the Kesgrave main drag, remains much as it was when the Barrows family left for Palm Beach twenty-three years ago. Jackson's, the local bar at the corner of Augustus and Center, has the same double doors. Fedd's Diner, across the street, where Maribelle and Caroline used to meet Samuel and Travis, is as faded as ever. Barrows remains the biggest store, spanning two doorways with their scripted sign in lime green, the latest logo. The place is busy with customers rushing in for coffee, lattes, lottery tickets. Raleigh notices mothers with babies or toddlers en route to Mommy and Me, playgroups. How Caleb used to snuggle on her chest, always content.

She texts Caroline. *Barrows is happening.*

That's been the case for ages, Caroline texts back.

The original storefront is heartening and sickening. Raleigh remembers when the store was a third the size, before Reed expanded it. When her parents spoke of little else and then became wealthier than anyone around. Raleigh was young and treated differently; respect mixed with blatant jealousy was palpable. From afar, the Barrows were envied: Lucinda and Reed, movie starlike, their daughters the offspring of a supreme couple. Maribelle told Raleigh years ago, when they first moved to Palm Beach, that she and Caroline had been whispered about at Pinestream. Because although Lucinda teaching English was fine and acceptable, being entrepreneurial while a wife and mother was forbidden.

Not that it stopped Lucinda. On weekends, she would bring Raleigh along to Reed's square upstairs room above the first Barrows. She'd wear six bangle bracelets at a time, silver dipped in gold. They clanked whenever she raised her arm to emphasize a point.

Heading north, away from the shops and restaurants, Raleigh reaches the Kesgrave Library with its brick front steps and garden path trimmed with shells. Aunt Bryant used to call it charming, but Lucinda wouldn't have it. *Charming,* she said, *no, there is no charm there. Paris is charming, Palm Beach is charming, parts of Connecticut. Don't be fooled by the cockle shells on the library path.*

Beside the library is the town hall, where the police department and mayor have offices. Inside the replacement cedarwood building, the hallway has jarring lights. Arrows are painted on the wall for directions to the county clerk, beach badges, and police station. Kirby Kirks, son of former mayor/present-day mayor, waits for her. He looks exactly as he did the last time Raleigh saw him. He was a friend of Samuel's; the two of them used to stop by to see Maribelle. He's older and still taller than most men she knows—maybe six-foot-five. He's skinny like he was but there's this phantom pot belly lurking. The kind Lucinda is always commenting on.

"Is that you, Raleigh Barrows? I haven't seen you since my father was mayor. He and your dad used to eat hot dogs together at Radio Days every Wednesday. He was a cool dad—so was mine. They were similar. Really tough and strong, y'know?"

His voice ought to bring it back to her, to trigger something. Instead Raleigh shakes her head. "I don't remember any of that. I'm the youngest, so I know nothing." She'd like to add, "Please give me details," yet she can't. Instead, she thinks of Porter and her last visit to Kesgrave, how she felt and what he meant to her from that first meeting. Porter, who finds her life complicated, who doesn't know she's here.

"Hi, Kirby." Her voice is high pitched. She tugs on her jean skirt.

"What are ya doin' in Kesgrave? I used to see Samuel sometimes. I guess he covered this territory. How are your sisters, your mom?"

"They're fine. They send their regards," she lies.

"C'mon into my office."

The sun seeps through the dusty venetian blinds. The mold around the corners of the room makes it dingy. There's the reek of stale cigarette smoke. Her head hurts.

Kirby wears a cheap-looking cotton blend button-down shirt. Raleigh dislikes the color—fatigue green—and his khaki pants don't fit right. On the filing cabinet are two Mars Bars; he must be a snacker. There can't be much to do as mayor.

"Whadya want to ask me? Our families were Kesgrave natives back to our great-great-great-grandparents. Here's a picture I wanted to show you. Reed and Bud. And my dad. Fishing. What they loved most."

He points. Three young men, the photo almost in sepia but not deliberately, the frame a tarnished metal, maybe pewter. "Humphreys and Barrows," Kirby says. "They had the convenience stores in Kesgrave and were about to open one in Panama City before Bud died. Then it became Barrows. You know the rest, right?"

Outside, black vultures are circling. When Raleigh was little, she was petrified of them. Lucinda would point out the other birds, the brown pelicans on the piers, blue herons, mockingbirds. She'd sing, "Hush little baby, don't say a word, Mama's gonna buy you a mockingbird." Her sisters sang it when Lucinda had no time.

"Not really, no I don't know," Raleigh says.

"Well, it was a big story in Kesgrave, a bad accident, it lingers. Or so they say."

"What happened exactly? Can you tell me?" Raleigh forces herself to ask.

"Not certain." Kirby sits down at his desk, the chair squeaks. "My dad wasn't with them that day. He was here, in his office. Whatever he knew, and I think he knew it all, he never said a word. He wasn't going to let it get into his head, didn't want to stir trouble. He liked both Bud and Reed."

Bud Humphreys—a dead man whose memory won't die. Raleigh has been hearing about him her whole life, not from her mother, but from Aunt Bryant. At her house there are pictures of Bud with Reed, holding up their prize red snapper from when they came in second place, reeling in a sixty-pounder in 1987. Pictures of Bryant with Bud, sailing a Flying Scot.

"I guess Bud liked the water."

"Oh, yeah." Kirby raises his arms over his head, stretches. "That's why it's strange how he died."

"I thought it was an accident." Raleigh's anxiety is ratcheting up.

"Bud was in his dingy. He was found hurt, y'know, his

head. They say he must've slipped going down the bank and ended up there."

"Was there an investigation?" Raleigh asks. A second later, she feels she's betrayed someone. Whom would that be?

Kirby shrugs. "We were in grade school, I don't know . . . Samuel, Travis, your sisters, and I went to the funeral. Bryant fainted, that I remember. Your dad picked her up and carried her out. We were watching, gawking."

"She still talks about him. I doubt she ever got over it."

"Well," Kirby says, "there are accidents every year. That's how it goes. Look at Samuel Walker, in a boat since he was a boy in Kesgrave. How'd that ever happen in Palm Beach? Same thing, really. Who can explain it?"

Who indeed? She thinks about Samuel heading out in his Riva Rivamare despite the storm kicking in. Yet the question of how Bud died is very unlike that. That storyline is vague, although she's sitting in Kirby's office, in search of it.

"Do you know anything more?" Raleigh asks, as if she's a reporter.

"Not much. No one else was there. Like I said, only Reed and Bud, by the river that day. I heard my mother and father talk for years about what really happened. Everything splintered after that."

She needs to get out of his office, away from him—except Caroline told her to dig, to learn, for their mother's sake. She should have done mindfulness before this meeting. Kirby pushes back in his mayor's chair, his Adam's apple moves about. He waits.

"Did you ever ask your father what he thought had gone down?" Raleigh asks.

"A few times. I mean, it haunted him."

Haunted him. Either Kirby won't say anything more, or he doesn't know. She wants to leave, have no further conversation with him. She steels herself to be patient, for the facts, if they exist. Some morsel, a lead.

"Kirby, I'm in Kesgrave to learn about my family."

"Don't you know who they are?"

Raleigh shakes her head. Her mother and both sisters feel incredibly precious to her. "In part I do," she says.

He whistles. "Around here, people talk about Bud Humphreys. Nobody forgets."

Chapter Twenty-Six

2026

When Lucinda stares into her Trifecta Pro Vanity mirror, she despises what she sees. Despite her best efforts short of a facelift—Botox, Thermage, filler—turning sixty is shocking. After belonging to the coterie of preened and groomed women in Palm Beach gloss all these years, she's failing. Her endless style—freshly colored hair, mani-pedis, designer shoes and wardrobe, bags, jewels—isn't holding up. She's off course. Is she aging out? Is that why she feels less noticed and less included at card games, luncheons, member-guest golf?

At least tonight suffices. She and William are due at Jolie and Ned's for drinks—they're hosting four couples—then off to the Geerad's for a dinner party. Her dress, a Brunello favorite, is understated, a sleeveless midi in a rose shade. Clothes truly are costume, while overdressing, a tried-and-true adage in Palm Beach, no longer seems as constant. Life has become more casual wherever she goes. Which Lucinda scorns as she peruses her enormous closet with its racks of color-coded dresses, sweaters, skirts, pants, tops, and blazers. She's even put her stilettos out to pasture recently.

William knocks on the door. He sounds ready to leave, anticipatory of the evening ahead. Lately he hasn't been the best sounding board. Whenever Lucinda mentions her birthday, or her sense that she isn't invited everywhere, or the Maribelle-Raleigh feud, he goes back to his latest David Baldacci read or his iPad. He knows nothing of the letters. Instead, she highlights the other dramas, in search of her husband's support. Why else did she marry him? During the good times, there is little need for him. She married him to avoid being shunned as a widow, sure, beyond that, she married him to remain visible, to be a couple on an island that values the template. And for a confidante/advisor on the off chance she might solicit his skills one day.

"We should be off," William says when she opens the door. Lucinda almost resents how unperturbed he appears, a man with time on his hands and no worries, unscathed by his wife's troubles. William looks well because he is not a deep thinker. Lucinda smooths the front of her dress; the fabric is fine, elegant. She's wearing a triple strand of graduated pearls with a diamond clasp and drop earrings (so old they're in again) that Reed bought for her the day Barrows made its first million. *Barrows.* She has been Lucinda Barrows for decades; it's her safeguard, her leading light, her orbit.

"I'm ready."

"Rosie gave me this. She said it was hand-delivered." William gives her the envelope, a clone of the others.

Angst rises, infective. Lucinda places it on the nightstand. Isn't he suspicious at this point? Apparently not.

She does her best Palm Beach half-smile. "Shall we?"

Seeing is believing, isn't it?

MIDNIGHT. During an evening where Lucinda should have been pleased, she had instead counted the hours until her return home to read the letter. Walking into the main bedroom, peeling off her clothes, is a relief. William, asleep, makes those once-a-husband-always-a snorer sounds. Lucinda tiptoes into their vast, overly mirrored bathroom with the view of the Intracoastal. She's in a pale blue silk nightie that she owns in every pastel shade from Pallie's on the Avenue. She looks best in dimmer lights. When she brightens the room in order to read the latest letter, her reflection changes, her skin more slack, those dreaded jowls show. Back to who she has become.

William has opened her bathroom door halfway without knocking. "Lucinda?"

She's startled, her heart starts squeezing. "You frightened me, William. I thought you were asleep."

He opens the door wider. "I was."

The envelope is on the countertop, the color out of place in the whitest of bathrooms—marble, quartz, glass. Their eyes on the damn thing, the air is humid despite that William has the temperature at sixty-eight for sleeping.

"What is being sent that Rosie keeps giving you? Why are you not yourself?"

Not herself. A good way to put it. He has to get back to their king bed, with sheets and a coverlet from Matouk. She needs another Xanax to read the latest letter. He seems slighter tonight, not strong or hefty enough to absorb what's happening, even if she wanted to share it. Would it help, would William be there to save the day?

"William, it's late. We're tired. It was a fun night. These are papers from the lawyers for Raleigh's divorce, sent to the house since I've not been at the office lately. You know I'm preoccupied . . . the parties ahead for me, and Maribelle has come home . . ."

"Wouldn't Estelle or someone from Barrows bring these documents over?"

"I suppose, but instead they've been hand-delivered." She's nauseous from this conversation or has eaten bad food. Possibly both. Lucinda puts her head against William's chest. He doesn't feel safe or protective, exactly; he's simply a man she married who must get some rest. She kisses him; it's the right gesture. He lowers the bathroom light, code for bedtime.

"I'll be right in after I scrub off my makeup."

Once she's certain he's asleep again, Lucinda patters down the hall to the guest wing and closes the door. She opens the sixth letter, hoping each time she'll find the clue to who brings them to her door. And why? What is the point, what do they want? No one has asked her for anything. She's being tormented, taunted, with no request for money. She wishes they'd ask—she would pay them and be over it. She could wash it away with fresh clean cash. She would be free of this.

FAME

My photos began selling for real money the year you were born, in 1996. I became known, visible. When you were about four, things really took off. I was represented by an impressive gallery, and people bought my work, commissioned my work. I became part of the downtown art scene. Some nights I had to be out, showing up, a part of it all. When I came back and the sitter left, I'd go to your room and watch you breathe. I'd remember the Apalachicola Bay oysters, wild roses that grew in the salty air. I'd remember early spring sunsets over the Gulf of Mexico, that last day I saw my brother. I was never going home. When you came along, it justified my path out. And I was in the news—there was this demand for my work. I was compared to famous women photographers like Diane Arbus and Lisette Model. Critics said I was a street photographer. Either meant I had talent.

No one from Kesgrave had ever tried to track me down. Nor had I tried to reach out. I was preoccupied with taking original photographs, depicting real life. I was asked to do portraits for celebrities and famous families. I agreed, along with photographing society weddings. It paid for your private school and college.

I made new friends, ones without stories and cover-ups, people who wouldn't choose me if they knew. I was careful, cautious, so they learned nothing and never would. There would be no confession, no woeful reveal to put me on the pity list.

Every time I had a show, there was a crazy demand for more. Then there was you, so dear to me, life changing.

She has broken her own rule: Read nothing, text nothing, watch nothing that stirs you up late at night. There will be no peace, no way out afterward. The air is stifling despite William's circulation method—windows open during the day, carefully sealed by 6 p.m. when their sophisticated cooling system starts up. Undoubtedly the alarm is set, Lucinda would have to pad around upstairs to avoid triggering it. Besides, she rarely works the thermostat; who knows what could go wrong. A sleeping pill—she had that prescription filled only last week. If she gets through until morning, she'll be okay.

Chapter Twenty-Seven

1994

TWILIGHT IN KESGRAVE after Bud died is dire. The sun sinks over the Gulf in charcoal and mustard color streaks, something she hadn't seen before. Her hands are shaking, she has to clear her head. She thinks maybe she'll give birth any moment.

Her girls are arguing in their bedroom about Barbie and Ken. Maribelle holds up a worn, hand-me-down Barbie while Caroline has an equally tattered Ken in her hands.

"Gimme Barbie," she says. "Please? I don't want Ken."

Maribelle shakes her head. "I don't want Ken. I'm older, so you can't have Barbie. We'll put them in their car."

Caroline starts twisting Ken, twirling him by the arms. Lucinda wants to stop her, she should, as the mother. Before she does, Bryant arrives back at the house, standing in the doorway of the girls' room.

"I'm sorry if I'm late. I went home to change and brought back a few things in case you go into labor, Lucinda."

"It felt like it was about to happen," Lucinda says. "Now I'm afraid I'll be in this state forever."

Bryant has this very unpregnant look in her Levi's and knit black shirt. She's wearing Lucinda's cowgirl boots from Walmart that had become tight. Bryant, who has lost her fiancé, appears as the good witch in a dark tale, in any tale.

"Girls, girls," she says in that soothing tone. Gently she takes both Barbie and Ken away. Lifting them up, Bryant turns to Lucinda. "Is this the best we can do?"

"Of course not," Lucinda says, although at the moment it matters little.

Bryant turns back to the girls. "How about we try a puzzle, a challenging one. Or Clue? We can start a game." She is acting preternaturally normal, it's bizarre.

Her daughters are hesitant. "No, thank you, Aunt Bryant," Maribelle says.

"What about a lanyard? We can braid it," Bryant said. "I bought this for you girls a few days ago, before Bud . . ."

Maribelle and Raleigh huddle together, uncertain what to do.

Bryant, the martyr, takes a paper bag out of her worn book bag and lays out yellow, green, blue, and red strands of vinyl. "Ready?"

The girls come close, interested. Outside, the sky is getting streakier, stranger. A familiar popping sensation, Lucinda has felt it twice before when her water broke. A clear fluid runs down her legs and onto the wood floor.

"Reed?" she shouts.

He comes in from the kitchen. His hair falling across his forehead in jagged pieces, like it hasn't been combed. His overalls smell like the river.

Bryant notices. "Are you alright, Reed? Because I can go with Lucinda to the hospital if you'd rather stay with the girls."

Lucinda and Reed lock glances. Only a half hour before, they were alone with Ruth-Ann. They pressed a brown bag filled with money into her hands and sent her out the back door.

"Bryant," Lucinda says. "I'm not sure how you'll take care of my girls while Reed and I get going. I mean . . ."

"I'll be okay," she says quietly. "Your girls are like my own. They'll be good company."

Lucinda's contractions are starting. Reed heads into the hallway, opening the front closet for her overnight bag, packed two days ago. Lucinda is about to give birth, yet this sense of ruin surrounds her and Reed. She leans in, kisses Maribelle then Caroline, knowing in the time to come it will take every ounce of grit to be herself. She begins to quietly cry, so unlike her. Both daughters are staring.

Maribelle is crying too. "We know you'll be back with a baby, *our baby.*"

Lucinda straightens up.

Bryant nods. "I'm taking care of the girls—it's fine."

"Thank you, Bryant." Reed doesn't look her in the eye.

Bryant hugs Maribelle and Caroline. "We'll bake brownies, we'll paint shells."

Reed is leaning against the wall. "Let's go—we've got to get on the road. If I speed, it's an hour to the hospital." He tries to wink at the girls. His face is broken in pieces, he's broken inside. "We're bringing a baby home for you. Any last votes for a girl or a boy?"

"Girl, girl!" shouts Maribelle.

Caroline shakes her head. "Boy! Boy! I want a brother. I'll teach him things."

Reed turns to Lucinda. "Ready?"

"I am." Her voice smaller than it has been in years. She is exhausted and about to give birth. In the hall mirror, she sees she is hollow. "Thank you, Bryant. Thank you."

"Of course. I hope it goes easily. Again, we're fine."

Bryant is empty, in the room and not there. Lucinda has no one else to watch her girls while she delivers. Bryant and Bud were meant to stay together, a long-ago plan.

Her contractions are quickening when they rush in Reed's Chevy Cheyenne to the main roads. Lucinda pulls in those long breaths to slow down the contractions. She thinks of Bud dead; she knows an investigation is to follow. Her baby will be born anyway—that's how it is.

Chapter Twenty-Eight

2026

Raleigh drives the Jeep along the back streets toward the west side of Kesgrave. She is en route to her cousins, fraternal twins Tom and Luke and their younger sister Ginger Barrows. Locals, they graduated Pinestream and are exactly Maribelle and Caroline's ages. She has no sense of who they've become since Lucinda and Reed's tale of triumph over adversity equaled having no past. If only she could nail the facts, it would be freeing. Although she doubts it could break the spell of Lucinda.

"After this, it's a wrap," Caroline calls to tell Raleigh.

"A wrap?" Raleigh asks. Although it has to be, her sister has carefully managed her time.

She stands facing the Gulf from her hotel suite. While this visit to Kesgrave to dig for the key to Lucinda is dicey, there are views of the Gulf, the river, the bay. She's seen little of this and has one day to finish her hapless task.

"Remember," Caroline says. "These were hip brothers. I did everything they wanted me to, from slugging beers to getting stoned at parties, to listening to Counting Crows."

"I do remember. I thought they were epic," Raleigh says.

"Keep saying whatever you have to and don't carry a notebook, Raleigh."

"Why not?" Raleigh has one in her tote and is hoping it won't offend anyone.

"Be discreet. Cousin Luke could prove useful," Caroline says before she rings off.

Useful. Only Caroline would treat Raleigh's trip like a business venture where she works for her. Yet they know, the three sisters, there has always been some frantic energy around their mother. Raleigh saw it as a child—Lucinda sitting at the dining table, poring over the books, planning their escape. Maribelle had Samuel; their dyad was consuming. Caroline had Travis; they worked on being "the couple." Raleigh was little, everyone and no one watched her.

The only one left at home when they arrived in Palm Beach, Raleigh was her mother's protégé. She and Lucinda ascended together. As a teenager she was too busy with her highlighted, waist-length hair, jean shorts, Ugg boots, and silk camisoles, to pay attention to her mother's maniacal maneuvers. They were both busy. Now she has to know what her mother has done.

THEY ARE WAITING outside Tom's house, leaning against the pillars on the front porch. Raleigh had no idea he'd done well enough to live in a McMansion with a wide veranda. Standing nearer she sees how weathered the white shingles and green shutters are; the wood in places is swollen. The windowsills might collapse. Tom, Luke, and Ginger are in jeans and sneaks, no designer denims nor Adidas running shoes, as in Palm Beach. The brothers are bald with shaved heads, a nice touch. Ginger is blond without nuance or varying shades. No one is as tall as Raleigh remembers. They have those deep blue eyes; their freckles have faded. How could she have lost touch with them? They once mattered so much. Growing up in Kesgrave, Barrows to Barrows, there was this important cousin vibe. She last saw them twelve years ago when they came to Reed's funeral. No one came to Samuel's; they just sent flowers. Maribelle was offended.

Odd how it wasn't until months after Samuel was buried that Raleigh cared who had been there and who had not. Who in the Panhandle gave a fig about traveling eight hours by car to show their respect? Was that it?

SEATED IN A SEMICIRCLE, Raleigh is on a pull-up chair, Tom, Luke, and Ginger on the couch. The upholstery is a dense blue print, heavy on flowers and leaves. While it's Tom's house, Ginger pours the Arnold Palmers, ice clinking per glass. Raleigh is patient, like there will be a reward for segueing out of small talk. Meanwhile, they're knee-deep in catch-up.

"You're divorcing?" Ginger asks. She remains fetching although she has lots of thin lines on her cheeks and forehead. Raleigh wonders if there's a place to get Botox in Kesgrave. Probably not, but if there is, Ginger is not a client. She's wearing dangle earrings in silver, maybe pewter. Lucinda would call them cheap looking. She'd say, "Don't wear earrings if they aren't passable," meaning fine looking, whether costume or not.

Ginger tilts her head. There is a stone in the middle of the filigree—not peridot, instead a peridot lookalike. "Didn't you marry your college boyfriend? Wasn't he at Reed's funeral with you?" she asks. "He was very attractive."

When Ginger raves about Alex's looks, Raleigh feels it's disloyal to Porter, as if anyone would understand.

"Yes, and we have a son together, Caleb, who is five. Caroline's girls are growing up so quickly. They're ten and twelve."

"That's about how old Tom and Luke's kids are," Ginger says. "Tom's girls are nine and eleven, Luke's son is thirteen."

Although she doesn't, Raleigh should remember their children's names, ask after them. Ginger is waiting for an acknowledgment, some mild enthusiasm. Raleigh conjures up a smile.

Ginger tosses her head. "Maribelle has no kids, right? I have twins, Ellie and Daisy. They're only six." She starts scrolling on her phone for photos.

Tom holds his hand like a crossing guard. "Later."

"I imagine your mother's still running the show?" Luke asks. He's the scruffier of the two; his shadow beard doesn't look deliberate or tended to. He's got a gravelly voice.

"She would be, Luke," Ginger says. "Cousin Reed's gone a long time."

"Adeline, our mother, says your mother was always running the show," Tom says. He's the taller twin, with a more chiseled face. Didn't Caroline once tell Raleigh she'd fixed Tom up with one of her friends, and he never called her back after he had his way with her?

"Excuse me?" Raleigh goes to the bookcases. They're sparse, some cookbooks, a few history titles, including one on Washington, next John Grisham, James Patterson, Elin Hiderbrand. Four frames stand against the books. The first is of butterflies, mostly monarchs, then a frame full of moths, then spiders, and finally beetles. She might throw up.

"Our mother didn't appreciate how bossy Lucinda was," Tom says.

Luke is fiddling with his phone, looks up. "Spotify?"

No one answers, then Raleigh says, "Sure, Spotify."

He taps his screen, plays "Losing my Religion" by R.E.M. "Shades of 1990s," he says.

After a beat, Thomas says, "I get it, we're here to revisit the past."

"Actually," she says, "I've got a few questions."

"Is this for Maribelle's magazine, *PB Confidential*?" Ginger asks. "I googled it. I see it's only local, about Palm Beach, West Palm . . ."

"No. She hasn't been involved with the magazine for the last few years. I've come about my mother. I'm trying to puzzle some things together. She's turning sixty. I thought maybe I could find something. I might write a poem or a speech to present that would include details from her life in Kesgrave."

Ginger is watching her closely, as if she doesn't trust her. "You could have done a Zoom with us for that."

"I wanted it to be authentic," Raleigh says. "I wanted to see everyone." She sounds lame enough that everyone pauses.

"Hey," Tom says. "She had a good reputation as a teacher. I was in her class where no one wanted to read *The Great Gatsby*, not even *Frankenstein*. She hooked us—she made the books interesting, her talking about it. We felt grown up and smart. Some of the boys called her 'the babe teacher.'"

"I remember her clothes. We have pictures. She was so young, her mid-thirties with two daughters at Pinestream already," Ginger says.

Everyone is still. Luke chooses another song—Jefferson Airplane, "Don't You Want Somebody to Love." Tom laughs. "Are you channeling our mothers?"

"Sort of," Raleigh says.

"Well, what I remember is how Adeline and Lucinda would get together and dance and play their favorites in Lucinda's kitchen. The cousins would be having fun together. You were a baby, Raleigh."

"Yeah, and they'd order pizza and laugh. Too happy to cook some mediocre meal," Ginger says. "It was random—after a really fun time, months could go by where we didn't see each other, except in school. I heard your mother blew hot and cold."

Raleigh remembers Cousin Adeline from Thanksgivings. She was plain but doing her best in sweaters and jeans, boots. They'd go to the cousins' house, and on the car ride back, Lucinda complained the food had no flavor, not a pinch of salt and pepper, that Adeline was pushy. It always took place at Adeline and Phil's since Lucinda had firmly closed her kitchen for such events. She wasn't going to reciprocate. On occasion, Lucinda and Adeline went to Apalachicola to shop together, it depended on Lucinda's mood. In retrospect, was anything ever right or ever enough for Lucinda?

"They smoked a lot of cigarettes," Luke says. "Adeline still smokes. Now she lives in Naples. She left the Panhandle six years ago."

"I'd say our moms saw each other until the Barrows shit went down. Probably friendliest when Barrows was a general store. We'd go for the beef jerky and M&M's on Saturday," Ginger says. "What we lived on . . ."

"What happened? What went down?" Raleigh asks. "I don't know. I always say, I'm the youngest of the Barrows."

"You know our grandpas were brothers," Tom says. He

runs his hand over his bare head. "The business got broken up because your grandfather, Reed's father, was pushing for that."

Luke shrugs, turns off the music. "Everybody knows. Everybody around town, anyway."

"Nothing was the same. It was because of Lucinda, according to our mother," Ginger says. "She had a strategy. She wanted Barrows to go way beyond the Panhandle."

The room feels gummed up, their anger festering. The more Barrows locations appeared around the country, the more the cousins in the Panhandle resented her family. Especially Lucinda.

Luke looks uneasy. Raleigh wishes she and he were the only ones in the house, talking it through. He was always the most sympathetic, her favorite of the cousins.

"Luke, what do you think? I'm not sure what Ginger is alluding to."

He stops, stands by the fireplace. "What are you asking? If anyone liked Lucinda? How shrewd she was and why our family put up with her? Only because Barrows was good for Kesgrave—it brought business here. The problem was the second Barrows store in town and the surrounding property."

Tom shakes his head. "She talked our father out of holding on to his half of the land. We've been told it started with her, she wanted Reed to buy out our side. She got some appraiser to say the land for the second Barrows was useless. It wasn't right, she wore everyone down."

They despise Lucinda. Her witty, sophisticated mother who willed herself to be a Palm Beach lady, a founder and preserver of life as she imagined it. "I have never heard about this," Raleigh says. "I'm sorry, really."

"Yeah, well," Luke says, "once she and Reed were the sole

owners, they sold the land to some developer from Tampa or Orlando, or somewhere, for a killing."

"Wait a second, where is this property?" Raleigh doesn't know. Caroline knows, of course. As does Travis. Anyone who pays attention to the company.

Tom swigs his drink. "It's the strip mall on Lincoln and Mason. It's profitable."

"A wise move to have left town," Luke says. "No one had to see them. Your mother and father never came back. It was Samuel who came to check on the property, and someone else, some field guy from Destin."

"The Barrows stores are a legend in Kesgrave," Tom says. "So we never could say anything. Why make Barrows look bad when we are Barrows ourselves?"

Ginger raises her hand as if they're in a college seminar; it's her turn to speak. "I know how Mom said that Lucinda could steal anything—a boyfriend, someone's ideas, a part in a high school play, land, whatever she put her mind to. She had delusions of grandeur. That someone as clever as Lucinda Matthews wouldn't have been pregnant young except she nailed Reed by doing it. Remember, she was very poor. You know that, don't you?"

"No, I don't," Raleigh says. They aren't right about anything. Her cousins are bitter, bordering on twisted about Lucinda. "I'm wondering if you have this wrong."

Ginger starts laughing, Tom joins in.

"We aren't confused about anything," Ginger says. "It was clear Lucinda had to have another life."

Luke is staring at his sister like she's gone too far. "Ginger," he says.

"Thank you, Luke, it's okay. I've got to be going," Raleigh says. She'd rather return empty-handed, anything to ditch this cousin who has taken on her mother's rage against Lucinda.

"Hey, Raleigh," Luke says. "Don't leave upset. We'll switch the conversation."

She looks at his hands, remembering how Luke would drive around town on his Honda sportbike when she was in third grade. He was the coolest boy in Kesgrave, after Samuel.

"That's fine," she says. Yet she's had enough.

"I heard you met with Kirby Kirks," Tom says. "Anything you want to ask about that?"

Raleigh hesitates. "He spoke about Bud Humphreys."

"Yeah. Our father told us there was an accident years ago, maybe thirty or more. Bud Humphreys died," Luke says.

"Our father thought he'd have a shot at part of the Barrows plan after Bud was gone," Tom says. "Reed must've promised him, and Lucinda cut him out."

Ginger moves to the middle of Tom's living room. "I heard Mom begging Dad to talk to Reed, to get to work at Barrows. She said he shouldn't be so proud and that Reed owed him. Dad said nothing. At the end of it, our mother said, 'Lucinda is a liar, a fucking liar.'"

Raleigh feels ill, like when she caught Covid back in the early days despite the precautions she had taken. And not eligible for the antidote.

As she leaves for the airport, the rain has started, coming down sideways, hitting everything hard. The flower beds will be saturated, battered. She factors in the hours from her cousin's doorstep to the Uber ride at the other end, until she'll be home. For the first time ever, she has no desire to stay in Kesgrave.

Chapter Twenty-Nine

2026

A LONGER THAN NECESSARY return flight to West Palm Beach, connecting through Atlanta. Raleigh is nauseous, as if she's eaten a triple stack of chocolate chip pancakes on a dare. She once did that in college, and it took her weeks to recover. A self-inflicted experience, which makes it not that different from what went on in Kesgrave, what she learned about her family. Her earlier trip to Kesgrave she was hopeful, invested in her paintings and decorative shells, handselling her art. That was when she idealized the place while today she is disheartened. Although she gleaned a great deal, she is missing the last part of Lucinda's story.

Digging deep into her less than stellar family—what does it accomplish? What does Caroline intend to do? Raleigh has newfound empathy for Lucinda, who, at sixty, should be concentrating on the life in Palm Beach that she's carefully created, her friends and family. Lucinda isn't herself, her eyes dart about, she's has this habit of nervously tapping her forefinger around her thumb on her right hand. The very woman who warned her daughters to sit on their hands rather than gesture. Yet it isn't Lucinda's unraveling per se; it's what it means, how it's come about. Raleigh feels grimy, as if she didn't do laps at 6 a.m. in the hotel pool for clarity then salt-soaped and loofahed her body. No matter what her mother's story is, it has sullied things. Raleigh feels forever looped with Lucinda's gritty, unknown skeletons.

Turbulence moves through the cabin. Raleigh looks around at everyone getting on with their day. Some passengers have their shades down. When they left the ground she Lysol wiped her seat, armrests, and tray table. Now she vigorously does another round. Then starts surfing for a film, scrolling through the offerings. Although it's March, a Christmas movie would be the right choice, a fine distraction.

Raleigh takes her vegan leather notebook out of her tote to begin reading what she's written from Kesgrave. The moment she lands, she'll share it with Caroline.

CAROLINE SIGHS. "Basically, you're back with gossip, when I suspect, and Maribelle suspects, that someone is hunting Mom down. We need *leads*."

That isn't exactly how Raleigh's mission to Kesgrave had been framed.

"You said to see what I could find out. Here it is. Mom has quite the reputation. Everyone talked about her and Reed, like some larger-than-life legend. They were a big deal, two successful people who turned their backs on the Panhandle."

Caroline is tapping her hands against the desk in her library. Raleigh feels defensive, sent in a vain pursuit. "You and Maribelle were older when we moved. You would remember. You guys could have gone to Kesgrave and snooped around."

On the bookcase is a collection of their father's tennis and golf trophies from Longgreens and the Harbor Club, charity awards—The United Way, The Dale Hospital, Boys in Sports—with Reed's name etched at the top. Her sister took possession of these once Lucinda married William and didn't want them showcased in her home. Reed. Had he lived, it would all be okay, if Samuel were here, things would be better, or so Raleigh sometimes believes. Travis is weak to put out fires; he hasn't the wherewithal nor an ounce of artistry. Whatever this entire mess is, he isn't to be counted on.

"I took pictures of pictures while I was there." Raleigh holds up her phone. "Of Lucinda and Reed with Aunt Bryant and Bud when they were young."

"We have the same ones in a box somewhere," Caroline says. "I wonder what went on this exact day in this very photo? Do we know? No."

Meaning Raleigh got lost in some jagged dream world, unnerved by her cousins, by what people had to say, while Caroline hoped she'd find clues.

Caroline starts pacing, to the wet bar and back again, without pouring wine or a drink. Although Raleigh's entire trip is worth less now, she opens her notebook, looks through the pages.

Maribelle arrives, tossing her bag and straw visor onto the Eames chair. "I'm sorry, I thought only you and I were meeting today, Caroline. I came because you asked. Seeing Raleigh, that still doesn't work. If she's in a room, I walk out. Unless Lucinda is there." Maribelle is in yoga pants and a sleeveless T-shirt. Her arms are tannish, like she's forgotten to wear sunscreen lately. Too LA—the old Maribelle wouldn't have worn this in her home gym with a trainer. There's that thin scar on her forehead from the time she and Caroline pushed each other. They were ten and eight, playing "Princess for a Day," a favorite made-up game. Maribelle hit her head. As the story goes, Lucinda insisted Reed rush Maribelle to Pensacola to a plastic surgeon. A smaller scar was the result.

Maribelle starts stage whispering to no one. "Her level of selfishness—an ongoing problem. "

Raleigh clears her throat. "I hear you, Maribelle. *I* was selfish? I loved Samuel, while you *pretended* you did. It's selfish to hold on to someone you don't love."

"Stop it, both of you," Caroline says. "What we're dealing with is important. I don't care about your grievances or if you aren't speaking. There's a great deal at stake here. Raleigh's back from Kesgrave, that's why we're meeting. We're here for Lucinda."

"Of course, Caroline. Except I have to go," Maribelle says. "I didn't expect to be with Raleigh."

"I agree. I have to go, as well—I have Caleb today," Raleigh says. Her voice is less sure; she might not mean it. She's starting to cry.

Maribelle stares at Raleigh "I won't ever forgive you. No matter what you try to do to make it up to me."

Raleigh nods. "That's okay. If you accept me, then we go forward. Forgiveness is not required."

No one speaks; the tension is palpable. Caroline storms in front of them, a referee at a basketball game. "Okay. Take two. We're here for a reason. It's not about either of you. It's bigger. It's critical."

Her two sisters have flipped. Caroline is the more sympathetic, while Maribelle is harsh. Raleigh keeps on crying.

"I'm grateful for family meetings. After Samuel died, we went through his things together, remember? In Maribelle's vast walk-in closet." Raleigh says.

"What I ask myself whenever I remember, which is every minute in Palm Beach, is what Samuel was doing that morning. What was he *really doing*? Why wasn't I good enough? Why wasn't Alex good enough for you, Raleigh?" Maribelle asks. "I second guess so much."

Caroline takes a lip gloss out of the pocket of her pink pleated golf skirt. "Lucinda taught us that second-guessing is a terrible waste. That we go forward. I'd like you both to get over it. Move on. That's what we do." She speaks in that corporate voice. "We have a situation on our hands."

Raleigh's phone dings. She dares to lift it from her bag, glance at it.

"Raleigh? Short of an emergency, there won't be any calls until we finish."

"What if it's about Caleb?"

"Caleb is with Rosie. He's more than okay." Caroline sounds like she's talking to willful employees, those with attitude.

Raleigh drops her phone back into the bag. Maribelle takes off her sunglasses, clears her throat.

"We've seen Lucinda is not herself," Caroline says. "She's getting worse."

"Staying in her house is upsetting," Maribelle says. "A few days ago, she was rambling. She asked if I remember that she drove us around when Caroline and I were in grade school, that she did that mother bit better than anyone knows. She told me she understands why people lose the will to live. She said some things are unforgivable. She wishes she were religious. She might start going to church if she makes it through the next few weeks. Yesterday she took down a framed picture of us fishing on the Apalachicola when Raleigh was a toddler."

Raleigh bites her lip. She needs an Advil, water, something. "The religion part is shocking. Did she really say that?"

Maribelle nods.

"With me, she talks about being popular every minute unless it's about my being the custodial parent for Caleb," Raleigh says. "She curses the lawyers on the team."

"You know how none of us were allowed to have a stain on our clothes, a wrinkle? She's messy, careless," Maribelle says. "She's distraught. She sneaks off to pop Xanax. She looks like hell. She's in some creepy state, like she's a stranger."

Caroline winces. "With two parties coming up for her birthday. Plus her obsession with being the best—her reputation."

"The real issue is her cover-up, what she's hiding," Maribelle says.

Raleigh nods. She's chewing her fingernails, a habit she kicked in ninth grade. Maribelle is twirling her hair around her right index finger, a habit she kicked in twelfth grade. Caroline is pacing again.

"The letters definitely have to do with Kesgrave," Raleigh says. "Does anybody know what she could have done?"

Maribelle turns away first. "I'd say she's done some crazy shit in Palm Beach to get where she is."

"Mom's suffering—she must've done something bad," Caroline says.

"You mean steal someone's money? She cares about money," Raleigh says.

"Or maybe an identity," Maribelle says.

"Why would she do that?" Caroline asks.

"We don't know. She's furtive. She and Aunt Bryant," Maribelle says.

"They are," Raleigh says. "In Kesgrave, everyone wanted to know what happened the day Bud died. Do you guys remember?"

"It was awful, so sad," Maribelle says. "We were younger than Caroline's girls are now."

"I've blocked it out," Caroline says.

"Right," Raleigh says. "Well, I keep wondering when this will be over, when things will be better, straightened out."

The three of them are quiet, each staring at the Intracoastal. At another exquisite Palm Beach sky.

Caroline puts on her take-charge-of-the-meeting voice. "Here's what I'll do. I'll put up the money, pay off whoever is threatening Lucinda. You'll both sign a note, an agreement, and pay me back later. I could do it tomorrow, if we only knew who it is."

"That's very generous, Caroline," Raleigh says.

"We don't know who to pay off," Maribelle says.

Caroline sort of huddles with them; she's in the middle. "We need to save Lucinda, save everything. Have it go away."

They stand together, as if it's a coven and they're brewing potions. Either triple goddesses or the witches in Macbeth.

AFTER RALEIGH goes upstairs to the guest suite at Caroline's, she rereads what Ginger said in Kesgrave. *Reed owed him. Dad said nothing. Then our mother said,* Lucinda *is a liar, a fucking liar.*

Her phone dings. From Porter: *Rethinking our conversation. Are you around?*

Chapter Thirty

2026

RALEIGH CUTS THROUGH the pool area where those who lunch at Swifty's favor Lilly Pulitzer shifts in hot pink and green, aqua and lavender, oranges and tomato red. The assorted men are more quietly dressed; it's less impactful. The women, old, young, in between, exude a similar determination. While appearing to peruse the familiar menu, through their sunglasses they're eyeing the crowd. The low humidity this afternoon is like a drug, everyone is sharper without effort, pleased to linger.

She moves across the terrace into the empty indoor bar area. It's intermezzo; late lunches are finishing, cocktails have yet to begin. Being here at the Colony Hotel reminds her of Reed, how incredibly polished and elegant her father was, how he owned any room he entered. The Colony was a place her parents frequented. It occurs to her she ought to be careful—not that she knows anyone who would stay at the Colony besides Porter. Yet among those who lunch it's another story. A memory of Samuel and their excessive caution washes over her.

Porter is waiting, exuding what is coveted in Palm Beach: an athlete, a beautiful boy to man, someone who knows money and doesn't talk about it, someone who always wins.

Reed never liked Alex—what would he have said about this one?

"I'm happy to see you," she says. She means it but can't shut down her thoughts. He looks so good, a gift that's guided him his whole life no doubt. Since Raleigh was a teenager, the mothers have whispered she's too pretty for her own good. Is that what they would say about Porter? Mainly she wants to fall into his arms. His skin is an invitation.

"Are you?"

She nods, looks down at her sandals, adjusts her mini shift.

"Let's go." He's speaking softly as if they're rehearsing for when people will be around. They'll be prepared.

"Are you worried?" she asks. What would it matter to Porter? He's single, he's from some other sphere. A time traveler she's falling for.

"Not exactly." He takes a room key out of his shirt pocket, waves it around. "Shall we?"

They don't speak in the elevator, she wishes he would kiss her. No matter what, Raleigh wants the hours ahead with him.

"A STANDARD ROOM, no ocean view," Porter says. "Only the penthouses have that."

"I don't care."

"Meaning that night in Kesgrave was fine?" His mouth is close to her ear.

"Fine," she sighs.

He leads her to a celadon wall and starts kissing her fiercely. As if a thread has been lost, with no guarantee of the next time, kisses that won't stop. He tugs the starched coverlet aside and undresses first, quickly. He's even better naked, his incredible body like the statue of David at the Uffizi in Florence. He carefully takes her dress over her head. They lie down together, the sheets and pillow shams smooth against her back.

He's vanquishing any memory of any other man. He's remarkably sexy. He'll never get old, be fatherly with a paunch belly. Would he look out for her, be protective? She ought to leave right now—there have been enough who failed her. Alex, Samuel. The sorrow. Is Porter only about sex?

Then he's on top of her, his skin against hers, a promise they trade. His three-day beard scratches slightly. Like that night in Kesgrave only better. The feel of him this near is cherished, inviolable.

AFTERWARD he leans back on his side of the bed, pulls her close. "We live in this room together."

"Do we?" She's praying it could be so. If only her life was hers alone.

He strokes her arm, puts his right hand over her heart. There's no space for the custody story, Alex's bullying, Lucinda's ambitions, Raleigh's affair with her dead brother-in-law. That she could pry free her names, separate Raleigh Barrows from Raleigh Morton. To be simply Raleigh. As if that could ever be enough, as if she ever deserves forgiveness.

He moves his head; he's drifting off. She loves how he breathes, measured, steady. Around him there's a serenity. The curtains billow; the air is in small swirls. He's drawn the covers up to their shoulders.

"I'd like to know more about you," he says. "Everything."

She should ask, "What about you, why are you in Palm Beach, why were you in Kesgrave? Are you stalking me? Do you know who I really am?" Caleb—she ought to explain Caleb in some detail. Except the facts, on both sides, could ruin everything. He might roll up a joint. His eyes might or might not be medium gray. He could rob her. He's that mysterious.

"No . . . no, you wouldn't," she says.

"Are you sure?"

"I'm sure," Raleigh says. "What about you?"

"Who am I? How much do you need to know?"

She shakes her head, flicks it from her conscience as Lucinda has trained her about any unpleasant thought or discovery.

He's watching her face. "Come closer, Raleigh." He pulls her to his side; they kiss and it begins again. She's a moth to a flame; he is like no one she has ever met. If she painted him, viewers would ask, *what is this? Has your work become about myth, is this a Greek god?*

She chooses Porter as much as he chooses her.

Chapter Thirty-One

2026

ANOTHER YEAR, the annual charity events are converging, one's calendar laden with expectation. Of course, Barrows has two tables at the Animal Rescue Ball, held at the spanking new Arts Center of the Palm Beaches. Few would miss being seen and noted this evening. Since it is near Lucinda's birthday festivities, she has not pressured her friends who are showing up for her soon enough. She has carefully selected family and "outer rim friends" to fill the chairs. That would include William's sister, Deanie and her husband Tad, who live in a gated community in Boca. And their two thirty-something daughters, sun worshippers with that weathered skin effect, and their husbands, both complete yawns. She's rounded it out by asking Estelle to bring Roy, her longtime partner who is on a cane; her son, Neil, a former rocket scientist at NASA; and his wife, Aylet, who also works at Barrows in accounting. The family table, inner sanctum per usual, includes her three daughters plus William, Travis, and Bryant. Although Maribelle isn't keen on it, Jacquie Quince of *PB Confidential* and her squeeze are there as well.

"Mom, I don't want to be with anyone from the magazine," Maribelle said when Lucinda told her the plan two days beforehand via a mandated Zoom call with her daughters.

"We're purposely including Jacquie and her date," Lucinda explained. "Because no one knows what's ahead. We want her at the table. She'll feel special."

"This is awkward." Maribelle's tone was hissy.

"Everyone wants to be at your table. It's always been so," Raleigh pointed out. "Is this the best we can do?"

Caroline tossed her head. "Are you defending Maribelle?"

"That's rich," Maribelle said. Still, she and Raleigh locked eyes for a brief moment.

Lucinda smiled her steeliest Palm Beach smile, reserved for a crisis at Barrows or on the cultural circuit. "Stop it."

UPON ARRIVAL, Lucinda eyes the ballroom with its swaying damask draperies, crystal chandeliers, and Palm Beachers filing in. Guests are grabbing champagne flutes from the servers as they move closer to the center of the cocktail hour. Voices are rising, the space feels oxygen depleted. What is apparent is the color scheme—the women are in black or white, long or short dresses, the men wear tuxes. The room is without color; no one is wearing a gold lace Michael Kors, a magenta Roland Mouret, a cerulean blue Talbot Runhof midi-dress. Even Lucinda's own guests, her table fillers, are in black, which she chalks up to being devoid of taste and imagination. Lucinda tugs on the waist of her vibrant floral print Oscar and taps the toes of her red Louboutin pumps. Has she lost her mind? Is this a color schemed party and she missed the memo? An almost-erased, long-ago sinking sensation starts, one conjured by a social misstep.

Bryant, late, arrives in one of her poorly fitting lace sheaths. Predictably, she hasn't gone on the Avenue or to Royal Poinciana Plaza for a fresher silhouette—longer, looser, an occasional hem that dips in the back. Her hair is in that everlasting tortoise clip. What she has gotten right, weirdly, is the black and white specification for the evening. She has gone so far as to be wearing black with white lace trim. Lucinda has to admit to this first, if unintentional, victory for Bryant.

"How is everyone?" She flashes a florid smile. For the fiftieth time, Lucinda wishes that William had a friend from his grad school days, a golf buddy at Longgreens, a bridge partner who would sweep Bryant off her feet or at least deflect her attention.

"We're fine," Caroline says, sounding precise, crisp. Her black dress works.

Raleigh, in a black crepe dress with bell sleeves, drapes her arms around Bryant's shoulders and hugs her, bordering on too private a display to be public. Maribelle gives that "we're in this together" smile when Lucinda walks over for a mutual air kiss. Jolie swishes by in a black satin mid-length cocktail dress that Lucinda also owns. The night is maddening.

Maribelle, in her off-white mesh dress, looking markedly Santa Monica, faces Lucinda. "I assumed you knew it was a color-mandated event, Mom. I mean, my dress is a little au lait for this strict dress code."

"Thank you, Maribelle," Lucinda says. "I'm fine. Surely not my biggest problem."

Maribelle rolls her eyes. "I'll bet not."

It's uncertain how any of her daughters view the evening. For Lucinda, that queasy sensation, part unease, part imposter syndrome, gnaws at her. As if there are mice at her feet, she's jumpy, miserable. Very alone in this, she's slipping in a quagmire where it was once solid ground. A place where being a Barrows guest in Palm Beach, for a dinner party or a tennis match or a charity bash, has always been a coup. Is she merely imagining Molly Inters along with Collette Nayers gliding past her without eye contact or a reverent pause to greet her? The idea of it is stupefying. Lucinda momentarily forgets how elusive her life is lately—how scrutinized she is. *Money.* As Barrows thrives, possibly sold one day, there will be no question of her status. She will be among the wealthiest of them all. Yet not in real time; not this minute.

William is at her elbow. "Are you alright, Lucinda?"

Suddenly it makes no difference that he's developed a small paunch and is balding, how he doesn't stand as straight anymore. His eyes are the brightest blue tonight, he remains a shade over six feet. He's kind to her daughters. Many wanted him when his wife died and his son moved to Brazil (always good news), and she won that round. Besides, he knows next to nothing about Lucinda's secrets, let alone when she is transparent.

She clears her throat; she needs a drink—or more. She expected tonight to be a distraction, a chance at fun. "I am, William. Although I'm astonished. I've worn the wrong thing, and it feels very strange."

"That's it? You seem deep in thought, uncomfortable. You aren't happy. We could go home—you could change. I see the ladies are in black."

"Or white." Lucinda pauses. "No, thank you, I'll stay. It's a little late for this mistake. Everyone has seen me, and who cares anyway?"

"You are always outstanding to me, regardless of any fashion rules," he says. "Be content, Lucinda. Your birthday is coming up soon. That will be the main event."

William takes her hand; his is cool and dry, another plus.

He leads her to their table, where every one of the women including her daughters have let her down. Was no one able to make a comment—from Estelle to Caroline—to have mentioned it, pointed it out? For the conversations that fly about wardrobe, venue, and who will be where, there was no such remark or reminder. Someone from her inner circle, from Bryant to Jolie, might have said, *Bizarre, is it not, that five hundred guests will be in black and white at the Animal Rescue Ball this coming week for one of their first big evenings . . . every woman following a mandate?* Nothing—not a word.

Lucinda leans into William, and together they are seated. Is it her imagination, or are the other guests staring, as if she's the has-been, the one who no longer counts, who is so tone-deaf she isn't simply in another color, say beige or a medium blue, but a bright print dress? She digs her fingernails into her thighs, what she did after Reed refused to leave Kesgrave while she was an outcast. A technique she used when everyone whispered about her. At local spots—the bowling alley, the movie theatre, family dinners at Burger Delight, her children's dance recitals. A searing doubt rushes through Lucinda, followed by her determination. Although appearing less socially is trying, she's been through much worse; she'll survive this episode. She looks around the room, suspecting the wardrobe faux pas was deliberate and she has been specifically snubbed. Somehow the invitation sent to her was missing the card detailing wardrobe. Someone on the committee wanted to see her disgraced and humiliated, someone who wishes to take everything she's worked to achieve. For that, Lucinda is irate—and worse, regretful. Regret, what she has always considered a form of despair.

Chapter Thirty-Two

2026

LATE AFTERNOON the next day, Rosie and Daisy stand in Lucinda's kitchen at her La Cornue eight-burner range, busily cooking. Seeing them makes Lucinda question why she had to remodel her kitchen last year, it seems irrelevant, excessive. Unless she is entertaining or Rosie is poaching eggs for breakfast and serving lattes, the kitchen is usually "closed."

"I'm sorry, are we expecting guests?" she asks.

The two women exchange glances.

"We are, Mrs. Barrows," Rosie says. "We have your family coming tonight. You gave me the menu weeks ago. Some kind of celebration for your company."

It comes back to her, a dinner for the two new openings of Barrows—one in Sarasota and one in Mobile. Estelle's inefficiency is annoying; why hasn't she reminded Lucinda? Worse, she might have and Lucinda wasn't listening. If only Lucinda had an interest in being with her family at the moment, yet it's the opposite. She dreads any intimate gathering, anything with people who count for her. Her head hurts. Last night's black tie is still fresh. Being chipper and graceful with her own family seems arduous.

"Enough. I'll leave you to it," she says.

Daisy scrolls through her phone. "A few changes,

Mrs. Barrows. Maribelle is vegan now, and Mr. William has requested osso buco. The girls want spaghetti and meatballs, and Caroline has said gluten free, dairy free. We have gone to Publix and used Instacart for the right foods."

"That's fine, Daisy," Lucinda snaps. "You'll figure it out."

The two women exchange glances again.

"We have, Mrs. Barrows," Rosie says. "We're tweaking, nothing else."

Not only does Lucinda not want to be at a sit-down dinner tonight, she's actually missed it on her calendar. In her new mode of semi-high on Xanax and deeply afraid of what's ahead, she no longer feels powerful; her house appears archaic, her style obsolete.

Sunlight hits the double sink filled with pale pink and lavender orchids. Lucinda comes near to watch the Intracoastal, which is glassy, quiet at this hour. The water is gray. A slick cigarette boat passes by, the driver honoring the speed limit—what Samuel couldn't do. Samuel—inconveniently dead while needed for a semblance of calm, if ever it was authentic.

"You had wanted that butternut squash recipe served at Buccan?" Proving her prowess, Rosie holds up two gourds of summer squash. Frozen, precut cubes would be such time savers, except few housekeepers or chefs in Palm Beach would go that route.

Lucinda nods. "I suppose I did." Leftover Xanax and vodka slosh through her bloodstream. She's floating and sinking at once.

Rosie gets it. She turns off the burner where hot water simmers. "Mrs. Barrows, I'll come upstairs with you."

Out of nowhere, Rosie is stout. How could this be, at a time when the world is on Ozempic or Mounjaro? It can't be right. Not under Lucinda's roof. The other scenario is that Lucinda has not noticed Rosie's weight shift. She seems to be missing salient occurrences.

Rosie is about to hold her elbow.

"Oh, Rosie, I'll be okay," Lucinda hears herself say. She manages to leave the kitchen, drifting up the staircase to her dressing room to costume herself differently.

Rosie watches, close behind, like she's a spotter and Lucinda will tilt backward, become one of those fallen diva tragedies.

"Rosie, I said I'm fine," Lucinda says, not quite believing herself. Rushing ahead, she closes the door. Alone at her dressing table, she scrutinizes her profile, both sides. Her upper lip appears deflated although six weeks ago she had a "lip flip."

Beneath her makeup and a tray of fashion jewelry, earrings, watches, bangles—what she throws on for a manicure, the bank, food shopping—is the latest envelope. Daisy had brought it upstairs right before she and William left last night for that disastrous black tie. By now she knows the lyrical cadence used in this series, honed for her, deliberately meant to stir her up, intimidate her. Still she opens every delivery, drawing her to the reveal, the threat ahead.

THE TRUTH

I would have been slated for the next boy/man, destined for young, local Kesgrave motherhood, had it not been for that afternoon.

In the nineties and for decades before, there were three ways to be stuck in Kesgrave—the sunsets and beaches that mesmerized, the boys who seduced, or the weight of your family name. The men were shrimpers, carpenters, boat captains, gardeners. Some women taught school, others cleaned the motels and hotels or were secretaries. If you were lucky your family owned a store or a service, maybe a diner. Boys to men, girls to women, tugged along like string cheese.

No one aspired to much—except my older brother Bud and his best friend Reed. You see, now I'm ready to name names. After Bud turned down a free ride to Florida State to pitch baseball and Reed refused a scholarship to the University of Florida to play linebacker, they were hell-bent on their "business plan." They were eighteen and in a hurry, bulkheading by day and helping out nights with our father's store—Humphreys, the one store you passed from any direction, wherever you were heading, at the intersection of Route 12 and Highway 7. Everyone drank back then, only boys, men and old timers got flat-out drunk. Sometimes I hope that Reed and Bud were inebriated that day, and their judgment was off.

Lucinda, Bryant, and I skipped it altogether. Lucinda was very pregnant with her third, Bryant was soon to marry Bud and watching her weight. I wanted to be a clear-eyed photographer and had to be sober. I got work however I could—confirmations, communions, christenings. I took pictures of the famed dual sunsets over the Gulf of Mexico and the Choctawhatchee Bay, selling them in tourist towns along the coast.

> Even before the drowning, the three of us shared this grief and sadness. It lay beneath like it was our legacy while we acted chipper, almost happy. And here in New York City, in the East Village where I've raised you, given you the best life I could, I've made sure you would not be a part of the thread and would not know.
>
> What we did as girls in Kesgrave was never ours. Any wins belonged to our fathers, the men. Until that happened.

Rather than file this in her safe with the others, Lucinda ought to burn the letter, burn every ugly installment. She intends to, in the infrared searing zone of her Hestan outdoor gas grill, on her terrace overlooking her mini-Versailles gardens. In the impressive Palm Beach home on the Intracoastal that she and Reed bought with their hard-earned money. After she figures out why they're being sent.

Chapter Thirty-Three

1998

LATE EVENING. Lucinda and Reed are on the deck of their new house, a house little better than the old one. Reed likes it, she finds it wanting, not exactly a step up, but by Kesgrave standards it's something. A Colonial with a wide porch, the fourth house in from the river. On Saturdays, Maribelle and Caroline follow their father along the banks, where he has fished his whole life. On Sunday afternoons, he takes them out in the Sea Nymph, the girls with their kid fishing rods, baiting the hooks with live shiners. Lucinda watches from the porch, giving Raleigh a bottle. *There's no point to this*, she tells herself over and over, *no point to this local shit. We aren't staying here.*

After the girls are asleep, she tells Reed, "We have to plan. We're stuck in this life. Nothing goes forward."

Reed stares at her. "What do you want, Lucinda? We're making money, opening a fourth location in Fort Walton Beach."

Everything about him has changed since the accident. His hair has turned from a wheat color to always looking dirty; his eyes, a slate blue, are murky; his voice isn't as strong. He remains tan and buff, hell-bent on creating Barrows. Behind the scenes, she shares her own vision for

Barrows while she substitute teaches, leaving Raleigh in the one preschool in town. When they combine her strategies with Reed's hours at the office, the mix pays off.

"We'll have more locations, I know it," Lucinda says.

"Look at what we have, we're at this house . . . with more room . . ." Reed says. "That's good news."

Lucinda shakes her head. "Not really."

"What do you want? You've got the girls, full-time teaching will pan out. Bryant's offered to help if preschool isn't good enough. Christ, she thinks Raleigh's her baby."

Lucinda sighs. "She does. She talks about how much she misses Bud, how much you must miss him."

Bryant, bereft, alone, is with them a lot. The least they can do is give her their time, their companionship.

"People hate us, hate me," Lucinda says. "How we're starting to have a real lifestyle. We have new furniture, replacement chairs. The girls have better clothes now."

"Isn't that what you want? For Barrows to make money?"

"Sure," she says. Although wherever she goes, on Main Street, in town, driving with her girls, there's the river. Anywhere, everywhere the Apalachicola is in her ears. She is never distracted from it, even if she wears headphones. She needs to be as far as possible from the incessant sweep of the water. Reed is oblivious, while for Lucinda, there must be an exit.

"Well, we're here, Reed. It's only a matter of time before it gets musty or moldy. We live in a damp, humid climate. We can do better."

"Use some fans. Open the doors, Lucinda, and nothing will be moldy. Use some vinegar, baking soda."

Doesn't he get that it's not only actual mold? It's airborne—it will suffocate them. He isn't ready to know, to put it behind, to chance bigger rivers, so to speak, unnamed travels, another place.

"Reed, don't you see? We've got to leave this backwater. We shouldn't stick around. We'll have a great life somewhere more . . . sophisticated. Fancy."

Reed whistles. The lamp on the side table reveals him as he looks tonight and in ten, twenty years. An attractive man who will grow old fast in Kesgrave. As boys to young men they're dashing, and then they're weathered and old.

"We . . . I can't stay here. Everywhere I go, every moment, it's about that day. Don't you feel it?" Lucinda asks.

"I have Barrows to build, my family to take care of, our new house, my new truck. There's not much time left for that," Reed says.

"Time? Do you believe I choose to think about it—that I'm not busy myself? I earned my degree—I can teach. The older girls are busy with friends, school, gymnastics. Any way I look at it, this is a hellhole. We've got to leave."

Reed is perplexed, frowning. "Where would you go, where would we go? Pensacola?"

Has he missed who she is, what she wants? Lucinda comes close to his chair and kneels beside him, so unlike her. She switches the lamp off, a milder, yellow light comes across the room. "I've chosen where we should go, Reed. I know what we'll do with our lives and for our girls. We are equal partners on these first four stores. We'll build it into a brand . . . I've been reading about businesses that grow, family-owned, from little to big."

The house is slowed down with their daughters asleep, not twirling about. Reed is listening, there is a chance that she is making an impression. Then he leans over, pulls her up and they're both standing. Like he wants to dance with her, his arms around her waist. She is persuasive. She once loved him very much; at least, she had to have him—she couldn't breathe if it didn't happen.

"Reed, I have a fine plan all figured out. We'll both work there, make Barrows into a large chain, a real family company. We'll keep our name for it and put Kesgrave behind us."

"I'm okay, okay as we are. This is our home."

Has he no spine? She isn't ready to point it out. The furthest she can take it tonight is to say this: *If we stay, you'll be a big man in a fishbowl. They'll watch your success. It isn't wise.* Lucinda will be cautious, patient. She is not quite up to the scene where she explains she's taking the girls, going with or without him, though she knows the day is near.

Chapter Thirty-Four

2026

In Lucinda's serene dressing room, Caroline's daughter Harper stares in the three-way rectangular mirror framed with exotic seashells, primping. "I need to have my hair blown out."

Her hair looks flawless to Raleigh in that preteen, luxurious way, except what does she know.

"For Jack's big birthday party tonight. I'm going with Layla and Steffi."

"Jack?"

"He's in our class."

"Harper, you do not need a blowout for your friends," Raleigh says. "Your hair is pretty without doing a thing. You have years to fuss with it."

"Lucinda says I should. I'm going with her to the new salon, Chez Dennis, at four o'clock," Harper says. "She wanted me and my friends to go before the Tate McRae concert too."

"Okay, sure," Raleigh says. "First, don't you have homework to finish before the weekend? If not, we could take a walk along the water."

Harper shakes her head. "Why is Lucinda much cooler than you and Aunt Maribelle and my mother?"

An intense light shines directly over Harper, a seventh grader already taller than her mother. One who prefers to go to bed later than her parents, and does her homework in no time flat in order to have fun afterward. She's the most perfect twelve-year-old Raleigh has ever seen. Her hair, almost to her waist, shimmers in honey shades. She has those high cheekbones that Lucinda obsesses over in old family photos when apparently everyone had them. Lucinda as a young mother, her three daughters, all endowed with that enviable look. Next, the eyes—wide set, green. Today Harper's expressions alternate between placid and hysterical, depending on the topic. Every tank top she wears fits as if custom made. Her dancer's body—how swiftly she moves into and out of the room and situation. *Just wait,* Raleigh thinks as she searches through Lucinda's various lengths of false eyelashes. *No one looks this good forever.* Few escape what follows: a boy crush that bottoms out, a friend who ditches you, family feuds, a mother who has trespassed.

As distracted as Raleigh is—she keeps checking her phone; Porter is meant to text a plan for them to meet—she's happy to be with her niece. Harper, on the cusp of being a teenager, exudes such energy and optimism. Before she moves into a preoccupation with beauty, belonging, followed by the boy/man prize. Raleigh envies Harper's last days on this side of naivete. What wisdom would she dare impart if Harper would hear her? Inevitably she's destined to endure every passage, regardless of the steps Caroline takes to protect her. Caroline is busy, fending for her daughters, for everyone. When the two of them were at a preview tasting for Lucinda's luncheon yesterday, her sister paid no attention to the food, let alone the table décor.

"Lucinda says it's important. My friends and her friends are at the salon. The first time we ran into Mrs. Trask—you know, the old lady everyone likes. The one who reads a lot of books." Harper struts around in her tank top and leggings, more dancer from New York or Boston than a Palm Beach girl reaching for the best times.

Raleigh gets a text from Alex: *A glitch in schedule on Friday.* Raleigh frantically texts back. *Please don't do this.* She pauses, considers it needy, deletes. Harper is also on her phone, her fingers flying across the compact keyboard like she's a pianist practicing her scales. When she lobbied for her own cell phone last year, confronting much hesitancy from her parents, it was Raleigh who was her staunchest supporter.

"Lucinda is almost here. She's in a hurry," Harper says.

"As always." Raleigh gathers her things. "I'm heading back to the studio to finish the Latiff mother-daughter portrait." Her phone dings again. For a millisecond she's lighter, believing it is Porter. Instead it's Alex again: *How about Thursday?*

Lucinda comes in, looks around. She has a stain on her short-sleeve teal cashmere sweater, and her cropped khaki pants look rumpled. Those camel-colored kitten heels, her favorite style, click across the planked wood floor. Total Lucinda, except her face is drained, and she's got lines on her forehead like someone raked a fork across it. Her energy is frantic and somehow dismal.

"Where's Rosie?" she asks.

"She's at Publix getting avocados. She isn't doing an Instacart delivery—they send them overripe," Raleigh says.

Harper points to the Biedermeier side table and waves a manila envelope. "She gave me this to give to you."

Lucinda's eyes dart from the makeup table to her walk-in closet, messy spaces thanks to Harper. "I'm sorry?"

Harper shrugs, gives it to Lucinda, and slides her book bag over her shoulders.

Lucinda tries a smile. "Let's go."

"What is it? Why are you carrying that like it's heavy?" Harper asks.

"Nothing, it's nothing." Lucinda tips her chin. "We can't be late." She stumbles over the area rug as her cell rings. She pulls it out of her bag, swipes right, redials. "Damn it. Estelle is trying to reach me."

She puts the envelope down. "Really?" She seems clouded over. Her voice sounds as if she hasn't had a sip of water or an Arnold Palmer in days. "Sure, postpone it 'til then."

"Mom . . . Lucinda, are you okay?" Raleigh asks.

Lucinda pulls herself into proper posture. "Do not ask me that ever again."

Harper tosses her gorgeous hair. "Grammy, I mean Lucinda, we'll be late." She leads them out the door.

Today Lucinda is driving her Porsche Cayenne SUV, parked smack in the middle of the paved circular drive. As if she's abandoned her vehicle there. Raleigh hears her mother rev the engine, much as she always does. She might rush out and volunteer to drive, not exactly thwarting their intentions but definitely questioning her mother's abilities. Lucinda would lose it completely, Harper would be inconvenienced in that preteen huff, Raleigh would be blamed for her precaution. It's only two miles down the road, she rationalizes, at thirty-five miles per hour to their blowouts.

After they are off, Raleigh lifts the envelope with her mother's name. There is no return address. People have broken into someone's mail before, although she isn't one of them. If she moves quickly to steam it open, the kitchen will be empty. Neither Rosie nor Daisy will be there.

A text comes in from Porter—what she has been hoping for. *In thirty? Meet in front of Bricktops for an adventure.*

Chapter Thirty-Five

2026

HAVING NEVER been in a car when he's driving, Raleigh finds Porter's style hypnotic. An extension of who he is. Smooth. Robust not bulky. Graceful, not weak. His face that she can and cannot forget since he floats through her mind constantly. If he were in line with the men she'd fallen for, he'd be leading. In fact, the line would stop with him. She likes the tight, neat turn he makes from Chilean onto the A1A heading south.

"I missed you." He steers with great purpose. His sunglasses cover his eyes.

Did he say that? After doubting her, her triangle with Caleb and Alex during their last shared conversation?

In the ten days since she saw him, things with her family have gotten worse, with no information or evidence, no hard facts of any kind to show for it. There's no reason Porter should know. Caroline would be enraged if anyone heard about it. Not that Porter exists in Caroline's orbit, yet she has to respect her sister's methods. Alone with Porter, confined to a car, in space and time belonging only to them, is enthralling. She imagines they are wrapped in diaphanous ribbon.

She'd like to say, "I missed you too." Or "Back at you." Something. Instead, she asks where they're going.

"Delray Beach. The Seagate."

Raleigh has a sudden pang of worry. Have Lucinda and Harper left the salon and arrived home safely? Is Caleb eating Pop-Tarts?

"Hey," Porter says. "You okay?"

She nods. They'll find her if they need to, won't they? She leans back in the Chevrolet Trax he's rented, a car William and Travis would disdain. Even Alex would make a snide comment, she suspects.

He's chosen the music, singing along like he knows it. Luba, "The Best Is Yet to Come."

"I remember this song," Raleigh says.

"It's old. My mother used to play it," Porter says.

Hers too, Lucinda's favorite. She would mouth the lyrics, dancing with Raleigh when she was small, in the living room, in Kesgrave. The river, that overwhelming melancholia her mother owned.

Porter pulls up, in line for valet. "Hey, Raleigh, it's alright." He starts kissing her, something he wouldn't do in public in Palm Beach.

She's pretending they're not down the road twenty miles; they've traveled together to the South of France, Capri, or Biarritz because they share a life.

FROM THEIR third-floor balcony, Raleigh watches the ocean. The beaches are wide, beachier here. He is behind her, leads her back to their bed. King size, pristine, white bedding. She wants it never to end. They're propped up, taking a break. He holds up his phone.

"These pictures are of my latest projects. Scroll down. I'm into sustainable green architecture. Minimalism."

"These are beautiful, Porter. So inviting." She keeps scrolling. "Why visit Palm Beach? I mean it's the opposite of anything minimalist or modern."

He pauses, takes the phone, searches for more photos, returns it. "I don't know. I wanted to see the place, the grandness, the Mizner homes."

She scrolls through again. "Everything in these pictures is clean, fresh." She imagines he's offended by ordinary designs. "How did Kesgrave come about? Not much about architecture."

He laughs. "I'll say."

"I can't believe we met there. What a fluke."

"I'll say. I'd always wanted to see the Florida Panhandle." He pulls her closer. She waits for a comment; she could write the copy: *Then I met you there*, or *we would have met anyway*, some such thing.

"Show me your work, Raleigh."

She stands up, wearing his T-shirt, and lifts her phone from the desk. Scrolls down and opens pictures of her three newest portraits. "These are in progress, to be completed."

He's examining them, taking much more time with her work than she did with his. "A far reach from the painted shells I first saw. You're very talented. Where does it come from?"

"No one in our family. My mother encouraged me, though. She bought me the sketchbooks, pencils, and watercolors. Later oils. I took lessons, art school."

"That makes sense."

There's an odd rise and fall to their conversation. Partly prosaic, partly loaded. A mystery, what isn't spoken. What does she know about him? That's what she always realizes. Does it matter? She had married a perfect stranger, later, she had an affair with a perfect stranger. Both men she supposedly knew well.

"How about you?" she asks.

"I always wanted to be an architect."

"Did your mother help?"

He looks at her as if he wants to add a thought then stops himself. "She did."

He starts the kissing again as if there is no need for anything more. Except there is. Already Raleigh anticipates the end of the afternoon, the separating of their bodies. Anything could come between them; there's empty space, many days exist without him.

RETURNING TO CAROLINE'S after Delray Beach with Porter feels stealthy. Violet and Nicole, like Harper, are out, Caroline and Travis are in the sunroom having a knock-down, drag-out conversation. She doesn't want to see them or to be seen. She needs to sneak upstairs and sustain the reverie of her afternoon. Their voices, Travis' louder than her sister's, boomerang across the honed marble floors of their quintessential Palm Beach home. The house becomes stagnant.

"Your damn mother, that's who," Travis says. "A woman obsessed with her reputation. She's a ruthless mother."

Raleigh stops behind the doorway, to the left. They don't see her.

"Excuse me, my mother? That's who you're blaming?" Caroline looks disappointed. She and Travis are dismal; their lounge wardrobes need sprucing up, even by Raleigh's yardstick. Travis' extremely drab T-shirt reads "Girl Dad," a Father's Day gift, undoubtedly. Caroline is wearing frayed, baggy sweats and a ratty white T-shirt. She's like a librarian who just got home from work.

"Yeah, Lucinda. The one and only," Travis says. "Don't all of us want the same thing? Well, except Lucinda, who wants money *and* respect—that Palm Beach lady shit. Are you going to defend her or admit she's been fuckin' strange lately? It's bizarre. She shows up at a meeting uninvited last week at Barrows and starts bossing Estelle around in front of four vendors. Nasty. The fourth vendor—new this year—was annoyed and pulled out. Since when does Lucinda work with vendors? She's a real spoiler, I'll tell you that."

"Please don't talk trash about Lucinda," Caroline says. She's pacing, moving faster in front of the potted plants in their lemony ceramic planters.

"I'm sorry, let me put it in a more polite, more Palm Beach tone. Your mother has no boundaries, she's intrusive, odd. With no other bag of tricks."

Caroline is definitely caught off guard. From where Raleigh stands, she has that detached, long-suffering wife look.

"What are you talking about? Is my mother holding you up in some way?"

"Well, she's a problem. She's come to the office for the last few weeks to go through files. She's frantic. Caro, is there something I should know? Do we have another Samuel problem?"

"I have no information. I swear, I haven't any idea."

How loyal Caroline is. She hasn't confided anything to Travis; he's simply onto Lucinda's strangeness. Raleigh notices how neither Travis nor Caroline has decent posture. They're worn down by the conversation, by the big gaps between what is and isn't said, the suspicions and defenses.

"Money makes men into monsters. That's what Lucinda says."

He glares at her. "You're making this about me?"

Another surge of loyalty washes over Raleigh. She suppresses a cough that would blow her cover and moves back from the door.

"Your mother acts like money is green except for Barrows money. Barrows money is soaked in gold. She acts like whoever she is counts more than anything else. She's tearing apart files for something."

Outside, the rattan furniture blows about the terrace. A nor'easter is forecasted on Raleigh's phone. Three days of rain, winds off the ocean.

"I can't do this, Travis. I can't wrap my thoughts around what you're saying. We should stop. Raleigh's due home. Violet and Nicole too."

"Do you know about Kesgrave? Do any of you know?"

Her sister stiffens, almost brittle. "What about Kesgrave?" She doesn't mention that she sent Raleigh there or what was learned, although it wasn't much. Except for a universal hatred of Lucinda, which seems to be an open secret.

Travis looks at Caroline with disdain, maybe pity. "You don't, do you?"

Hearing Travis say this, Raleigh considers bad husbands, the kind on Netflix or in novels she won't read after 10 p.m. They're frightening. The type she is divorcing. Worse than that, after eavesdropping, she suspects Travis is the one sending the letters to Lucinda.

PART THREE

And then there will be chances
Stretching before you like a
path away from home.

Chapter Thirty-Six

2026

Each morning Lucinda believes she is flying overhead, directly above her old self—the disciplined, in control, confident version. As the hours progress, she loses more of who she was. Today, like every daybreak, she is in her mini-Versailles gardens with her yoga mat. Lately it has become an ideal escape, a place where there is no tension, no expectation. In the last week she has begged off cards and golf, canceled a lunch with Jolie, and hasn't so much as met Bryant for a quick salad at Pizza Al Fresco. She ought to be happier. Her three daughters are together, if not exactly thrilled about it; Barrows continues to thrive; sixty is the new forty. Except as she sees Rosie trudging toward her, scowling, Lucinda's anxiety rises. Before Rosie says a word, she is filled with dread that another envelope has arrived.

"Raleigh and Caroline are here. They've gone upstairs to find Maribelle, Mrs. Barrows."

Lucinda is on her yoga mat. "Why? It isn't even sunrise yet. No one texted first."

Why is everyone coming to her home, once a safe haven—currently so utterly unsafe?

"I'm not sure." Rosie is agitated. Her shoulders won't lie flat.

Lucinda drops her Warrior II position. "I'll go check."

Her daughters' voices are rising when Lucinda climbs the staircase. She opens the door to the sitting room where they huddle in the center. Beyond the classic Palm Beach eye candy—wicker chairs, tropical prints in rich shades of green, Lilly Pulitzer throw pillows in hot pink on an off-white couch—is a standoff.

Caroline, dressed for one of her understated days in a medium-blue sheath and wedges, is taking deep breaths. She tugs on her string of pearls. Maribelle and Raleigh in joggers and hoodies, hold their coffee tumblers. All three are similar, the same height, narrow frame, the pitch of their bodies. Barring that, they are almost screaming at one another, Caroline is loudest. This Lucinda has not witnessed. They know the rule; no one raises their voices to one another. That this is happening sharpens Lucinda's instincts, sobers her up from her recent Xanax stupor.

"Hello, girls, did we have a breakfast date?"

"No, nothing on the calendar," Caroline says.

Lucinda should normalize the scene, ask everyone to sit down. Stupefied, frozen, she stays on the perimeter of the braided area rug, her Hokas touching the edge. Her daughters' eyes are iridescent, snappy. Their common cause is brewing. Lucinda's eyes are oddly vacant.

"We wanted to see you—together—for clarity," Maribelle says. "We're talking about Raleigh's recent trip to Kesgrave. I heard about it once she got back."

"Kesgrave." Lucinda tsks. "Ask Caroline about that. She arranged the visit."

Raleigh steps away from her sisters in order to deliver her lines. "Oh, Mom, we're not going to rehash the trip. We only want some facts, some details."

Raleigh, her youngest and most dreamy child, demanding information. Raleigh, the one who skipped the drama by being born afterward, while her older daughters absorbed the loss.

Lucinda shakes her head. "I don't know what you're referencing, Raleigh."

"Are you going to let us in on your secret, a story of yours—offer a clue?" Caroline asks.

"Caroline, stop." Maribelle calmly places her hand on Caroline's upper arm. Obviously she's the least emotional. "We're asking so we can help. We're on your side."

Lucinda is disappointed and surprised by her daughters' ambush. She'll need to be camera ready by eleven for the Rally Around Books Brunch at the Palm Beach Literary Society. Their presence, their mission, is meant to be reassuring. As if the reason for her recent fog—missing out on the dress code, being unfocused on occasion—is easily remedied. Unless they are like Bryant, who, in her mousiest voice, questions how Lucinda will manage her birthday festivities. Her girls seem in search of a confessional, an explanation. They'll get nowhere with that. What's apparent to Lucinda, since she's not yet succumbed to an extra Xanax this morning, is that if she tanks, every member of the family goes with her. Which means at the moment, her girls are trying to be in charge, and this is not appreciated. Rather it's beyond annoying. Nothing like this has ever happened before.

Caroline comes near Lucinda, posing for a supportive hug.

Lucinda steps back. "You should go this minute, girls. Before it gets late. "

"Why don't you tell us what you did, Mom? What happened in Kesgrave. Otherwise, I can ask Aunt Bryant or William," Caroline says.

"Mom! Caroline! Please." Raleigh has begun to cry.

Lucinda is silent. Suddenly she's lonely in her own home with her daughters. "I don't understand what you're talking about, Caroline."

"You must have done something," Maribelle says.

Lucinda is at the doorway. "Don't be so sure, Maribelle."

"I don't . . . we don't believe you," Caroline says. "Because the stakes are raised and you have no defense. We want to help."

Their distress over her is distasteful; it smacks of being a loser, a failure.

"I want the three of you to get on with your day," Lucinda says. "Our time this morning didn't happen. We were never in this room, having this conversation."

ONCE THE GIRLS DECAMP, their best intentions and suspicions gnaw at Lucinda. She dresses carefully, she is chic only because she had already selected what to wear. When it comes to makeup, her hopelessness isn't fixable despite that she's facile at covering blotches, lines around her eyes. No mascara or eye shadow will costume her sorrow.

At the bottom of the staircase is Estelle. Rosie has opened the front door. Estelle notices Lucinda and steps backward.

"Lucinda, I thought you had gone already. William asked me to come by . . ."

She's holding a gift bag from Seaman Schepps. From William, undoubtedly the Classic Link Necklace in Multi

Stone. Along the way, Lucinda coveted it. In Estelle's other hand she's holding a manila envelope.

"Strict instructions from William to bring this box to Rosie. You weren't supposed to be here. This was at reception when I was heading out. I'm sorry, I should have called first."

"Well," Lucinda says. "I do live here."

Rosie places them on the console table. "No worries. All good."

The moment Estelle leaves, Rosie walks toward the laundry room. Lucinda watches her, making sure she doesn't twist back to mention any household quasi-concerns. The Yukon potatoes are small, William's favorite blazer wasn't included in the dry cleaner's delivery. Once the coast is clear, she lifts the envelope and goes into the garage.

As soon as she gets into her car, she opens it.

THEIR SUCCESS

2021

In the early 2000s, I began to read about the Barrows. The family was underwriting charity events, donating huge amounts of money to certain causes. Lucinda and Reed and their girls were showcased in a Town and Country spread about the family. They mentioned being from northwest Florida, there was no reference to Kesgrave, the Panhandle, no reference to how far they'd climbed. The focus was on what an impressive Palm Beach family they were, how crisp, clean, and innovative were the stores, how exponentially the business had grown. I thought of my brother, who long ago had invited Reed to be his partner when our grandfather died and left him his stores in Kesgrave and his savings. Bud was the one who had imagined irresistible chain stores, magical 7-Elevens. Lucinda encouraged Reed to join in. She had been scheming her exit from Kesgrave since Maribelle and Caroline were toddlers. What is it they say about success—those who were indigent crave it until it is achieved, while those who inherit it throw it away? When I left Kesgrave, Lucinda Barrows couldn't afford an umbrella, and by 2010 she was wearing Hermès.

I was sickened. The company that was meant to be Humphreys (Bud) & Barrows (Reed) was everywhere. Instead Bud had been gone for years while Barrows stores flourished across the south, stores that had sprung from the cash our grandfather left to my brother. Lucinda and Reed were in society columns, photographed at charity events and fundraisers, including ones that tried to hire me for celebrity pictures. In Palm Beach, where they lived, they had become part of the inner sanctum. In each pose, they stared convincingly into nothingness.

By 2012, Lucinda's older daughters and their younger sister, the one I never met—the night I left, Lucinda was soon to deliver her—had become part of the charity circuit. Such pretty young women, seemingly tied to Lucinda's agenda, Palm Beach, a moneyed, rarified life. I looked up their addresses, I checked their homes on Zillow. I researched more—about their charitable donations, looking into what I could find about the company.

I remembered again the smell of the river. We had been best friends in a miserable Brigadoon. That we'd gotten out was fine, how rich the Barrows were—that was another matter. Once Reed died, I decided you had to know. He was less of a snake, not like Lucinda, with her fabricated fame. There was Bryant, my brother's fiancé the day of the drowning. I located her address in Manalapan. You would need to seek her out, too.

Chapter Thirty-Seven

2006

THE HOUSE in the estate section has views of both the ocean and the Intracoastal. An exceptional home that Lucinda has chosen for her family—to be admired, envied. She loves the island of Palm Beach; it is the right place to be. Yet after three years of relentless effort, she has made no progress socially. From the outside in, all is well. Raleigh, so beautiful she turns heads, is in junior high at the Academy. Lucinda's wardrobe is designer, including her bags, shoes, and jewelry. Maribelle and Caroline, beautiful as well, are ready to infiltrate the Barrows' new life after finishing college. There is no talk of Kesgrave—as if it never happened. As if they've been beamed, Star Trek-style, to paradise.

"We live in Palm Beach now," Lucinda says at Sunday brunch one morning when they are assembled. She and Reed sit like royals at either end of their long sleek dining table. The weather is brisker than usual and she's decided they'll be indoors. Daisy is serving Eggs Florentine and cut pineapple on Wedgewood dishes—Lucinda's latest acquisition. The vine-pattern linen placemats and napkins are Frette, the cutlery from Tiffany. Still Lucinda is displeased. She is excluded from Palm Beach circles. "People are watching, waiting for us to fail. The stakes are high here. We need to win, to do better than anyone else. You have been taught manners, taught how to think for this very day. I'll need each of you to infiltrate."

"Are we rallying the troops?" Reed asks. He might be bemused, Lucinda is not.

"We are happy, aren't we?" Bryant asks. Always the Pollyanna in the story, no matter the tale.

"Happy," Lucinda repeats. "Happy. Well, we could be happier. We could have more friends and be invited to parties, galas."

Although Raleigh appears bored, she is listening. Maribelle and Caroline sit poised, ready for their mother's instructions for the next steps.

If only her daughters would appreciate Lucinda—for her looks, her style and savvy, her lavish life. Yet if they did, she is aware they're not enough to sustain her anyway—worse, depending on family feels lackluster. She hasn't come this far, coached Reed in building Barrows, to be neglected.

Because it is Sunday, Lucinda opens *The Daily Sheet* at the table and recites the recap of charity events and private parties in an eighteen-mile radius. As she references what they've been left out of, she calculates what is worth pursuing and what is not. Nothing far west, north, or south, she believes. Only organizations where she knows of the women at the top, causes that are popular and well received.

"Why not write checks for these charities?" Reed asks. "Why not volunteer your time and hand out your money?"

Lucinda narrows her eyes. "My time?"

She makes a valid point; she's at Barrows, unofficially and instrumentally, two or more days a week. She has a grid system on expansion of the company, telling Reed what is beneficial and what is not. Her work at Barrows in Palm Beach is more complicated than back in Kesgrave. There, she kept it quiet while she taught school and raised her daughters. Here, she is an anomaly—she goes to work, she has an office. Few women in the crowd she aspires to are working. They play cards, tennis, golf.

"I'll tell you what, Lucinda," Reed says. "We'll write checks for some local charities, give them a million each—ones that you choose. The caveat is that you'll be put on the board. That will be our starting point, and from there, doors will open to clubs, parties, chances for you to chair galas."

Lucinda smiles her victory smile. She rattles the social pages of *The Daily Sheet*, closes it up. "Girls, what charities sound important to you?"

Reed winks. Lucinda will get what she wants. *Money is everything* has been her mantra for a very long time.

A MOTHER-DAUGHTER theme in Palm Beach carries great weight. Lucinda sees the Academy mothers with their daughters on the Avenue after school, shopping in the vias, spirited, bordering on jolly. Raleigh, her only daughter young enough to be useful, isn't interested. She longs for adventure; she is crunchy, worried about the planet. Her stint as a teenager is more challenging than Maribelle's or Caroline's ever was. There is no conversation, discipline, or object lesson that sinks in with this daughter. Raleigh cries at night for Kesgrave. She misses her friends there, the river.

After everyone has left the table, Lucinda corners Raleigh, who is reading Aldous Huxley by the pool and sits at the edge of her daughter's lounge chair.

"I hope that you are happy here, Raleigh."

"I am not, Mom."

Lucinda spreads her arms open. "Tell me, what is lacking?"

Raleigh looks around as if she isn't seeing what Lucinda sees. "A lot that I care about."

For the progress Lucinda has achieved, it cannot be that her daughter isn't on her side, ready to make the leap for her. Daughters are commodities; women showcase the winners and downplay those who aren't. Reed has just agreed to pay for their entry ticket, and Raleigh must do her part. Lucinda takes off her Ray-Bans and looks into Raleigh's eyes.

"I swear we will be a team for this, Raleigh. We can work together to make our mark."

Raleigh pauses. A single, orange-breasted bird is flying low, skimming the pool. "Okay. Okay, Mom."

Lucinda would hug her if only it were her nature. Instead, she leans toward Raleigh. "One day, when you need a favor, I promise I'll be on your side."

Chapter Thirty-Eight

2026

Raleigh and Aunt Bryant tool around the West Palm Beach GreenMarket, flitting from stall to stall. Midmorning on a Saturday, the bikers are out. Runners and walkers are finishing up. A cloudy day for this time of year; humidity hovers but hasn't yet risen. As if the air could ever turn crisp in south Florida, a new climate rising out of the old. The color of the water, reflected by the sun, is a soupy gray-blue. Raleigh has jet lag without having traveled. The young women in biking shorts or cropped leggings and sleeveless crisscrossed tops remind her that even the youngest get older.

Aunt Bryant has a wad of cash in a Parker Thatch sling around her waist. She's in a good look, Vuori black wide-leg workout pants and T-shirt, trending and non-Palm Beach for Aunt Bryant. Every vendor nods and smiles at her, noting her empty recyclable bag, soon to be filled with purchases. Apparently she's a regular who loves to shop. The crowd is assorted, different languages are spoken. Aunt Bryant tugs on her straw hat, then pats sunscreen from a small tube on her face and hands. She leads Raleigh to the north side of the marketplace and on to a jewelry stall.

"First let's look at the beach shifts and jewelry. After I'll need to get fresh vegetables for dinner tomorrow night.

Single ladies only. Taylor Trask, Dionne Mettes, and Grace Kates are coming over, and we're grilling." Aunt Bryant holds up a bangle, slides it on her wrist. "Why does someone need real? Incredible, no?" She places it back on the narrow table that shows other equally appealing bracelets along with two rows of earrings and pendants. She holds up a pair of earrings, glistening pale blue stones. "What do you say, Raleigh? They look like aquamarine." Aunt Bryant smiles at a young woman at the stall. "I'll take this pair, thank you, that's all. Unless you would like something, Raleigh."

Raleigh shakes her head. She tries to imagine Lucinda shopping here. "Has my mother ever joined you at the market?"

"Yes, once I brought her. She told me there was no way she was squeezing melons or avocados, and she had enough fashion jewelry. She said as a reward for her hard work, she only wanted to own the real thing."

"That sounds about right," Raleigh says.

At almost noon they head to the other side together. Beyond the market is a view from the west side of the Intracoastal along Flagler, the marina to their right, filled with superyachts. Across is the island, what used to be the only place to live if one aspired to a moneyed life. But no longer, now the idea includes West Palm, facing east.

Although Raleigh wants to tell Aunt Bryant about Porter, her aunt should go first on any announcements. "What is your news, Aunt Bryant? Wasn't there something you wanted to tell me?" She sounds stilted, she's doing a Caroline imitation at a Barrows Christmas party in Central Florida, that arm's length way of being.

"This part of the Intracoastal, near these docks, makes me remember. It never goes away," Aunt Bryant says.

"I know," Raleigh says.

"About Bud, always. How he died on the Apalachicola, back in Kesgrave."

"I'm sorry," Raleigh says. She always says it when the topic comes up and her aunt seems to mourn again. Complicated grief, isn't that what it is? When a person suffers such loss, she is stuck—unable to get on with it and forge another life, a second chance. Unable to be soothed, the longing that great.

Aunt Bryant takes off her hat. "What I wanted to say, my news is, that I've bought a place, here in West Palm Beach, along this strip."

"Really? For an investment? You'll lease it out?" Raleigh asks. She tries to fathom her aunt separate from her home in Manalapan, with the dock and the pool and the ducks who walk her property.

"No, no, I've put my house on the market. I'm moving to West Palm, to the Bristol. The building has such services, the accoutrements . . ."

"Aunt Bryant, you like having a house. You swim every day in your pool, walk along the path with your neighbors. Those kind ladies."

"I'll have other neighbors," she says. "I'm sure your mother will consider me a defector. I'm not. I'm being modern—I'm moving on."

"Moving on?"

"Exactly."

"Did you tell my mother?"

"I am telling you first, Raleigh."

"Well, it will be a blow to her. The two of you are attached, a support system. She's going to be very displeased, I think."

"I realize that," Aunt Bryant says. "I've made up my mind, though. I'm ready. This apartment is what I want. I'm starting fresh by crossing the bridge. I won't be very far away." Her aunt looks different. She is young/old. She's been let loose.

"Why did you decide now?" Raleigh asks.

"Maybe it has to do with Ruth-Ann."

"Ruth-Ann? What does that have to do with moving from the island to West Palm?"

"Well, I learned that Ruth-Ann died. I never got to see her again, never looked her up, googled her, found her somehow. To me, Palm Beach is a continuation of Kesgrave. I'm always hanging onto the Barrows family, always the old maid auntie. Not if I live in the Bristol. I've *chosen* this. Your father . . . your parents . . . bought me the house I live in. Your mother has called the shots for years. This is my choice—the Bristol, West Palm."

There goes another family member, so to speak, behaving out of character. They begin walking at a clip. Aunt Bryant's decision is a standalone. Raleigh will wait to confide about Porter, that she's fallen for someone, a lone traveler who's come to town.

Chapter Thirty-Nine

2026

"WHY ARE YOU EARLY?" Lucinda asks. "Aren't we going to be sitting together for say three hours tonight? That litany of speakers every year at the Arts and Media Ball is exhausting."

"True." Bryant is at the three-way mirror in Lucinda's walk-in closet. Lucinda is smoothing the front of her dress. Honey color with pale flowers, rather out of character, although she's pleased. Lately, with the snubbing that Caroline assures her is not the case, a brand-new dress feels rewarding. She hasn't popped a Xanax—she's that sanguine about tonight. Her T-straps are high, and she ought to switch, except for the effect. "I like those earrings."

"I bought them yesterday with Raleigh at the GreenMarket in West Palm."

Lucinda squints to see. "Did you? Are they real?"

"They are. Blue topaz."

"Ah, well, no one will guess." Lucinda sniffs. "They'll assume they're aquamarines."

Bryant moves to the settee and casts the throw pillows to the side, crosses her legs.

"Don't you want some hair spray, a brighter jacket, a scarf, since you're here?" Lucinda asks. She might push harder; the Barrows family needs to be extremely tasteful tonight, and Lucinda cannot have any flaws. Only yesterday she believes she was slightly ignored at Longgreens after playing women's doubles. Unless she was imagining everyone racing out and on to their next thing. "You can borrow a few tennis bracelets, those with diamonds, not the diamonds and emeralds. I haven't been wearing them this season, no one will suspect. "

"I'm fine, Lucinda. I'm happy with my dress, my jewelry."

"Are you, Bryant?" The two of them could shop the closet right now, improve Bryant's entire effect.

"I said I'm fine." Bryant's voice is dry, her tone unfriendly. "I've come to tell you what happened yesterday."

"Is everything okay? Does this have to do with my children, grandchildren?" Bryant's visit is annoyingly loaded, adding to how drained Lucinda has been for weeks.

"Yesterday I parked far from the GreenMarket. Raleigh offered to walk back with me—a bit off the beaten path, near Flagler, and I said no need. I was alone, trying to find the car, and this young man showed up."

Lucinda looks at her phone; they have ten minutes before they get in the car with William to not miss the cocktail hour. "And?"

"The crowd was behind us, so it was kind of isolated. He wasn't someone we are familiar with, no one's son or stepson. He was vivid, reminding me of a male lead sauntering across a stage. I thought I'd seen him around with a young group. Then I realized he was the man who was at The Marlybone Club and caused a stir at the start of the season. People whispered about him, what it meant to have a newcomer who gets attention. *The architect*, women were whispering."

"I don't remember."

"Well, he was walking toward me, waving. Close up, he couldn't have been more than late twenties, maybe."

Lucinda smacks her lips together to seal her lipstick, powders her face with that translucent green powder that Caroline swears diminishes rosacea. "Did you search for help? Honestly Bryant, what is the point?"

"He knew who I was. He'd come to talk to me. He had this very sure smile and held out his hand, gallant and awkward. He said he's the architect who's come to learn about local buildings. Do you know about this?"

"I do not. Should I?"

"Up close, not in a crowded club, I saw it right away. How he reminded me of what we liked when we were young. Broad shoulders, tall, sort of streaked blond-brown hair. We would have called him 'larger than life.'"

"Ew, where are you going with this? It doesn't sound like you." Lucinda lifts her Judith Leiber vintage clutch from the side table. She and Bryant both look well in the gold diffused lighting. She wishes she could transport it to every evening event in town.

"How I'm describing him, does that ring a bell?"

"I've no idea, Bryant."

"Are you sure? He reminded me of someone from a long time ago. When I told him, he said, 'Do I?' with this polished smile."

"Okay . . ." Lucinda sighs. They should not be late.

"That's when I told him what you don't even know. That I believe in spirits . . ."

Lucinda is only half listening; Bryant needs to move it along. "Spirits? I never heard that."

There's this wild, exuberant look about Bryant. "I totally do. Spirits—like Bud, like Reed."

"What are you talking about?" Lucinda asks.

"After we crossed Flagler and looked out at the yachts, it was his voice. At first I thought it was absurd. I hadn't heard anything like it in so many years. I felt this repose." She's euphoric, smiling broadly. Bryant is acting weird, it unsettles Lucinda. Apprehension runs through her, worse than when she gets the goddamn letters. What she hasn't felt in years, in decades. Since Kesgrave.

"He reminded me of Bud, Lucinda. He could have been our son. I might have had a boy like this. He could have been mine."

More dread, as if Lucinda is about to have a CT scan with contrasts, and the dye that feels like a hot liquid has been shot into her veins. She's squeamish, she has to sound neutral. "I'm not sure what you're talking about."

Bryant is swinging her arms, storming the closet. "No? Are you sure? I know what you did, Lucinda. How dare you. *How dare you.*"

Suddenly Lucinda is stricken, she's ice cold. William must have lowered the AC in the last seconds. She must be calm. Hopefully she's packed her Xanax for an emergency, of course she has.

Bryant's eyes are blazing. She's been transformed. A woman wandering through time who holds her head up high. "We're the only two in this room, Lucinda. Why don't you tell me the truth? You owe me that."

A knock on the bedroom door. A rat-a-tat loud enough they hear it despite the confines of the closet that borders on a decorated prison.

"Lucinda? Bryant? What are you ladies doing up there?" William calls out. "Let's get in the car. We have to be on the road."

When Lucinda passes Bryant in the hallway, she whispers, "You'd best be careful what you say and to whom you say it."

Bryant catches up, brushes against her shoulder and thigh. "I think not. I'll say what I want. I'll be civil to you in public. I'll play your sidekick until your birthday parties are over. Just remember, we aren't finished. Not by any means."

Chapter Forty

2026

FOR A MOMENT when the front doorbell rings, Lucinda hopes it's Maribelle and she's simply forgotten her key. Earlier she texted she was off for a doubles game at the Harbor Club followed by shopping at the Royal Poinciana Plaza. William is at golf, naturally, while Raleigh is at Pilates or hot yoga with Caroline. Jolie is at lunch at Longgreens with her Saturday mah-jongg game, ordering a chopped salad with grilled chicken breast, vinaigrette on the side. Lucinda, overwrought from Bryant last evening, hardly slept and begged off. That Bryant is no longer her ally is staggering. Their closeness, somewhere between sisters and best friends, is in ruins after a lifetime together.

She sits on the terrace of her main bedroom, a space so large it covers the entire library below. She watches the Intracoastal as if she's a tourist who has never seen the boats. The house feels notably quiet. Could it be that both Daisy and Rosie are out mid-afternoon doing Saturday errands? She ought to say something, hint that they're taking advantage, especially since packages are being delivered for her birthday festivities to come, and someone must be home to log them in. Three group gifts—a cashmere scarf from Hermès, a small Dior bow bag, a Foundrae extension necklace. Single gifts—a massage at the Eau, a facial at the Breakers

Spa, a Miu Miu card holder. *Noblesse oblige*, Reed would say about the ultra-rich, out to impress each other. Lucinda appreciates it; she has succeeded by working ceaselessly for this life. These gifts, proof that her unrelenting efforts and positioning have paid off, might assuage her fears. Yet ever since the letters began, she ceases to feel certain. Her chronic anxiety is worsening. Maybe she has impostor syndrome; she's read about it.

Some days are better than others. High season in Palm Beach, back-to-back fundraisers are an interruption. In two hours, Gigi will be coming to the house to do hair and makeup. For Lucinda to be camera ready for the Mothers and Children Gala. "Opulent fundraising," Bryant calls it, although she's been on the board for years, along with her volunteering. "I'd rather just write the check than be seen." Even if Bryant's approach is more noble, Lucinda, thanks to Reed, has always viewed charity as an easy entrée. Write the check and voilà—success. Except now, Lucinda is frayed, vulnerable. Tonight is for Bryant's charity—Bryant, who has turned against her.

To distract herself, she scrolls through her phone, rereading about Mary Lily, Henry Flagler's third wife. How she and Henry Flagler, twenty-eight years her senior, created the Palm Beach season. After Flagler died, she married Robert Bingham, a friend of her brother's. A year later she died suspiciously, described in the headlines as "foul play." Lucinda shivers.

The doorbell is still ringing. Self-trained to not shout "who is it," she resists. Instead, she holds onto the banister, her flip-flops slapping on each step as she descends. Her house has that fresh scent of Palm Beach, the mood luxurious and restful. What a deliberate effect: Lucinda, a beauty seeker, created this home, this life. She passes her smoothest, curated rooms for hosting, white couches to her right, the library with natural tones to her left.

She hopes it's not a neighbor. She's in yoga pants and a baggy black T-shirt. The sunlight tosses these geometric designs onto the wood floors. At the landing she opens the door, although she knows better. He nods, takes off his Ray-Bans. In the driveway, a ten-speed bike leans against the wrought iron gate.

"Hello, Lucinda." He's speaking with great purpose.

She knows the rules on strangers and random violence. "I'm sorry, have we met? You're crossing the line. This is private property."

"Crossing the line? I don't know about that. We have met. At the Marlybone, at Longgreens."

Lucinda shakes her head. "Have we?" She feels old, weary. The dread begins again. Up close, she realizes she's seen him in passing, an architect studying the houses and vias, young women swooning over him—Ingrid Gee's daughter, Georgia, and her entire group. This cadre in their mid-twenties mostly work in fashion and design. They come back to Palm Beach in season from cities, New York, Chicago, LA, and work from home. He's been mentioned during a Saturday bridge game—a charming Ivy League outsider, up for grabs. In theory he could be passed among the single and divorced daughters. In contrast to the local boys, he would appeal to them. He's wholesome with flecked eyes, sturdy in that long, broad-shouldered mode. Sharper, more standalone.

She takes a deep breath. She's been through enough;

she'll manage. *I can cope*, she tells herself, it's her mantra, the one that has gotten her through. "I don't think we've been formally introduced," Lucinda says.

He shifts his weight, watching her. "I'm very close to Raleigh. Did you know that?"

Raleigh? This isn't the person she's alluded to. Hasn't Raleigh been asking for an audience with Lucinda for weeks, to talk about a man, that he's different, special? Some such jargon.

"I did not," she says.

"She's great, and Caleb is fabulous. You're lucky to have a daughter like that."

What is there to say? Her mind goes to Raleigh when they first got to Palm Beach, how she longed for the Gulf Coast, Kesgrave. She cried for her friends back home. She would write actual letters, with sketches, of course, and Lucinda would mail them.

"Raleigh is . . . unique." Lucinda puts her hands behind her back, touches the door, steadies herself.

Porter seems pleased. "That she is. By the way, she has no idea I'm at your home. I checked her schedule and made sure. This conversation you and I are having has nothing to do with Raleigh."

"I'm sorry, how did you meet Raleigh?"

He puts his Ray-Bans back on. "Kesgrave. We met there. A few months ago." He waits a beat.

That sickening fear starts, like she's in quicksand. "Why were you there?"

He shrugs. "To see the place, understand better. May I come in?"

She ought to have listened to William, who said to train

watchdogs. Her daughters had agreed. Maribelle suggested a few rescue dogs. There was a dog who was very appealing, a Dalmatian. One doesn't see them around anymore. Caroline offered Supy, Maribelle and Samuel's yellow labrador, who lives with them, but Violet and Harper are attached to her. Years ago, Reed had wanted a pair of Dobermans to guard the property, to avoid this type of danger. At the moment, she has no dog to sic on this stranger. It's best to speak politely by the entrance. On another lovely afternoon in Palm Beach—excluding her stalker who seems to care totally about her youngest daughter.

They are less than three feet from each other, It's dizzying. She's sweaty, and she is never that. "Maybe not today." She tries to look cordial anyway in case a neighbor passes by, which is uncommon at this hour—mostly everyone does an early morning walk or run and moves on to their country clubs on weekend afternoons. The grounds and house feel desolate, as if everything has deteriorated out of nowhere and is boarded up, no trespassing allowed. Although to anyone else, it remains her captivating, coveted home. She sighs. "I'm sorry, maybe next time you'll come for lunch. For now, it would be best for you to leave."

He smiles. His teeth are very white; his upper lip to nose ratio is in balance. Few people have this feature. "Let me introduce myself. I'm Porter Sanford."

An unfamiliar name. She nods, relieved.

"You don't know, do you?" Porter asks.

"Know what?"

"We have been introduced. You paid no real attention. I don't blame you. It was at the Heart-to-Heart fundraiser. You had a table, you were busy."

His presence is beyond unsettling. She expects someone to walk in—William, Maribelle. Where the hell is Rosie?

He leans on his left leg. "How about the letters, have you been getting those?"

Lucinda recalls the feeling, that moment that destroys what is, trades promise for darkness. "I have." Her voice isn't hers.

Porter smiles again. Making it worse since it is not some toxic gesture, not menacing. "Well, then you know who wrote them," he says.

"I do. I've known from the start."

Her rose bushes bob in a strong gust. She needs a Xanax, although she did take a half tab an hour ago. It would be unwise to call the police—*that* she knows. This young man likes Raleigh; he is a darling around town, he is at her doorstep for a reason.

"Porter, maybe you should go. This isn't a good time. I have someone coming for makeup, hair, for a cocktail hour and dinner . . . a charity . . ."

"I understand. Just one last thing." He clasps his hands together, waiting for the right beat to make an announcement.

Lucinda looks around in case someone is pulling into the garage. Where is Maribelle? She is expected by now. "Sure," she says. He's got to leave and she'll text Raleigh, asking about him. Then Bryant. No, not Bryant, who has chosen to not be slightly on her side.

He's staring at her, possibly counting to himself. He must be a swimmer, a runner—maybe he does triathlons with that lean, flat-waisted effect. He is softspoken; he seems thoughtful, artistic. She gets why Raleigh is entranced. Her daughter knows nothing, only what she feels. No backstory, merely this disarming young man. From anyplace. The fact is, he's at Lucinda's doorstep, deliberately sent. Aren't there too many stories in Palm Beach of buried pasts, hidden truths? This one is hers.

"Ruth-Ann, right?" he says. "We both know that's who wrote the letters. I believe . . . I think she had meant a great deal to you, Lucinda."

Porter lifts a burlap bag he's put on the ground, takes out a manila envelope. "The final installment."

The same envelope as the others, the same handwriting. He clears his throat, about to open it and start reading.

Lucinda takes shallow breaths.This can't be happening. "I'll look at it later. I've got to get inside."

Porter politely holds it out to her. "I'm family, you know, in that Kesgrave way, the Panhandle way."

He is replete with good manners, good looks, style. Raleigh might be in love with him. "Excuse me?"

"Yes, well, I was asked to bring you these letters, one at a time, personally delivered. I hadn't a clue, not until they were left to me. I was supposed to read them first, then bring them to you. That's why I'm in Palm Beach, not only for the architecture, although it's quite something. That's why I was in Kesgrave recently."

He's unnerving her more as his visit goes on. Her heart squeezes, reminding her of being in the Panhandle, like someone is standing on her chest—the years she waited to get away at any cost. How long she has lived with this. What no one can know, especially Bryant. "I see," she says. "You might have overnighted them to me if it was that important. You didn't have to be the messenger."

"Ah, but I did. As I said, I was asked—instructed to."

"You should go." She takes the envelope from him.

Porter steps away, facing the path bordered with anemones and bluebells. "That's fine." He turns back for one last glimpse. "Lucinda, Ruth-Ann was my mother."

LUCINDA STEPS into her foyer. The emptiness in the house is worse; no one has arrived home. She heads into the library and locks the door. In the desk drawer she's stashed a few Xanax. She takes one, opens a small bottle of Perrier from the bar, washes it down. The shelves where she has filed fiction—literary, historical, and commercial—and nonfiction—memoir, narrative, and biography—create a pseudo tranquility. The art books have their own section with titles on Sargent, Corot, Rembrandt, and contemporary artists from Miró to Picasso to Julian Schnabel. Every gesture is ironic, a charade that she is a truly well-educated sophisticate. Who is she fooling? She begins to read.

VENGEANCE

2023

No matter what I've written, it wasn't easy turning my back on Kesgrave. I loved not only the place but everyone there. My darkroom, how I'd set it up, meant everything to me, along with the tides and the riverbank at every season. How it overflowed those spring mornings, we were young together, laughing. There were riptides, there were our families, entwined for generations, like the branches of the long leaf trees on Mill Road.

Once the veneer was shattered, I still would never have sought them out. Except with their level of fame and fortune, what they did to me was a bargain. Sending me off to New York was easy, painless for Lucinda and Reed. No promise was made to me, no compensation beyond my ticket out and ten thousand dollars pressed into my hand that night. I'd been young and too frightened to negotiate, to threaten. I wanted escape, a chance to become a famous photographer, whether Bud was dragged out on his dinghy or not.

I blame myself. I fueled Lucinda's lies by leaving. I made it easy for her and for Reed. Years ago I read that Reed had died. Lucinda was in charge, if she hadn't been all along, beneath the surface. I knew it was time for me to leave this last letter for you. If you've read up to this point, I am gone—it is one of those letters.

You are my son because I left Kesgrave. You deserve the rewards of what my brother, your Uncle Bud, set out to do. Carefully go through this second set of pictures from my Nikon 35Ti—what I had in my pocket that day. Use a magnifying glass if some aren't completely clear. Nothing is as important as this.

As I wrote at the start, once you do, you will have a moral compass. You will decide on retribution.

Chapter Forty-One

1994

LUCINDA likes that Bryant helps out with the girls; there's no question it works. Ruth-Ann isn't expected to pitch in. Nor does Lucinda ask her—there's no pointed request for Ruth-Ann to take the girls to Walmart or the movies on a Saturday afternoon. Ruth-Ann is the baby among their created family—Lucinda and Reed, Bryant and Bud. She's not maternal, she's Bud's little sister. It should have changed when Lucinda started having her children. It might have, yet Ruth-Ann has that calling. She only cares about her photos, meaning she's unlike every other girl in Kesgrave. Being artistic and ethereal is complicated. Ruth-Ann covers it up well enough when she must, at town picnics, Fedd's Diner, when she runs into her high school friends.

Only a few weeks ago, she announced her plans to go to college in the Northeast, Moore College of Art & Design in Philadelphia, School of Visual Arts in New York, or Rhode Island School of Design. How does she know about these places, Lucinda wonders. She both admires Ruth-Ann's purpose and knows the weight of yearning, of escape.

Tonight, after Reed grills hamburgers and the girls are asleep, Ruth-Ann corners Lucinda. The others are on the porch, watching the fireflies, talking about little. The tape deck plays Guns & Roses' "November Rain." Bryant and Bud begin a slow dance.

"Help me, Lucinda, help me get out," Ruth-Ann whispers. "I have the grades. I have talent."

Lucinda's third child, due in the next month, flutters around inside her. Ruth-Ann, in the soggy light, is graceful, desperate. She has a chance, something neither Lucinda nor Bryant have.

"Sure, I'll try," Lucinda says. She smiles, but she's sick inside. Being trapped is worse than regret, worse than guilt. She isn't jealous by nature—she's wildly ambitious without any place to park it. Who would believe her view of what life should be like? Ruth-Ann is pristine, a free spirit. She isn't stuck; she isn't someone who fritters her life away with some local boy. Lucinda knows the trappings. She lives them. For Lucinda and Bryant, Ruth-Ann is their fictive sister. She needs someone to propel her forward, to believe in her. She ought to take her pictures of storms, fishermen, high tides and move them out into the world. Away from a town where no one cares.

THE ENGINE IDLES the next morning when Bud comes over to get Reed in his pickup truck. It's a Saturday, Reed is saying goodbye to the girls.

"What will they do today?" he asks.

Lucinda shrugs. "Something. I'm damn pregnant, so I don't have much energy. We'll figure it out."

Reed is still promising them ice cream with dinner when Lucinda goes out to Bud's truck.

"Your sister is destined for something else," she says.

"She's fine. Ruth-Ann will figure it out. She'll help in the office for now," Bud says.

"She deserves more, Bud," Lucinda says. Her baby twists inside of her like it's on a trapeze. She gasps.

"There's plenty to keep her busy. Look at how the stores will do, Humphreys and Barrows. Look at what's ahead."

"Not for Ruth-Ann. That's no life for her," Lucinda says. *Another narrow man*, she notes as she watches them drive off.

Later, when Ruth-Ann comes by with her two cameras around her neck, she brings Drake's Coffee Cakes for the girls. Bryant is due to come over any minute. A day much like the others.

On their path to the river, Lucinda unfurls the girls' kite, hands them the strings. "Run together and you'll go faster." The kite tails twist, Bryant rushes to straighten them out.

Lucinda speaks quietly to Ruth-Ann. "You're right, there's no reason for you to stay and marry someone who washes cars. Pumps gas. You are gifted, you deserve to be released. I'll do what I can."

Chapter Forty-Two

2026

ALTHOUGH RALEIGH put down her paint brushes for the Handel family portrait when the 'urgent' text came in and sped to West Palm, Porter is already at Flagler Park, waiting. He stands by the bulkhead, the water lapping in a quiet rhythm. He's in tennis shorts, staring at the superyachts. It's overcast, he's squinting, possibly more appealing than ever. There's that tousled effect, like young male models in ads, on billboards. The good features, shadow beard, broad shoulders.

"I'm glad you came, that it worked out," he says.

"I was alone, not with Caleb. I raced over."

She might have taken a fast shower, changed from her yoga pants and sweatshirt. Yet she sees how serious he is. His face set like that night in Kesgrave when a call came in and he left. He takes her hand, leads her to a bench. The wind is blowing at their backs as they face Palm Beach. A couple about their age is there, blaring Neil Young singing "Heart of Gold" on a cell.

Porter waits for them to pass. "We have to speak. There's something I need to tell you."

Raleigh does an involuntary shiver, afraid that his news will absolutely undo her. Everything could change. The fear that they won't be together sluices through her being.

"I do too," Raleigh says. "I need to tell you something."

"Okay, sure. Who goes first?"

Neither says anything as two catamarans pass by, followed by a speedboat. Again that image of Samuel on his Riva Rivamare fills Raleigh's head, she wills it gone. What she has to tell Porter is in real time, not what was.

"I'll go," Raleigh twists around to face him. She wishes they were kissing on this bench, not about to trade confidences. "We don't really speak about how we grew up. I mean, only in bits and pieces, not actual details. It's not like you know about me, or my mom, my sisters, what happened to my father. And I don't know about you." He's listening with care, it makes her fretful. Besides, she dislikes explaining the Barrows. She's shied away from it her whole life. "Our mother oversees everything since our dad died. My middle sister works at our family business as CEO, and her husband is CFO. My eldest sister's husband worked there until he died."

Porter nods; he's with her. No questions thus far.

"Anyway, our mother is into being important in Palm Beach. I don't want you to judge her—she's just invested in it. Lately she's been threatened. She thinks someone is out to ruin her, and she's unraveling. I've never seen her like this, I feel terrible for her. She's loopy, taking anti-anxiety meds. I can't stand it."

"You don't know who this is or why?" he asks.

"No, no, I don't. No one does—my sisters and I have no idea. She hasn't told anyone. She's being blackmailed or something, Porter, it's frightening. Whoever it is, why bother some sixty-year-old woman, whatever she did? My mother, we call her Lucinda most of the time, we've had our moments with her, but she's our mother."

He's looking out at the Intracoastal, not at her. His jaw seems tight, he's clenching his teeth. Is she meant to go on, reveal more?

In profile he says, "A big hurdle for everyone."

There's this sense she could be with him always, never fathoming who he is. That he went to Yale to be an architect has been shared. Yet she could lie in his arms the night long and not know if he has ever smoked, whether he drinks, or how many women he's loved, how many have loved him. If he is an early riser, lifts heavy weights, goes for yearly check-ups. What foods he would cook at home, not through Uber Eats or room service. In their bubble he is magical, in real time maybe annoying. Or worse, he might not understand her, let alone her implausible family.

In theory, Porter is entitled to hide anything he wants. He's met Caleb, has learned about her divorce, knows nothing of Raleigh and Samuel, of her break with Maribelle. Had Raleigh not been at Lucinda's yesterday and witnessed her mother's vast despair, she might not have revealed any of it.

"We count on Lucinda, our mother."

Porter is still watching the water. "This will work out, Raleigh."

"No offense, but why say that?"

"Things work out," he says. "If she's being blackmailed, she'll settle, make it go away."

Fluish, that's how Raleigh feels; a migraine is about to set in. The sky has this wavy quality. They're outside, yet she needs more air. "Things work out, things like this?" she asks. "I'm sorry, I've gone on and on. I know you wanted to tell me something. Probably major."

Porter looks at her. "No, that's fine."

More boats go by. Pedestrians, more music blares on a phone. This go-round it's Phish singing "A Life Beyond the Dream," music she and Porter listened to at the Colony.

"I'm the one, Raleigh. I want you to know."

"That's ironic. I mean, bittersweet. Here we are talking about Lucinda and you say this to me."

"Raleigh, listen. I'm the one."

Timing and lighting—one never knows when the best or worst things will happen. Isn't that what Lucinda has warned her girls? While Porter is sounding romantic, if that's what he means, it's bad timing while critical.

"Yes, I believe you are." She's speaking softly. "I know you're the one."

She kisses him, he kisses her back, then stops.

Porter sighs. "Listen, Raleigh, that's not what we're talking about. This is important, you have to have this information. You are the last to know."

Raleigh sucks in her breath; the migraine is becoming full blown. "The last for what, to know what? Are you married, with someone else, a long-standing monogamous relationship? Are you polyamorous? Are you . . . not in love with me, and it's one-sided?"

"None of that."

"Okay, then what is it?"

Porter takes Raleigh's hands in his. The bench feels cold; there's no more sunlight. "I'm the one who sent the letters."

She has never seen him write a note. Does she know his handwriting, who is he writing to? Raleigh frowns. "Letters to whom, Porter?"

"To Lucinda. To your mother."

The Intracoastal stops existing. He stops filling the space

beside her. She is solitary, trying to comprehend. "Please, make this understandable. Please, Porter."

He stands up, begins pacing along the path. "The letters. They're from my mother, Ruth-Ann Humphreys. She'd written them to me to read after she died. With instructions to bring them to your mother."

Ruth-Ann. It comes back to Raleigh, the photographer friend of Aunt Bryant's and Lucinda's. Only Aunt Bryant mentions her, not Lucinda. A woman Raleigh never met. Her head is pounding, imploding at her temples. She has Caleb tonight; she has to process what Porter is saying, grasp it, contain it. No wonder Lucinda has been so surreal.

"Wait, maybe I've seen one of your letters in a manila envelope without a return address. One afternoon I was at my mother's when it came. I didn't get to read it. It was dropped off."

He's looking at her in this tragic way. "That's about right."

"What do you want from me? How could you do this, to any of us?"

"I was in Kesgrave for some research. I met you. I had no idea who you were. I fell for you right away. It wasn't supposed to happen."

Right. Except his face, his eyes, how he's standing straight, show how alone he is, crushed beneath. Anything, everything that is and was about him remains crucial to her.

"Okay, I'm trying to absorb this, Porter."

"What I want, what my mother wanted for me, is my share, what I'm entitled to. Bud, your Aunt Bryant's fiancé, was my uncle, my mother's brother. My mother was there."

"Your share? And where is there?" She despises this conversation. Worse, she despises what he has done while he still matters. She stands, ties her sweatshirt around her waist. "Porter, I have to go. I can't be with you. I am a Barrows. I need to leave."

Raleigh crosses Flagler, rooting through her bag for the linen handkerchief with embroidered hearts from Aunt Bryant. She holds it to her mouth and throws up.

Chapter Forty-Three

2026

Sislie Denton's plan—to host a table of ten at Coco's for a pre-birthday lunch for Lucinda—is a generous gesture. Yet Maribelle's iciness toward Raleigh lingers, putting Lucinda on edge. Caroline, strategically seated between her sisters, twists from one to the other for conversation. With what Lucinda has endured these past few weeks, she's annoyed at them, especially since one of her long-standing friends in Palm Beach has graciously put this together. "An intimate luncheon ahead of your birthday" is how Sislie pitched it. Over two months ago—another life ago, really.

Nonetheless, Lucinda and Bryant sit across from her daughters, while Jolie Danes and Jayce Wiley, bookended by Gabriel Sim and Aurora Brents, engage in Palm Beach tattle. *Grill Night . . . casual these days . . . whose daughter just had triplets . . . did the Dolton party have one band or two?* For Lucinda, the sheer lack of depth in their conversation is a panacea. If only it were more than a diversion; if only it could be her life. Instead, she watches—Maribelle is immutable, Raleigh seems defeated, while Caroline works doubly hard to appear charming, carefree. Lucinda craves a steady state, no letters, no feuding daughters, no threat of falling from grace. In this hour, she is with friends and family. She fingers her pill box in her green Gucci Jackie bag, knowing an extra chip of Xanax is always on hand. For the first time since Reed died, she senses she has no buffer.

BY THREE O'CLOCK, everyone stands in line to retrieve their cars, moving on to the rest of their day. When the young, athletic valet swiftly drives up in William's Bentley Bentayga, Lucinda is counting how long until she's by herself. At least forty-five minutes since she's foolishly offered to drive Bryant—who Ubered there, inexplicably—back to Manalapan, and Raleigh has chosen not to drive back with Caroline.

Lucinda looks to her right at Bryant in the passenger seat, in her rearview mirror at Raleigh. "Everyone buckled?"

Raleigh clears her throat. "I'm glad we're in the car, the three of us. I wanted privacy."

"And so comfortable. William always drives such elegant cars." Bryant speaks in her pleasant noncommittal tone. As if she's not known what William drives before today.

"I wanted to tell you both . . ." Raleigh stops, starts to cry.

Bryant reaches back to find Raleigh's wrist, holds it. "Raleigh, what is it? Is Caleb alright?"

Lucinda heads toward the Royal Palm Bridge, expecting this route will have less traffic.

Tears glisten on Raleigh's cheeks in that soapy movie style. "Yes, it's not Caleb." She sniffles. "Remember that I have someone in my life? I've been telling you, alluding to it."

"You have," Bryant says. "I don't know much. I hope he's good to you, Raleigh."

Lucinda hits the gas by mistake, then brakes. They thrust

forward in their seats. She could comment that someone ahead is unpredictable. She says nothing.

Bryant keeps going. "I hope it's good news after the nastiness of Alex and the divorce. You deserve to be happy. We *want* you to be happy."

Lucinda and Bryant equal one cheerleading squad when it comes to Raleigh. Any of Lucinda's girls or grandchildren for that matter. The focal point where she and Bryant are best as advocates.

The traffic moves like molasses. Lucinda has to get out of these Manolos that used to be comfortable. Her weight could be shifting, which is why they aren't in her future. "Want to tell us about him now? We're at the longest red light."

Raleigh is still crying. "Well, he knows you, Mom, and he knows you, Aunt Bryant."

Bryant smiles. "Really? That's lovely. He must be a Palm Beacher. Whose son is he?"

"Whose son is he? Is that what you asked, Aunt Bryant?" She starts crying louder.

"Raleigh, take a moment," Lucinda says. She edges into the right lane, her signal ticking.

Raleigh slurps her tears, blows her nose.

"Please, Raleigh, nothing can be so terrible. Start by telling us about him. What he does, where he's from." Bryant says this in that extra soothing tone.

Lucinda presses on the gas, although she doesn't want to be stopped for speeding. She tries to see Raleigh in the rearview mirror. "I have the air conditioning on," she says, then presses a button and brings all four windows down a third.

"I don't feel well," Raleigh says. "I'm nauseous."

Bryant, jutting her chin forward, gives Lucinda these

pointed looks. "Let's see what Raleigh has to say about this young man."

"I rode in this car because I wanted to speak with you both. This man, the one I care about. I met him in Kesgrave."

Although they're on the bridge, the car ahead has stopped out of nowhere. Lucinda hits her horn. "What the hell?"

"Please, be careful, Lucinda." Bryant morphs into *I should have been a nurse* voice. "Is he from Kesgrave?" She continues with that tone.

Raleigh tosses her head, pats her eyes. "No, he's not. I met him there when I went the first time this year."

Bryant gives Lucinda one of those conspiratorial side glances. As if she doesn't know where it's going and on red alert. Lucinda looks away. She won't accept any other shared news; she's beyond drained.

"We could pull over and park," Bryant says, as if she's the only sane one in the car.

Raleigh crying softly, points. "Over there?"

Lucinda steers toward City Girl Consignment. She maneuvers the Bentley like it's a dump truck, back and forth, into a spot. No one says a word. When they're parked, Lucinda and Bryant face the back seat where Raleigh sits in the middle.

"Who is this man, Raleigh?" Lucinda asks.

"You both know him. It's Porter. Porter Sanford. That's who I want to be with—that's who I'm with."

Lucinda gasps. She's about to be ambushed by Raleigh and Bryant.

Bryant starts gasping, equally astonished. She shakes her head. "Porter?"

"I planned to ask you after my birthday about your boyfriend and when can we meet him. Now you're saying it's Porter," Lucinda says. "Porter is *blackmailing* me."

Raleigh sits up straighter. "I know. He told me. I just found out. I don't believe it. Why would he do that? What is that about, Mom?"

The one glass of prosecco has gone to Lucinda's head, or worse, it hasn't yet. She isn't able to process the question. "It has to do with the letters," she says. "You know, the letters I keep getting from him."

"What surprises me is that this is who you love, Raleigh," Bryant says.

"I love him. I totally love him." Raleigh begins crying again, sloppily.

Bryant does one of her sympathetic nods. "We love whom we love."

Lucinda bristles. "Love? How could you love him after finding out he's your mother's blackmailer, Raleigh? Isn't that quite enough reason to *not* love someone?"

Raleigh takes down her window completely.

Lucinda hits the master button, puts it back up. "Nothing goes beyond this car."

Each of their phones ding. Texts are coming in. Women with shopping bags, are passing by William's Bentley. Different ages, threesomes, strolling along. Sometimes they link their arms, speaking quietly. Not beleaguered; rather, they meander around town—Worth Avenue, Royal Poinciana Plaza, to South Dixie. Unencumbered, free-spirited.

"It's getting late. We'll keep this conversation among ourselves. Your sisters, William, none of them need know anything," Bryant suggests.

"That's self-evident," Lucinda says, annoyed with Bryant. "Is there anything more to discuss?"

Raleigh shakes her head. "No, not now."

Bryant clears her throat. "Maybe it's best if we drop Raleigh at Caroline's. I'll go on with you to Manalapan, Lucinda."

"I'm sorry, I'm not feeling well," Lucinda says. "Let's have Rosie or Daisy drive you back, Bryant. Or an Uber."

"I have to get to Caroline's," Raleigh says. "Caleb is being dropped off at five by Alex. I promised Harper and Violet I'd do a 'shop the closet' for some parties they have on the weekend."

As if it's merely another post-lunch afternoon in Palm Beach. There has been no earthshattering bulletin, no significant shift in their lives.

CAROLINE RUNS OUT to the car when Lucinda pulls up. "All okay? Raleigh texted like forty minutes ago that she was en route. The girls are waiting."

Raleigh opens the door. Caroline gets a call and walks away.

"Wait, not yet, Raleigh, another minute," Bryant says, which is surprisingly instinctive. "There is more to say."

"Yes, that's true," Lucinda says. Her tone is sober, concise. "Please stay in the car."

The door closes with a thud. Raleigh sighs. "Sure."

Again both Lucinda and Bryant face her.

"I do a great deal for you, Raleigh," Lucinda says. "I pay for your team of lawyers to fight Alex's absurd custody and alimony demands. It's a costly divorce to start, and his request puts it into the stratosphere. I'm funding a substantial trust for Caleb. I've not asked you to repay the 'loan' from when you and Alex closed on your house."

Lucinda pauses for the dip in the conversation where Raleigh thanks her for being so giving. Instead, her daughter runs a lip gloss across her lips without a reply.

"Porter Sanford, whom you profess to love, be in love with, however it plays out in your life, is threatening to destroy my social standing in Palm Beach. He has access to some fictive letter collection about Kesgrave over thirty years ago."

"It has to do with Bud, Lucinda," Bryant says. "Is that 'fictive'?"

Lucinda narrows her eyes. "I'm speaking, Bryant. I, Lucinda, am explaining to Raleigh that Porter will destroy our reputation. It will affect all of us. In addition to harming my standing, he wants money. He claims to be entitled to a piece of Barrows."

"What did you do, Mom, in Kesgrave? Because he's a kind, honest person. I have never met anyone like Porter."

Raleigh is starstruck, smitten. Not that Lucinda misses what that is like, rather that it has nothing to do with the consequences. For a millisecond she remembers Reed, how it was. Bryant with Bud, the times together. Wasn't everyone kind and honest—wasn't she the only one with an agenda?

Caroline, on her cell, heads toward the car. Harper is with her, a wide lavender streak in her hair that is unnecessary. Caroline has changed to yoga pants that fit well. Their entire family will be ruined by Porter Sanford. Raleigh, the most fragile of her three daughters, holds the key.

"Give him what he wants, Mom, please. Please sort this out. Only you can do it," Raleigh says, sobbing.

Despite the wine at lunch and the Xanax whenever,

Lucinda shakes her head emphatically. "I see it from another lens. It's best if you reel him in, Raleigh. Tell this man who seems to have won your heart—to stop threatening me. That he ought to leave Palm Beach immediately."

Raleigh wipes her eyes and gets out of the car. Before she slams the door, she looks in at her mother and Bryant. "I doubt I'll do that, not until I know the facts."

Chapter Forty-Four

2026

If only the parlay with Lucinda and Aunt Bryant hadn't been. If only Raleigh could banish what was said and discovered. She walks through Caroline's foyer into her library, feeling physically ill. She'll choose a book—romantasy, chick lit, anything to quiet her mind

Violet, in a hot pink bikini, her long blond hair wet and flat against her head, swings open the double doors. "Mom thought you were here. Caleb's outside with us."

Violet's innocence. Raleigh tries to remember what it's like.

"That's great news. I'm following you."

On the deck, Raleigh is surprised to find Caroline, usually at the office at this hour, and Maribelle, who shows up and doesn't. Caleb bobs up and down in the pool with Harper and Nicole. When he waves at her and laughs, he seems much older than five. He's growing up; it is unstoppable.

"Mom, Mom! We're about to play Marco Polo!"

Of course they are—some things do not change. Corny as it is, the game works. Besides, it was never an "in" idea. Caleb might or might not have sunscreen on.

"That's perfect, Caleb." Raleigh wants to smile, her face doesn't move.

Harper, followed by Violet, dives off the board and

swims to Caleb in the shallow end. Beneath an umbrella, Maribelle scrolls on her phone.

Caroline spins around, puts her hand over her cell. "You've joined us—I'm soon to be off this work call."

The air is clean, the sky a deep blue. They are framed in a flawless afternoon where nature could save them.

Caroline sashays over. "We'll chat while the kids swim."

Raleigh glances at the pool, everyone is preoccupied. Better than whisking Caleb upstairs, she wishes they could simply leave. The two of them would drive to Sprinkles for bowls of chocolate mint chip ice cream. Porter would meet them there per usual. Except they are on hiatus; she knows who he is, what he's done. This is where she belongs, with her sisters and the children, defending their mother. If only she didn't miss him, crave his company.

As if telepathic, Caroline raises her voice and claps her hands. "Nicole, the kids can have ice cream sandwiches by the gazebo. Maybe some iPad time."

Maribelle looks past Raleigh. Without proximity to Lucinda they are not exactly warm and inviting. Caroline walks with purpose to the chair next to Maribelle, motioning for Raleigh to join them. Raleigh takes a scrunchy from her bag and gathers her hair.

"A few things to cover." Caroline begins in her corporate Barrows office voice. "After Lucinda dropped you off, she called. I thought the three of us would hang out with the girls and Caleb. It sounds like crazy shit is happening. We have to talk first."

"That's odd," Maribelle says. "We were at a luncheon for Mom not an hour ago. What could go wrong so fast?"

"Mom was cryptic about new developments. I also think she wants our vote—proof that we support her."

"Developments? What, is this an investigation?" Maribelle asks.

"If only it were that easy," Raleigh says.

"Well, we already know how Lucinda has been acting. She's skittish," Caroline says. "If nothing else, we've banded together."

Maribelle appears bored and weary, not sold on the concept.

Caroline stares at her. "Maribelle, please," she says. "I'm about to ask for your thoughts, memories. There can't be a cold war with Raleigh."

Maribelle sighs. "Okay, sure. Are we continuing with what started in Kesgrave when we were in grade school?"

"We are," Raleigh says. "Do you remember a friend of Aunt Bryant's and Mom's called Ruth-Ann?"

"With her cameras?" Caroline asks. "She wore combat boots and jeans, bright color sweatshirts—she acted young. She didn't pay attention to us."

Maribelle sits straighter. "She would be snapping photos of us—we were her practice subjects. She and Lucinda used to laugh. Aunt Bryant too. She was there, y'know, a lot."

Raleigh leans in. "What else do you remember?"

"Outside there were nature pictures, inside for close-ups. A bunch of Mom in profile. I guess she was a photographer—one in the making. We were young when she was doing the pictures. I was nine or ten, Caroline was seven or eight—we didn't really care."

Raleigh wants to take her notebook out of her bag, but there is a momentum. When it's over she'll get into the pool, swim laps, sort it out. "Who was she, who did she become?" she asks.

"I have no idea," Caroline says.

"I don't think we ever saw her again after you were born," Maribelle says. "I asked Lucinda and Dad about it after she sort of disappeared. Later there was an elective photography class offered in tenth grade. I heard Mom talking to Dad about it, saying they shouldn't encourage me, no one needed another Ruth-Ann. I assumed she'd moved on and they'd lost touch."

"We had pictures she'd taken on the mantle, and later they were gone," Caroline says. "I'm not sure, maybe when we got to the big house—in Kesgrave—on Sequoia."

"What's the connection?" Maribelle asks.

Finally, the salient question, the one Raleigh has been expecting. She has to do this without tears. Stronger than she presents on a daily basis. "I told you I'd met someone, a new guy. I first met him in Kesgrave," she says.

"That's sort of strange," Caroline says. Her phone dings, she glances at it, back at her sisters. "The Kesgrave-Palm Beach axis isn't a frequent occurrence."

"I really like him . . . more than that. I care about him," Raleigh says. "He's an architect. He went to Yale. He's curious about the houses, the buildings built in Flagler's day."

"That must please Lucinda. She loves credentials," Caroline says. "Wait, I know who he is—good looking and refined, isn't he? Everyone throws themselves at him. The forty-year-old divorcées, fifty-year-olds and up."

"Well," Raleigh says, "I've been with him. I'm seeing him. That's the man I wanted to tell you about."

"Who can one trust? Surely not the men we sleep with. There you go, Raleigh, yet again with a man governing your life." Maribelle directs this at neither sister, her tone cold. If she ever forgives Raleigh completely, her anger will linger.

A southwest wind is frothing up. Out of nowhere the temperature is falling.

"There's more to it," Raleigh says. She wishes she didn't have to share the rest, that this would be ample for one day.

"Go on." Caroline is paying attention.

Maribelle adjusts her sunglasses, checks her phone, looks at Raleigh.

"Anyway," Raleigh keeps on, "this guy, his name is Porter. He's Ruth-Ann's son."

To the south the middle bridge is up; a group of white ibises is by the dock. Cumulus clouds are covering and uncovering the sun. Caleb's voice gets louder; he's crying about his stubbed toe. Nicole, a fine nanny, soothes him, offers some pretzels. Raleigh could rush over, yet she doesn't leave her sisters. They sit stupefied.

"Wow, that's a coincidence. No wonder Lucinda's falling apart. Did you tell her?" Caroline asks.

Raleigh breathes deeply. She's a beginner on a trapeze, and there is no safety mat beneath. "He told her first. He's threatening her. He's her blackmailer."

More silence. The sisters are in that coven again except without any potions. No ace up their sleeves.

Caroline coughs, drinks water, coughs. "I'm sure Mom wants him gone. I'm sure she's beyond hysterical about her reputation, Barrows, every one of us. We have to work together, figure out next steps."

"What makes it go away?" Maribelle seems sad.

"That depends on what Lucinda wants," Caroline says.

"Or what she did," Maribelle says.

Raleigh wants to fall into them as if they are a human hammock. The despair in Lucinda's face today, Porter that afternoon at Port St. Joe, the Panhandle. "Hasn't that been the question all along?"

Chapter Forty-Five

2026

After Raleigh's confession, Lucinda and Bryant are silent the entire ride to Manalapan. The winding drive south along the A1A with water views of the Intracoastal. It has always seemed long to Lucinda, including on a good day, which this is not. When she pulls up to Bryant's house, a waterfront estate, she has sunken into major despondency.

Bryant slams the passenger door. Were Lucinda not so weary and defeated, she would remark that William doesn't appreciate anyone slamming the doors of his Bentley. Why bother? Bryant is insisting there is more to discuss and that time is of the essence.

She hasn't been to Bryant's in an age, and if she could collect her thoughts, she'd note how lovely and elegant it is. Reed did this for Bryant over twenty years ago. Reed—who was Bryant's lover in the loaded Lucinda/Reed/Bryant triad. They co-existed, each of them profiting from their arrangement. Today more than other days, Lucinda wishes Reed were alive. He knew everything; he had her back. She's painfully on her own as her past unravels.

Lucinda follows Bryant into her study and pours herself a few ounces of vodka at the narrow mid-century bar. Bryant tosses her bag and cropped jacket onto the love seat. She's watching.

"You're assuming I've become a lush," Lucinda says.

"Actually I don't care, Lucinda. I'd say it goes way beyond that."

A tip-off that Bryant's grievance is imminent. The vodka burns Lucinda's lips. It's tiring being hypersensitive, high strung, and no longer as tough-minded as she once was.

Lucinda holds her glass up. "Your views of the Intracoastal—I forget about them. They're special, truly. To houses in Manalapan."

"I agree, such good views. You've probably forgotten since you're rarely a visitor," Bryant says. "Manalapan is popular. I hope someone appreciates it like I do since I've put the house up for sale."

"Have you?" Lucinda asks. "That might be an invigorating change." She can't imagine what she's expected to say. Bryant's house listing can't be the topic of conversation with Lucinda asking where she'll go. Lucinda's essence is endangered by an intruder whom her daughter loves and Bryant finds beyond scintillating.

"I'd like to move to West Palm, on Flagler, one of the new buildings."

"That's an idea." Lucinda sounds patronizing, tinny. "Too bad you can't leave the island."

"Raleigh said you'd feel like this. She is the only person who knows my plans to move to the Bristol."

The Bristol. Even if the two women recover from a serious breakup, the Bristol will lure Bryant away. She'll love the building, the lifestyle. The seesaw of it—how Bryant was up and Lucinda was down when they were growing up in Kesgrave. Lucinda had nothing while Bryant had plenty—sweaters, dresses, shoes, hair ribbons. Ruth-Ann and Bryant were family friends while Lucinda worked to become inner sanctum, to count. In Palm Beach, Lucinda has held the power until recently. If Bryant moves off the island, Lucinda will be without her. Despite how her life has many layers and has sustained her, Lucinda feels shunned.

"You aren't able to do that," Lucinda says.

"Ah, I will. Things are changing." Bryant points. Lucinda sits on the chair across from the couch. While everyone loves white couches and chairs in Palm Beach, Bryant's level of white is severe. Her study and her living room are sterile. How ironic that she and Bryant are the ones left to live, with Bud, Reed, and Ruth-Ann gone. "You know Lucinda, I wanted children with Bud. I adored him. When he died, I lost everything."

"I know," Lucinda says. "I tried to make it up to you. Reed did too. He wanted you to have a pleasant, comfortable life."

"I imagine Bud, Reed." Bryant says. "Porter looks like Bud. I'm sure you saw it at once."

There's no commenting on this loaded remark. Lucinda wouldn't venture a thought. She practically slurps her vodka.

Bryant's Tiffany bronze clock on the mantel chimes, a gift from Reed, Lucinda suspects, as if that carries weight now or ever did. Bryant is at the bookcase. She finds an envelope in her stack of art books.

"Here, read this."

Lucinda refuses. She needs a Xanax. If she takes yet another, she won't be in shape to drive home. She could potentially harm someone or herself. She could be pulled over—police patrol the A1A, and that would be mortifying. It would move quickly through her circles, fodder for gossip at the card games. Still an outcome of no consequence compared to what she and Bryant are up against. She places her two-thirds-full glass on the coffee table. "I'd rather not," she says. "I've gotten enough letters from Porter. In fact, when I met him, I believe he gave me the last one."

"This one is out of sequence, as I understand it. He gave it to me the day I met him by the GreenMarket." Bryant remains standing as if it's a rehearsal and tomorrow she'll be the recipient of a medal for her humanitarianism. She has had such accolades, although Lucinda has had more. They will both be destroyed by Porter and the letters. The family will be. Doesn't Bryant realize this?

Again, the rising fear, an anxiety so fierce Lucinda could fall backward and crack her head open on the porcelain wood-style tiles. Yet survive to live with less—to be ratted out and ruined. Since Ruth-Ann's letters ascend, more deliberately "out to get you" each time, Lucinda senses the letter Bryant has will reveal what the woman must never know. What Lucinda has spent decades safeguarding. "We ought to be a team, Bryant. We ought to squash this problem—these letters and Porter's threats—immediately."

Bryant brandishes the letter. "Is that what you suggest? Let me read this."

THE PHOTOGRAPHS

It wasn't winter but felt like it. The river was very cold. I was watching when they fought. They pushed at each other, it became vicious. They'd forgotten or didn't know they were best friends, almost brothers. They were caught up, oblivious to being in a public if empty place. I stood and watched what men do to one another. No one saw me. I began to take photographs. I caught every angle, every move of what Reed did to Bud. Lucinda was pacing. Her face, always perfect, was wretched. She put her hands beneath the mound that was her baby, trying to protect her from heartbreak.

A half hour later we were back at the house. Bryant was in the yard with the girls on the swing, innocent. "You saw nothing, Ruth-Ann," Lucinda said in that cool glass of water voice. Reed came into the room carrying a paper bag. I knew it was cash—he'd always told my brother he kept a lot of money in the house. He handed it to Lucinda. "There's nothing to say to anyone. What happened today will never go beyond this room," she said. "I'm sure you understand." An odd shadow fell over her. Reed stood behind, looking like he'd been trampled on. They had become contaminated.

"I'll go to the police with these photos," I said. "You will not," Lucinda said. Reed didn't speak. He was a bent man now. He needed Lucinda to prop him up.

"Bud Humphreys just drowned. Your brother drowned. Another boat accident in the Panhandle." Lucinda stared at me. "No one will ever know anything else. Understood?"

She dangled the bag. "This is your ticket out, finally, far from Kesgrave, Ruth-Ann. But before you take the money and Reed gets you to the airport, you'll give me the film." She came over, put her finger on the Canon hanging around my neck. "Once you hand over the film, you'll have plenty of cash. You have wanted this—your ticket out of Kesgrave, to study photography in a city up north. You have a gift, Ruth-Ann. Your photos are unforgettable."

Lately books have come out about trauma, how a witness writhes afterward from what she saw. For me, it was not only what I saw but the deal I cut, that I fled. The secrets fester and harm. What if I was broken and left Kesgrave, walking away from everything? We had been one family and then we were finished. We were undone.

Bryant places it back in the envelope. "It's not only that I know what you did. I have evidence."

"These Ruth-Ann rantings that she compiled for her son aren't exactly evidence," Lucinda says.

"We have to help Porter. He deserves something. He's dear to me, Lucinda."

"You met him once, Bryant. What do you know about him?" She takes a sip of vodka—she has to. "He's out to harm us."

"Harm? I don't see it as you do. Porter wants money, he deserves something. He's Ruth-Ann's son. It was supposed to be Bud and Reed together. The company was theirs. And Porter loves Raleigh. She loves him."

Raleigh's eyes, that's what comes to Lucinda's mind. Since she was a girl, those wide brown eyes, saucer eyes. The rounder, more enchanting they were, the sicker she'd be the next day. Flu, strep, fever. Today she had that look, otherworldly, on the brink.

Barrows comes to mind next. How the company grew from the start with Lucinda's insight. In the years since

Reed has been gone, the company has flourished. Quadrupled in sales. It will go public.

"There have to be conditions, Bryant. Porter doesn't have total power, does he? He'll have to sign documents swearing he'll stop threatening our social standing." Lucinda looks out at the Intracoastal. The harmony quotient is high; it can't be duplicated. She remembers the river, that morning, Reed and Bud. Her panic, Raleigh kicking inside her, about to be born.

"Do you believe it's that easy? I suspect Porter will say sure, give me half of everything."

"Half?" Lucinda does a dry cough.

"Whatever he wants," Bryant says.

"We won't know until we negotiate," Lucinda says. "I'll have to speak with our lawyers. There will be terms. There will be an NDA."

The dredging up of the past, Ruth-Ann, all of it vile. Lucinda moves to the glass doors, Bryant follows. They look out together, as if they could reclaim the drowned men. Bud in his dinghy on the river. Samuel on his Riva Rivamare. Countless men, countless bodies of water.

"Lucinda, let me add—I doubt there's room for negotiating," Bryant says. "We need to save face."

They're beside one another, both overwrought, heartbroken for separate reasons, dovetailing to survive.

"Well," Lucinda says, wishing she could light up a cigarette, having not smoked in over twenty-five years. "There's always some room, a piece worth preserving, a price to be determined."

"No, it won't be like that," Bryant says.

"I'm not sure why," Lucinda says. "Are you with me or against me?"

Bryant who doesn't drink, opens up the Grey Goose and pours herself a glass. "I'll need to know one thing, not that anyone else will."

"Okay."

Bryant takes a long sip. "For years while I was entertaining your husband and godmother to your children, I've wanted an answer. Not that it would change anything—or maybe it would have changed everything. I never asked. Then Porter came and blew up our lives. What I need to know is why? Why were you at the river that day?"

In the shortest silence before Lucinda answers, she's at the river again, her entire life divided into Kesgrave and her caravan out. To Palm Beach for another chance.

"I'm sorry, Bryant. I won't answer. Not yet."

Bryant is at her desk drawer. She takes out a cigar box, old, withered. "Lucinda, I have the photographs. The pictures Ruth-Ann took the day Bud died. Porter went to Kesgrave for these. Ruth-Ann had buried them somewhere. I don't know where, or how they were preserved. He retrieved them. He has another copy, I'm sure. You and I have to give Porter the money, shares, whatever he wants."

Duplicate sets of photos. Regret, like poison, seeps into the room. Lucinda says nothing.

Chapter Forty-Six

2026

Raleigh knows Lucinda will ask—demand—that her daughters and Aunt Bryant come to her house after the birthday luncheon ends. That it was a great success, an exquisite production choreographed by Kit Carter, makes it a steeper crash and burn. What a relief it was to be distracted with live theatre, a chance to breathe free of the letters and Porter. To be transported from Lucinda's mess of these past weeks to Lucinda's stature in Palm Beach today.

As if it's roll call, Maribelle, Caroline, Raleigh, and Aunt Bryant sit on the wrought iron love seats, facing one another. Lucinda's mini-Versailles gardens, where beauty and misery reign. Aunt Bryant lifts one of the sun parasols from the umbrella stand and opens it up, a Monet water lilies theme with vivid blues and lavenders. Everyone is still dressed up since a command appearance left no time to change into slouchy cottons. Predictably, Lucinda is the most jazzed and outfitted. Anyone would admire her melon-colored silk dress, Kelly bag, kitten slingbacks. She borders on being draped in jewelry, the yellow diamond solitaire from Reed, tank watch from William, a heart locket she recently bought herself on the Avenue, a favorite among the three sisters. Lucinda's focus and stardom are a major relief. What hangs over the family, regardless of Lucinda's ability to turn a corner, is only about Porter.

Maribelle begins. "Lucinda-Mom, you wanted us together to talk about what you call a high-stakes situation. Before we start, let's toast your sixtieth birthday and the array of accolades today. What a celebration! Every guest was genuinely delighted to be there, feting you."

Aunt Bryant stands up. "What more could one ask for than the chance to punctuate the good times? That's why today was grand. And Saturday night will be the grand finale!" She does this folksy arm gesture. Raleigh expects she was like this in Kesgrave. When she, Lucinda and Ruth-Ann were young.

No one cheers, although they should. Lucinda, under better circumstances, would be relishing this. Instead, she's contemplative. At least she isn't drugged or high, her go-to of the last few weeks. Raleigh shifts her weight on the love seat. Whatever Lucinda's mode, it's making her jittery.

To have achieved what Lucinda has reminds her of the nights in Kesgrave before the move to Palm Beach. Her parents whispering in their bedroom, she outside the door unable to quite capture the words. Lucinda's voice more strident, fighting fiercely. Now again there is that kind of urgency. Raleigh knows this. She is that third-grade girl again, left alone with her mother at the center. This time Raleigh is completely invested. She loves Porter.

"We have an issue," Lucinda says. "Everyone knows how Porter is out to wreck me, meaning us, bringing our downfall in Palm Beach. I'm counting on Raleigh."

"Downfall is a dramatic description," Caroline begins. "There's always a remedy. It always comes down to money to make it go away. We have lawyers, and we are strategic."

Maribelle nods. "Doesn't it depend on what happened, what's about to happen because of Porter?"

"Right." Aunt Bryant places her parasol on the ground, twirls it, lets it fall forward. "We have to consider what he's asking for. As well as where Raleigh comes in."

Lucinda kicks off her pumps, paces the open patio in front of them. Her chignon is loosened; her shoulders aren't back in her usual exaggerated pose. "I'm asking you, Raleigh, to seize the chance to work this out with Porter. His mother laid it out before she died and left her blackmail letters as his road map."

"That was the deal, wasn't it, Mom?" Raleigh asks. "Her silence."

"Yes, absolutely," Lucinda says. "Ruth-Ann signed off. She promised when she left Kesgrave." She's jutting her chin forward like she used to do when Maribelle and Caroline were in high school and broke curfew or smoked cigarettes.

Caroline practically jumps up from the love seat. "Raleigh, for our sakes you'll have to fix this. If Porter is so important to you, negotiate the terms. We'll bring in the lawyers, of course, have papers drawn up. An NDA for certain. Porter will need his own lawyer. Let's get this right. None of us will lose our standing. That's what we want, the best result."

"That's doable, isn't it, Raleigh?" Maribelle faces the Intracoastal, not her sister.

A weather front is rolling in; the rose bushes and anemones bend and dip. Aunt Bryant tugs her sheer cashmere shawl around her shoulders. "He should be treated well," she says. "Porter is a Humphreys. He's Ruth-Ann's son."

Lucinda holds up her right hand as if she's a traffic officer. "Not so fast," she says. "We'll give him part of Barrows, the money too. However, the letters and photos have to be destroyed. No copies will exist. He'll sign off on that. There's a caveat—it's not negotiable."

"What would that be?" Aunt Bryant asks, using her calmest voice. As if she anticipates a deal breaker, as if trusting Lucinda to be fair and kind is a long shot.

"I'm considering what Reed would do. He would take care of Porter, but the past would have to be cleaned up," Lucinda says. "That means Porter has to leave Palm Beach. He can't be within a sixty-mile radius of the area. It's too risky. He might be at a party, a charity event, and he'll get to know people. He'll talk about it, unintentionally or on purpose."

Everyone waits as if they're discussing the latest fashion, the best halibut. A typical Palm Beach afternoon with nothing typical about it.

"I'd like to hear from Raleigh." Maribelle rallies. An olive branch, letting their sister feud go.

"If we're gathered here for me to work it out with Porter, I can ask him to stop the blackmail, the letters. I won't ask him to leave Palm Beach. No one controls someone's life like that. He's my boyfriend. He's an architect. He's kind to Caleb. I love him, and I want him here."

Lucinda sits down on the love seat between Maribelle and Caroline. Aunt Bryant and Raleigh are aligned and directly across.

"That's the best offer after what Porter has done?" Lucinda asks.

The air around them feels dirty, tainted. There's a thick quietness; the world is splitting. Lucinda's eyes have no light, and her mouth curves downward.

"What did you do in Kesgrave, Lucinda? We're entitled to know," Caroline says.

"I know what happened in Kesgrave," Raleigh says. "I understand it better than anyone."

"Excuse me?" Caroline says. "You weren't born yet."

"I've spoken with Porter. Plus, I know what it is to trespass." She leans across the coffee table toward Lucinda. A woman whose outfits, jewelry, home, work, charity, and hosting, costume who she is. It must follow her no matter how much she has accomplished. Where would that take her at sixty years old on the eve of her birthday, in a town where she must belong, where women believe her thoroughly constructed canvas? An infinite sorrow covers Raleigh. She is an inch from unspeakable loss. "I'll help you, Mom, but only if you help him."

Lucinda nods. "I want him to leave town, Raleigh, and destroy the evidence. That's the proviso. The rest is easy—the money, the shares of Barrows."

Lament rises in Raleigh. "No, I'm sorry. No."

"Raleigh!" Caroline says. "How unlike you. You and Porter can go anywhere. There are plenty of places—South Beach, Lauderdale. If the two of you last."

"She has Caleb, Caroline," Maribelle says. "Raleigh's trying to be named custodial parent."

"As if that's set," Caroline says. "Porter is the next guy, anyway—next and next. What is it that makes this permanent?"

"Girls, please," Aunt Bryant says. "Stop this."

Again, no one speaks.

Maribelle stares at Lucinda. "Mom, did you kill someone? Was it Bud?"

Raleigh tilts her head back to take in the clouds. The sky has turned ashen. The Intracoastal, reflecting the sky, is the same.

Aunt Bryant stands up. What she will say is intended to affect each of them, it's palpable.

"No, that's not it," Aunt Bryant says. "Bud died in the dinghy."

Raleigh starts crying. "How do you know, Aunt Bryant? Why do you know?"

"Aunt Bryant was with us. Mom was so pregnant. We were in the back yard, remember, Caroline?" Maribelle asks.

Caroline nods. She, too, is crying.

Lucinda, the next speaker, stands. "There isn't a day that goes by where I don't relive what happened on the river. That's why this life, the one I worked for, fought for, dreamed up, counts so much. I didn't kill Bud. It was Reed—it was an accident. Bryant asked me why I'd gone down there. I went to ask Reed to come back to the house because I felt like I was going into labor. I saw it. They were arguing. Reed hit Bud, and Bud fell down. It was my idea to put him in the boat, to send Ruth-Ann away. We had two girls. Bryant's fiancé was gone. If Reed got into trouble, my children would have had no father. I did it for my girls, my husband, Bryant. For us to have a whole life. I saved our family, didn't I?"

Lucinda's lies, like her truths, have never surfaced before. Raleigh walks to her sisters, they hold each other, weeping. Lucinda and Aunt Bryant are side by side, facing the water.

Chapter Forty-Seven

2026

Lucinda is pleased with the glass lanterns and strings of light illuminating the driveway of the Boat and Oar Club. The club itself has a Gilded Age opulence about it, including the ornate crystal chandeliers throughout the first floor. After her assiduous research on the Palm Beach "season" at the turn of the century and with enough internet scrolls, Lucinda opted for ball length dresses and white tie.

Guests are announced by an actor impersonating a footman. There to greet them is the Barrows lineup: Lucinda, William, Maribelle, Caroline, Travis, Raleigh, and Aunt Bryant. Harper and Violet awkwardly stand by Aunt Bryant, smiling as they are acknowledged. Caleb, who made a brief appearance, has already been sent home with Rosie.

Couture gowns, bags, shoes, hair piled high or teased to add height. The men almost appendages to the women. No one needs to learn what the past weeks have been. The promise of moving on is intoxicating. William, who is standing remarkably straight, whispers to Lucinda, "You are respected. You have arrived. Look at the women, at your guests."

"Brava!" Bryant says quietly. "The tone of the evening is stellar."

Maribelle, Caroline, and Raleigh, busy smiling, doing

some short laughs, and air kissing, do not add a requisite remark. Nor would any of the bejeweled and dazzling guests attempt to gossip. The mood is festive. In Lucinda's vintage bag is her Xanax, although she is over it. The room is filling up with one hundred and twenty-five guests, there to celebrate with her. More importantly, to not miss a glamorous event.

AFTER THE COCKTAIL HOUR, they are led into the ballroom for dinner and dancing. Guests stand at the windows overlooking the ocean. There are floodlights, waves roll onto the shore. In the center of the room is a nine-piece band, performing Cher's "Believe" with a woman vocalist, about forty, in a gold jumpsuit. Some couples move toward the dance floor, others toward their tables, escorted by mimes. Lucinda low-level waves at Kit Carter, who zigzags about, double-checking on the lilies and votive candles, the precision of the place settings.

The mimes jaunt along in their leotards, ready to escort the Barrows family to their table. Raleigh sits between Aunt Bryant and Maribelle, with Maribelle flanking Lucinda on one side and Caroline on the other. William and Travis are across the table. Lucinda has placed Harper and Violet between them.

Lucinda motions to Maribelle, and she and Raleigh change seats for a moment. Very discreetly she gives Raleigh a small envelope. "This is for you, Raleigh."

Raleigh smells of the ocean. She is iridescent in a pewter bias-cut satin dress. A stack of delicate bangles covers her left wrist. As if she's cleaned up after a two mile swim.

Raleigh takes it. Her mother's initials *LBM* are on the back.

Alexandra Zee passes the table and holds up her phone. "Sorry to intrude, I couldn't resist this mother-daughter moment."

After she is off, Lucinda pauses. "A party favor, from me to you."

The band switches to "Another Night" by Real McCoy, a song Lucinda used to play for her daughters in Kesgrave. She would hold Raleigh in her arms and dance with Maribelle and Caroline.

"Did you request this, Mom?" Raleigh asks.

"I did not, but your sisters could have put it on the playlist."

Up close, her mother is as she was ages ago, in Kesgrave. The same ratio of smile to seriousness, her clear eyes. When Raleigh knew only how fiercely she protected her, her sisters, their story.

Lucinda takes her hand. "We do the best with what we have. That's how it is."

NO ONE NOTICES Raleigh moving to the end of the ballroom, out through a half-open slider, how quickly she reads in the light from the terrace. To the right she sees the entire length of beach; a full moon is rising over the ocean, the waves curl into the shoreline.

Dusk is falling. Raleigh spins around, knowing he is awfully close, recklessly near.

Discussion Questions: *Palm Beach Confidential*

1. Lucinda, a mother of three adult daughters, presents as perfection but carries a deep secret. Do you believe many women do this to varying degrees? What type of secrets?
2. Lucinda cares deeply about her image and place in Palm Beach society. How does this affect her and those around her?
3. Maribelle and Raleigh, the eldest and youngest sisters, are not speaking when the book opens. Whose side are you on and why?
4. This is the fourth of the Palm Beach novels. What is it about the setting that makes it distinctive and a part of the story?
5. Each sister has a specific place and role in the Barrows family. How would you describe Maribelle, Caroline, and Raleigh?
6. We witness many sides of Lucinda's personality. How do you feel about her?
7. Bryant and Lucinda have a complicated friendship. How do you interpret it?
8. Aspects of this story deal with survival for women, even in an exclusive place. Were you surprised to read about unhappiness and yearning among women of wealth and privilege? Why and why not?
9. As the novel progresses, we wonder more about Lucinda's choices. How do her daughters relate to her?
10. Were you surprised by Lucinda's decision and her truth?

Acknowledgments

I have long thought of and imagined the Barrows sisters and their mother Lucinda: their secrets, their longings, their place in the world of high society. And what they left behind.

I am grateful for those who have cheered me on this path (in alphabetical order): Helene Barre, Linda Berley, Meredith Bernstein, Brondi Borer, Cynthia Conrad, Beth Corn, Kara Feifer, Ann Fishman, Elena Hartwell, Amy Cecil Holm, John Lotte, Alice Martell, Sally McElwain, Elisabeth Rohm, Jane Shapiro, Judy H. Shapiro, Jonathan Stone, Jennifer Weis, Ellyn Williams.

Juliet Brockman for caring, Miles Brockman for his knowledge of Greek mythology.

The unforgettable team at Meridian Editions, led by Meryl Moss.

Katie Schaffstall and Alexa Lieberthal for holding down the fort. Rebecca Stowe for her editorial wisdom. Early, trusted readers.

Treasured family and friends always. Jennie and Elizabeth, my muses.

In memory of my mother, best critic, steadfast supporter, who adored the Palm Beach season.

For Howard Ressler, totally.

SUSANNAH MARREN is the author of *Between the Tides*, *A Palm Beach Wife*, *A Palm Beach Scandal*, and *Maribelle's Shadow* and the pseudonym for Susan Shapiro Barash, who has written fourteen nonfiction books. Those titles include *Estranged: How Strained Female Friendships are Mended or Ended*, *Tripping the Prom Queen*, *You're Grounded Forever but First Let's Go Shopping*, and *A Passion for More*. For over twenty years she taught gender studies in the Writing Department at Marymount Manhattan College and has guest-taught creative nonfiction at The Writing Institute at Sarah Lawrence College. Susan's books focus on the gender divide, how women are positioned in our society, and their innermost feelings about themselves as daughters, mothers, sisters, friends, wives, mothers-in-law, daughters-in-law, rivals, colleagues, and lovers.

www.ingramcontent.com/pod-product-compliance
Lightning Source LLC
LaVergne TN
LVHW091644100826
845152LV00007B/154/J